VOCATIONAL GIRL

VOCATIONAL GIRL

Rosa Mundi

Quercus

First published in Great Britain in 2006 by Quercus
This paperback edition published in 2007 by

Quercus
21 Bloomsbury Square
London
WC1A 2NS

A CIP catalogue record for this book is available
from the British Library

ISBN 1-84724-063-1
ISBN-13 978-1-84724-063-7

This book is a work of fiction. Names, characters,
businesses, organizations, places and events are
either the product of the author's imagination
or are used fictitiously. Any resemblance to
actual persons, living or dead, events or
locales is entirely coincidental.

Printed and bound in Great Britain by
Clays Ltd, St Ives plc.

10 9 8 7 6 5 4 3 2 1

Ninety-Three Days On

I RAN HOME, IN THE end. Not really ran all the way, I hailed a taxi: but it is fair to say that I fled for my life, who knows, maybe for more than my life, dressed only in Jimmy Choo cracked metallic silver four inch heels, no-crotch Wolford fishnets, beige cashmere jacket – sequined, Christian Lacroix, but well cutaway – and without my purse. Fear and anger propelled my flight. Mother told me once that I should never go to a party without the fare home: as it happened I had a folded twenty-pound note in my pocket.

The party – though that may not be quite the right word – was in Hampstead, a couple of miles away from where I live in Little Venice, by the canal. It's not really me to walk any distance by day let alone night, if only because my heels are so high, so it was just as well the money was to hand. Otherwise I might have killed the anger, decided escape was too much like hard labour, too much strain on the ankles, stayed, and been destroyed. I don't need hindsight to know that I was within a sulphury whiff of it.

I had borrowed the £20 from the rent money, which I hid as cash between the leaves of Wittgenstein's *Tractatus Logico-Philosophicus*, on the grounds that no-one else but me is going to open it. I'd put it in the pocket of the Lacroix jacket at suppertime on June 21st, having perhaps some intuition of what was to come – a feeling of adventure in the air on that midsummer's night – where it was to stay until 21st September, the date of my flight.

I do love Lacroix. Not just for the pocket, I'm in his debt for that, but the way the clothes make you feel so extravagant, dramatic and luxurious: textures surprise and delight, discretion and glitter exult in tandem. I like to think that's my style.

During the ninety-three days of my dealings with Alden X and his painter friend, Ray, I could not focus on Wittgenstein, nor even on Kant's somewhat easier *Copernican Revolution,* nor my twenty-four volumes of Jung's *Collected Works*. I was meant to be getting on with my PhD thesis on 'changes in the group psyche as created through faulty perceptions of reality as exacerbated by implicit distortions of meaning in the new lingua franca: Bill Gates' Microsoft'.

But during that summer, the year I turned twenty-six, if I turned the pages the words meant nothing: they hung alien and unconnected on the page. If I tried to write nothing came. It worried me. Can the life of the flesh so undermine the life of the mind that one loses all powers of reasoning? Or interest in them? Or perhaps it's okay to take lust and intellect in shifts, and not to try to live a balanced life and kind of synthesize your own Prozac, like you're supposed to do.

At The Front Desk

I WORK PART-TIME IN ONE of London's plusher hotels, the Olivier in Covent Garden, and it was there at my post behind the reception desk that I first met Alden, on June 21st last year. At eleven that morning I had checked in a Mrs Matilda Weiss and her party. She travelled with a posse of three – nutritionist, personal trainer and lawyer. She had booked into our Premiere Suite, 406, the others into cheaper rooms on the second floor. Mrs Weiss was a botox-happy Manhattan matron and socialite in her fifties, passing for her thirties, newly divorced, slim as a rake; dressed in taupes with heavy gold hung here and there. She was not a pleasant person, and caused trouble from the start, demanding instant personal access to the chef for her nutritionist; and installed in her suite, sent down to demand black grapes instead of the white ones in the complimentary fruit bowl, banging on that they were too acid. Takes one to know one; she'd know all about acid. Some guests never feel at home until they have registered a whole string of quite ingenious complaints.

Two hours later, at ten to one precisely, Alden came towards me in his wheelchair, broad-shouldered, energetic, cheerful, brown floppy hair, a man with bright-eyed film-star looks, though rather more in the square-jawed manly Warren-Beatty mould of yesterday, than today's softer, more troubled Tom-Hanks-ish look. Late thirties, I thought; wealthy. His suit was good, his wheelchair Italian and custom built. He had a paid companion to push it, a pasty young-old little man with an egg-shaped head, over-large, dark, watchful eyes and clammy hands, whom I was eventually to know as Lam.

I paged Suite 406 to tell Mrs Weiss that Mr Alden X was here for lunch and for my pains was rewarded with: 'Lunch – with that fucking crazy? He is joking? Tell him to shove his interior designs up where no sun shines, is that interior enough? Or can't he reach, sitting in a wheelchair?' and further words to this effect.

I held the phone further away from my ear but the contemptuous voice crackled on, the others now hearing it the better before I realised what I'd done. Lam frowned in concern – his lugubrious eyes seemed even panicky – but Alden just smiled and said quietly, 'Don't worry about it, kid. Just put the receiver down.'

So I did.

'It's an ill wind,' said Alden. 'Perhaps you'll have a drink with me instead?'

I had to say yes, but not because he was disabled

and might have interpreted any reluctance on my part as insult. I was curious. This is embarrassing, but I'm going to say it anyway: faced with a good-looking and vigorous man in a wheelchair one's mind instantly goes to practicalities: can he, can't he? Was he born like that or was there an accident? Will he get better or is it permanent? How does he manage? Does he confine himself to oral things; was the important part of him permanently limp, or even altogether gone? Perhaps it was part of his minder's remit to hoist his master on to all fours so he could perform? Or did he just lie on his back? Or... what? I wanted to know. I needed to find out. Because I'm a philosopher, and trained to ask questions about the world of phenomena? Or my natural curiosity, like that which killed the cat?

I said we'd have to wait for the concierge to come back. Max was down in the kitchens trying to soothe the chef, who was still miffed because of the earlier insult to his white grapes, a special purchase – they had a particularly fine flavour and delicate skins – flown in from the Andes or wherever they grow them in June. My shift was technically over at one o'clock, but if Mr—?

'Call me Alden,' he said. 'Alden X.'

– If Alden didn't mind waiting five minutes or so, my shift would be over and I'd be free, I said. Conversation with someone in a wheelchair is difficult. You have to talk down to them, as if they were a child.

I rather wished I hadn't said yes, and then felt guilty for wishing it. Also, I was slightly miffed because he hadn't asked me to lunch but only for a drink. I know the girl behind reception can hardly expect to be treated with the same courtesy as a guest, but even so these social distinctions can make you paranoiac if you're on the wrong side of them.

He asked me what my name was and I said 'Joan Bennet,' and added that I was only temporary staff. I had a proper profession. He asked me what that was and I said I was a nursery school teacher. I was working extra hours at the Olivier to pay for a course in teenage counselling. He said that sounded very virtuous and I said I was.

What else was I to tell him? The truth? That my name is Vanessa d'A. and I have a double first in philosophy, and while working towards my PhD I earn money best as I may? Nothing puts most men off like too much class or cleverness in a woman. It's still true: they need to feel they're your superior. Best to come over as a nurse or a teacher, and there are no disappointments; everyone knows where they are and cocks rise uninhibited.

I am virtuous enough, in my way. My mother once told me that the only difference between a professional girl and the others is that the first take money for sex and the rest don't. She's a lady vicar in the Church of England with her own vocation, so I take her word for it. She could even be a bishop one day if Synod ever gets its act together about female equality. I do not sell my body for a living. I see it as the temple of my soul, as my mother explains to me that it is, and so I respect it accordingly. It's just that a temple will need its roof mended and its doors and windows painted and the rest, which requires money. I am not cut out for regular employment. I'm useless with computers, and offices make me claustrophobic. I could set out to marry a rich man but that might have to limit my sex life, and I'm not ready for that quite yet.

I am what Max the concierge describes as a vocational, rather than a working girl. I like sex; I'm good at it, and sometimes I feel it's what I'm best at; what I feel I'm for.

Unaccompanied men, especially when in a strange land, are often at a loose end sometimes of an evening. Max the concierge will point them in my direction: not too often – but once or twice a week or so is acceptable. I am a nice girl, a good girl and an educated girl: my face stays soft and vulnerable and the corners of my mouth turn upwards, not down. I am a rosy sort of person: friendly: people stop me to ask me the way, knowing I can be trusted to give a true answer. Rather too rounded for a catwalk model, though with a little help from a seamstress I know I can get into their cast-offs: I have friends in the fashion houses. A little waist, full breasts, very long legs, shiny reddish hair – people ask me if I use henna but that's just the colour it is

– slim thighs, little feet and pretty hands. I have not much to complain about.

If men care to give me gifts for services rendered that suits me very well. A couple of hours a day behind the desk at the Olivier pays peanuts but is a good way of making contacts. The hotel gets an excellent class of clientele – prices range from around £400 a night for an ordinary room without a river view, up to £2,000 for a suite. We are a favourite with EU officials, NGO senior staff, wealthy Americans, UN magnates and Japanese tourists; nothing too flashy or corrupt.

If I had been born Japanese, my natural habitat would have been in a tea house, as a geisha. Nothing too vulgar, nor up-front, but if the clients feel like sex as well as conversation – well so do I, and should they like to give me presents, I don't have a problem with it: my rent is high and I have to fund my own way through college. In the long term the only place I see for myself is in academe. Meanwhile there are my clothes to pay for – I have a princess's taste but a commoner's income. I hope I don't sound too defensive here. Because I frequently have sex without requiring or expecting payment: although, oddly, men often prefer to pay than not to pay. The transaction is less value-loaded: no sense of emotional obligation is left drifting in the air. It is more like paying one's psycho-therapist: then it is clear that 'friendship' has been bought, and with a time limit.

In the Bound Beast and Bumpkin

ALDEN TELLS ME HE is a musician, an interior designer and an 'applied conceptual artist', and I say, 'Quite the Renaissance man!' Which is slightly over-clever for Joan, and Lam suddenly speaks up in flat, nasal tones: 'Mr X – true Leonardo,' just as I'd forgotten he existed. Then Max comes back, says it's okay for me to go, and nods us over in the direction of the bar of the Bound Beast and Bumpkin, a designer pub which crouches in the lee of the Olivier, where its staff meet out of hours, a few drugs are bought and sold and high-class hookers congregate.

Max is tall, grizzled, lugubrious and around fifty: he is dapper and neat and self-contained and wears a red carnation. Max has a smooth line of talk which keeps guests happy, and a dangerous glint in his eye which keeps staff docile. He is the outer and visible sign of the Hotel Olivier's dignity. His wife long since learned to live without him: his love goes to the hotel. He started as a bell boy and is now head concierge and doubles at reception if required; he is the link between the hotel and the outside world; he knows every theatre, every restaurant, every call girl in town; he bribes and blackmails in the hotel's interests; he has a hot line to the local cop-shop; he has his favorites amongst the cab drivers; he takes a modest cut from everyone for putting business in other folks' way, as is his due, and sometimes boasts to me about the tens of thousands he has in cash beneath his bed.

'Except,' as he says rather unnecessarily, being a wary kind of person, 'it isn't really under my bed.'

Max seems to like me. I dress tastefully, even modestly, I'm cool and efficient behind his desk, and if I find myself in Larry's Bar at the hotel with a guest, after work, it is with Max's permission. I am well-spoken: I don't attract the wrong sort of attention. He once told me I was good for the bar trade. We get top film and music people, even writers, scientists, all kinds of interesting sorts in, and super celebrity models too, so I took that as a compliment.

'Wheelchair access is better at the Beast than in Larry's,' says Max. It sounds ingenuous, but there is a subtext. What he means is that wheelchairs are not welcome in the hotel bar. The Olivier offers wheelchair access to all floors and public spaces, but the well-heeled public, though happy to pay lip service to the blind, the deaf, the dumb, the physically and mentally incapacitated, does not want its nose rubbed in disability when it has its hair let down, enjoying itself.

Better if Max had said nothing. I felt quite upset on Alden's behalf. He had already that morning been snubbed by Mrs Weiss, and humiliated in front of me. Now his eyes were bright as if there were tears brimming just behind them. Maybe he was just blazing cross, but hiding it. I resolved to be as nice to him as I could, and on our way to the Bound Beast shook my hair loose from its pins, undid the top three buttons, pushed up the sleeves of my white ruched blouse, and by the time I sat down opposite his wheelchair and was finally able to engage with him on the level and not from a height, I felt we were kind of pals, on the same side, almost joined together at the hip in some way. I smiled at him as if he were God's gift to women – which I could see that, were he not in a wheelchair, he might very well be.

'You have an interesting smile,' he said. 'You're not as obvious as you pretend – I like that.' His voice was quizzical, strong and low and had a slight Yorkshire growl to it. He was at ease, so I was at ease. I felt honoured to be noticed, to be more than just essence of girl, but girl with detail: girl fascination. But then I wondered if his flanks were thin and withered, or strong and firm like normal. How could I know? Would it matter? Probably not. As a child I used to rescue birds the cat brought in, befriend the bullied, adopt African children and so on. I've always liked lame ducks. But then he wasn't acting lame at all.

So I wondered what he wanted. A drink with a nursery school teacher because his lunch date had fallen through? Company, any would do, and that was that? He was hardly the lonely type though: so why?

Lam bought drinks and chicken sandwiches with cash Alden handed him, put them in front of us, then went and sat by himself at another table and read his newspaper, not resentful, but humble like Uriah Heep; the role made him comfortable. So he acted as servant and not some kind of companion. The Leonardo comment was incidental. And he seemed uninterested in me. Perhaps he was gay? He had a small mouth and a tapered chin and a plaintive air of incipient victimhood. I was pretty sure about Alden's sexual orientation and he was the opposite of plaintive. If he was a victim, he asked for no favours because of it.

'A tenth of the price and twice as good as lunching in your hotel,' said Alden. He had a good appetite: broad white orthodontist-teeth bit into thick chunks of fresh crusty white bread. I nibbled at the chicken, leaving the bread. Personally I would rather have lunched at the Olivier. The mayo here was too sharp, out of a jar.

'It's not my hotel,' I giggled, and he put up his hands in a no contest gesture and made a face and grinned, then shook his head. 'Thank you for keeping me company, Joan. God, that woman is a bitch.'

'I don't think it's nice to call any woman a bitch,' I said primly, in my Joan persona. His eyebrows rose a bit. 'How do you know her?' I said, changing tack.

'It's a business relationship,' he said. 'Is, was ... ? Probably still "is".'

There were two or three professional girls at the bar,

swinging legs, eating lunch, waiting for their pimps or the odd punter to come along, eyeing me and my new acquisition up, smirking and whispering behind hands, but not aggressively, perfectly friendly. They don't seem to mind me. I don't take business away from them, or only in such small quantity it scarcely affects the price of fish. Anyway, I put business their way from time to time, whenever I depped for Max behind the concierge's desk.

Alden told me he owned a design agency. It was called Arts-Intrinsick. I looked it up later that afternoon on Google. It was 'working towards a unified vision of art, design and sound', which could have meant anything, or nothing, but so far as I could see its mission was to bring together private art collectors, architects and 'sound sculptors to embrace the senses in a functional, luxurious and sophisticated environment'. Bullshit, it seemed to me but plausible enough to work. What did I know? In other words if you were a very, very rich divorcée like Mrs Weiss and liked to buy paintings and art installations as an investment, you would then employ Alden to create a state-of-the-art gallery within your own home, where you could display your collection to its advantage against a background of specially composed sense-enhancing music.

I had no doubt Arts-Intrinsick would thrive: there is plenty of free-floating money to be netted in the art world – especially if you are not an actual painter. I have a step grand-father, Lord Wallace F, grand old doyen of British architecture, and so I know all about that from him, and from my grandmother, who had the misfortune to be married to him for a time. Wallace was a horrid man, though his scathing dismissal of what he called 'art-world scum' and 'culture nomenclature' could be quite energizing; no doubt it would have included someone like Alden in it. I felt the more protective towards him, having to struggle not just against the handicap of his disability, but the contempt of the likes of Wallace while he tried to bring his vision to reality. Wallace had a point perhaps, but froth would be a kinder word than scum. But then I liked Alden and didn't like Wallace: judgment follows where emotions lead.

Alden and I chatted; we talked of our families. He came from a Yorkshire vicarage – had gone to grammar school – he'd played with the village soccer team, which suggested an accident later in life, but he was not prepared to go into details – the Royal College of Music, then fine arts at the Slade – he was multi-talented, evidently – a job with the Warhol Foundation – and then on to start his own business. No marriage. A light laugh – it wouldn't be fair: he couldn't have children. What about me?

I resisted the temptation to say I too came from a clerical family, only on my mother's side, and, as Joan Bennet, presented him with a portrait of a lower-middle-class Essex family – father an out-of-work printer, mother a social worker, two sisters working in a call centre, a brother in trouble with the police. I implied that I loved working with children: I was not ambitious, other than I wanted to make a difference, you know? I added for good measure that I was Plymouth Brethren, and he looked quite intrigued – a sect in which sex is a source of neurotic guilt, and where else, these days, can you find that?

For hit-and-run sex it is useful to be someone else: if you feel bad about it later for any reason, why then, it wasn't you that did it. If you get emotionally hurt, it is someone else who suffers. The kernel of you stays intact. I rather liked this Joan of mine. She had a cuddly, kind heart and would certainly go to bed with Alden, if that was what he wanted, if only out of compassion, because she was whole and he was not. She would not of course expect financial reward.

I would use Joan again: the thought quite stirred me. Being Joan as well as Vanessa added spice to the expectation of adventure. It was almost as if I could be both male and female: dom and sub, top and bottom, the one who did, the one done unto.

So, Alden was infertile. I felt restless on my chair. Why couldn't we just get on with this? But would it work? Men can be infertile for reasons other than mechanics. He would lie on his back: I could sit on top of him. If the worst came to the worst he could use a vibrator. Lam could run out for one, in the role in which he was now running backwards and forwards to the bar with whisky sours for Alden and over-sweet cocktails – made of crème de cacao, brandy, cream and nutmeg with two little umbrellas on top – for me, that seeming obviously the sort of thing Joan would drink.

Luigi the barman at the Beast, with his Robert de Niro looks, was ever one to foster intimate relationships in his bar; he had coated the drink with a thick layer of nutmeg, rather than the normal bitty sprinkle. Alden told me it was aphrodisiac and I pretended ignorance, which is usually popular with men, for the less you know the more opportunity they have to enlighten you. He gave me a full breakdown of the spice's chemical composition.

He asked me if I had a boyfriend, and I confessed that I had been engaged for four years to a Geology student who'd then walked out on me and married my best friend. A tear or two came into my eye. I really took myself in. He sympathised, and I said really, I was okay, but I'd given up on men. You couldn't rely on them, you couldn't trust them. He said, 'We men, perhaps we're not all the same.' I said perhaps I didn't know very much about them really.

He set about impressing me. One of his 'environments', he said, had been had been written up in May's Vogue. But his real passion was music, sound. He had had some acclaim recently – a ten-minute piece for percussion on Radio 3 last year, in a series called Minimalist Maelstrom – and he was currently struggling to deliver a twenty-minute commissioned piece called

Thelemy: The Silence of the Senses, again for Radio 3. He asked me if I liked music and I said I was quite keen on trance. He laughed and said that figured and reached out and took my hand and held it a moment. When we touched a spark of static electricity clicked and leapt between him and me. It was probably co-incidental – there was a new carpet in the bar – but it left me with the feeling that the energy ordinary people wasted walking round built up in some kind of inner battery he had, and was ready for use; his eyes were so bright.

He said he was an avant-garde man himself and I asked him what he meant by avant-garde and he said 'in the forefront' and I said that seemed a dangerous place to be, in the front line of the battle, and he said yes, that's what it was: he was in the forefront of the battle against stupidity and man's inhumanity to man. I would have asked him where women fitted in but remembering in time that I was Joan, not Vanessa, just nodded appreciatively.

Alden and Joan were really getting along together, rather happily together in fact. And then of all things the great diplomat Max came in, escorting Mrs Matilda Weiss who looked me up and down as if I was something the cat had brought in. She sat down at our table all conciliatory frowns and smiles and mwah-mwahs, simpering and apologising all over Alden. While they were thus engaged, Max gave me a very definite little nod towards the door, telling me I should leave, and since Alden had lost interest in my presence, so I did.

And I thought that was all there was going to be to it, and that I wouldn't see him again: I was furious. But Lam came out into the street after me with a message from Alden – an invitation: that if I was free that evening perhaps I would join him and some friends of his for dinner at home? 8.00? Wear something pretty? He lived in Hampstead and would send a taxi.

I hadn't felt so happy since I was six, when I saw my father walk in through the door, returned from a week away, during which time I was sure, quite wrongly, that he'd run off with the au pair. It was like waking from a bad dream to find your teeth haven't fallen out, the house hasn't burned down, and the world is a far more wonderful place than the disastrous one you have become reconciled to overnight. A sudden, gratuitous, lift of the heart. I gave Lam my address, and would have gone straight home to doll myself up, already working out what Alden's idea of 'pretty' might possibly be while I waited for the taxi: but Max had something else in mind.

Suite 402

A WELL-KNOWN CENTRE COURT TENNIS player was checking in when I left the Bound Beast and came back into reception. I will not tell you his name, not even the initial, but he is as famous for his sexual impetuosity as for the speed of his serve: over 140 miles per hour. His wife was not checking in until the next day. He was a shock-headed blond, stocky, lovely and healthy looking, and barely thirty. Women in the foyer were already huddling and staring. Max caught his attention and moved his eyes enquiringly towards me: I felt an involuntary tingle of response as I watched him look me briefly up and down and nod approval to Max.

'Perhaps you could help our guest up with his bag,' said Max. And so I did, though God knows the tennis star was young and strong enough to carry it for himself, the porter's desk for once was well staffed, and I was off-duty.

Max usually gives me some warning, and a free

range of options – yes, no, never, perhaps, what's in it, and some time to think about it – today for some reason he did not. But I chose not to make a fuss, and just went along with it: I wanted adventure. I had been thoroughly stirred up sexually and then dismissed, and I was still shaken. I owed Alden less than nothing, yet it was partly the thought that I owed him this to serve him out which drove me to smile my consent. Max gave the glimmer that for him passed as appreciation – a slight loosening of his impassive lugubrious features. I was often surprised that men found courage as they did to approach him regarding their sexual needs – but there's nothing like sex, I suppose, for stiffening the sinews.

I trotted ahead of the great Wimbledon server, carrying his bag for him with both hands. The expectation, amongst equals, that the male carries the burden for the female, is overruled when such class distinctions are at play. In the great scale of things my position as servant far outweighed any traditional rights as a female. I resolved to make a note of it when I got home and see if I could work these ideas into my thesis. The different meanings of serve: an internet server, a tennis server, a servant…

Had my hair been thin and grey it could have changed the balance, he could have said 'let me', but my hair was doing its glossy, tumbling thing since I'd taken out the hair grips earlier, and it's amazing the effect undoing a button or two on a staff uniform can have. We had crossed into the roles of the chamber maid and he the young master, and we were locked in.

I put down the bag – heaven knows what was in it, did tennis players do weight lifting? – and used the card to open the door of Suite 402. I heaved it inside and started on the usual spiel about the master switch, the air conditioning, how to call the maid to do the curtains, the Carreras marble bathroom floor and not to remove the non-slip pad, and so on, but my voice faded away because the famous tennis player was leaning back against the closed door with his flies already unzipped and his serpentine member moving upwards and outwards, a wilful, independent, questing thing. It was a blond's penis, moderately thick, but long and pale, with veins taut as if they were muscles, and impressed even me. All it had taken was three slight nods, Max towards me, his towards Max, and mine to Max, not a word spoken, and all this, within minutes, was not just possible, it was inevitable, already really happening. But such was the panders' art, I supposed, and why Max had so much cash beneath his mattress, or wherever he really put it away.

Not all women enjoy fellating, and many do it just for the man's sake, but I have more than broken myself out of that habit: I have come to love doing it. I like the feel of my lips being stretched, the incorporation of the chthonic male other into the mouth from which I speak, the head from which I think, the face which is my polite persona in the non-sexual intercourse of polite society. The teasing and honouring with the tongue, like the anointing of a priest-king, I revel in it almost – though never quite – as much as I do full penetrative sex in my cunt, where the superego is entirely absent.

The fact that you do this for a stranger adds to the marvel of it, and the religious reference in kneeling gives intensity to the obeisance, as if a god someone has whisked you out of the crowd for this moment of intimate selfless sacrifice, and will whirl you back into it again afterwards, some symbolic act of union accomplished, leaving you the more for it, not the less, and the rest of the world outside ignorant of the secret ritual, unknowingly saved.

I was on my knees in front of him, his prick in my mouth, which was steered by his serving hand wound firmly into my hair. First the tip to be circled, then the whole sucked and given up, sucked and given up. It tones the mouth muscles: keeps the lips firm and full. Now he pushed his pelvis forward into my throat, my head pressed against his flat sportsman's belly. I could scarcely breathe but that too is a discomfort one quickly gets to like, once one stops panicking.

Sex is a cheap way of escaping the compulsive nature of ratiocination. That is to say, in the language of everyday, rather than the language of my PhD thesis, fucking stops you thinking, and that can be a relief. But since blow jobs only take up half the mind, not the whole of it, there's enough room left in one's head, observing, for being one's own voyeur, and thinking discursively, even creatively. What I was thinking about now was ancient Babylon and the temple whores of Ishtar.

My father is a classical scholar of the traditional dusty and distant absent-minded professor type, and he had me reading Latin from the age of five and Greek at seven. He kept a clutch of books on the top shelf of the library, away from my eyes. These of course were the ones I later sought out when he wasn't in the house, standing on a chair and books to get them down. It was thus, when I was ten, that I'd first come across a passage by Herodotus about Ishtar's sacred harlots written two and a half millennia since.

'Babylonian custom,' he wrote, 'compels every woman of the land once in her life to sit in the temple of love and have intercourse with some stranger…the men pass and make their choice. The money that passes hands makes the act sacred, but its amount is of no consequence, the woman will never refuse, for that would be sinful. After their intercourse she has made herself holy in the sight of the goddess and goes away to her home; and thereafter there is no bribe however great that will get her. So then the women that are tall and fair are soon free to depart, but the uncomely have long to wait because they cannot fulfil the law; for some of them remain for three years or four.' I liked temple life. My vocation was to serve Ishtar today, and the Hotel Olivier was her temple. I was fair, not short,

I was comely enough to return home almost at once, but I preferred to leave it a while.

Herodotus also observed that many of the temple whores returned home to marry and have children, but that was then. Personally I'm for an academic career when this period of my life is over. I believe later Sumerian texts advise against marrying a professional temple prostitute, since she would tend to be too independent. That figured. 'Besides being accustomed to accepting other men, she would make an unsympathetic wife'. Indeed. She would make comparisons and that is hard for a man to take. Joan Bennet, the figment I had created for Alden the cripple's benefit, was a girl of little experience if not downright virginity. But she was an aspect of me, taking my shift at a sacred duty: I was no professional.

As I reflected on these things, the tennis star came, but went on and on – with all the stamina of someone used to world championships – until my knees were sore, my mouth began to stiffen and threaten cramp, and my interest waned. I was beginning to be bored. I made him come again, and gasping, removed myself and lay back upon the bed, half hoping he would take matters further to a different and less mechanical conclusion but he did not: his wife was joining him the next day and he probably liked to be faithful. For many men, like President Clinton, sucking doesn't count. In church car parks of the Democratic mid-west, bumper stickers were displayed during his time of trial taking,

in his support, the biblically arguable view that Eatin'
ain't Cheatin'.

But now my champion was on top of me, his
trousers kicked away, thrusting down into my mouth
from a more productive angle, unnaturally huge balls
banging my nose, and finally reason abandoned me
and I squirmed and gasped as he stretched and jerked
and shrieked and more semen spurted at 140 miles
an hour, and trickled down my throat and that was
– finally – that.

Freud said there was a vaginal orgasm (superior)
and a clitoral one (inferior) but in my experience there
is also an oral one, linked more to the imagination, the
shock and wonder of the event, than to any physical
stimulation. You observe it in the mouth but you feel
it in the vagina.

It seems rude to wash one's mouth out after such
an encounter so I desisted, rearranged my dress, as he
did, finished the guided tour – here is the television
wand, here the pay-movies card, here the spare pillows;
was there anything else you required, sir? – while he
retrieved his chinos, looked in his wallet and peeled off
two Centre Court tickets for Wimbledon.

'Men's Finals on June 28th,' he said, handing them
to me. 'You'll get fifteen hundred each on eBay. Unless
you want to watch me win.' Tickets were in great
demand. And he hadn't had to pay a single thing for
them. It seemed remarkably like cheating to me, and I
felt a spasm of indignation. But a goddess's servant is

required to accept what comes, and be grateful with noblesse oblige: no doubt rare Centre Court tickets sanctify the act as well as money, if not better.

The champion thanked me, asked me with albeit genial impatience to stop rambling on about the room – it wasn't the first hotel room he'd been in and he could see with his own eyes where the minibar was – ran his fingers round my mouth, iron-fleshed as they were from many a racquet handle, and assured me I was surely 'the best', whatever that meant, and I left. I was tongue-tied; I think I bowed first.

As I left 402 I passed La Weiss going to her own suite. She looked right through me as though I were not there: hotel staff are often invisible to the guests, like the wallpaper. She seemed quite pleased with herself. Perhaps she had managed to beat Alden's fee down in whatever project they were jointly involved in. I worried for him: I wasn't sure he was necessarily tough enough to look after his own interests. I was feeling sorry for him again. I remembered the way the stored energy had leapt between him and me – and the feeling of repletion that usually follows the closure of a successful sexual act had gone into abeyance before I even made it to the lift. I wanted Alden, though in what manner and with what choreography I could not be sure.

The stocky personal trainer, with neck almost wider than head, who was booked into 314 – a much cheaper room – opened the door of Suite 406 to Mrs Weiss, and he wore no clothes. That must have had plenty to do with her earlier reluctance to meet Alden for lunch. Nothing will do for some people, when they first set eyes on an hotel bed, but that they use it for sex. And some women become foul-mouthed while they're in rut.

Max held out his hand as I came down into the foyer and I gave him the two tickets. I don't do eBay. A friend of mine had her identity stolen from using it, and I am more computer-illiterate than she. Anyway, I can't stand a bargain: I like to pay full price. Show me two similar objects, one cheap and one expensive, and I go for the dear, investing it with some extra magic. If eBay has magic, I don't know what it is. And Max was expecting the tickets. That was why he had given me no choice but just told me, by inference, to get on up there quick before someone else got hold of them. Max is a Wimbledon junkie; he saw his opportunity and moved quickly. He would probably hand me, what? – probably a grand in cash in his own sweet time. We were, after all, partners, in a team.

I got off home as quickly as I could, with less time now to make myself 'pretty' for Alden.

Home

I LIVE ALONE, BETWEEN PADDINGTON and Maida Vale, in a much too expensive apartment looking over a canal. My London telephone prefix is 286, which in the old days when it was represented by the letters on the instrument dial was 'CUN': some wag must have been in charge of the allocation of codes a hundred years ago at the telephone's inception, because newly built Maida Vale was then where the grand pubs had music-hall acts on their cavernous ground floors, and more or less discreet brothels on the first and second, and the mansion blocks contained spacious apartments where gentlemen kept their mistresses.

I have tried sharing with other girls, but it never seems to work very well. I like my own space, and I don't put things away very often, except in the kitchen where everything is clean and orderly. Elsewhere you can't see a surface for the mass of discarded, once worn, or about to be worn garments, shoes, scarves, pashminas, beaded jackets and bags – I just love beads

– promiscuous jewellery and all the trappings of an admitted fashion shopaholic. But I like to think that all the mess that the eye falls upon has an aesthetic to it. Cosmetics, creams and scents are bought for the beauty of their containers – the contents, I find, are much of a muchness, but somehow if you buy the most expensive in the range it works best.

There are some good paintings on the wall, left to me by my grandmother Molly, the one who was married for a time to Lord Wallace F. They include a minor Picasso, a good Klimt and a tiny Chagall. I have managed so far to get by without selling these, though I am always in debt and persecuted by credit companies telling me what I know perfectly well already: that I owe them too much and am late paying. I just about keep things in balance as they are, but if I fell ill, or lost my looks, I'd be in trouble; the paintings would have to go. My problem is that I want to have it all – lots of money to spend, lots of time for my thesis, frequent thrills and plenty of security, sex on demand and respect from everyone – but there's neither time, space nor money enough for all of it. You have to choose, any idiot knows, but I can't bear to. To some extent I pretend otherwise: at least sex stops you thinking, and temple offerings pay the rent.

I like to think that the small room which I use as an office demonstrates the other more rigorous side of my nature. It is thoroughly Spartan, decent and plain. Stationery is stacked in neat piles, pencils are sharpened, notebooks placed in size order; the computer is state-of-the-art, the keyboard wiped with a cloth after every use. The lighting is efficient and the works of Wittgenstein, Jung and Kant and relevant others are to hand on custom-made adjustable Douglas fir shelves. It is my ambition to finish my thesis by the end of the Christmas holidays – I will go home for the season – and present it to my supervisor, Professor Freddie Wilques, first thing in the New Year.

I am quite a family person though you won't have observed much evidence of that so far; indeed, a Home Counties person. I was brought up in a country vicarage with Wellington boots and sit-up-and-beg bicycles in the hall, and an Aga in the kitchen to warm your bottom on. I always had a bottom that needed warming. My mother took Holy Orders some twenty years ago: my father the classical scholar, who has a private income much eroded by taxes, such being the way of the times, tutors children at home in maths and Latin. I have two younger sisters, Katharine and Alison, identical twins of seventeen, and child prodigies, both already at Oxford doing classics – prodigal like myself – and a little brother Robert, sixteen, who is no prodigal and still at school. My Joan Bennet family, the social worker mother, the redundant father, the call-centre sisters, the boy-in-the-hood brother, is their Essex equivalent. When telling lies I try to keep as near the truth as possible.

I read philosophy, and was the only woman in my

year to get a First. I graduated when I was twenty-one, four years back. Men usually get the firsts, not because of male discrimination against the female, or so Professor Wilques assures me, but because the bell curve which relates to academic intelligence is flatter in men than in women. Women cluster together in the middle ability ranges: men stretch out to either side, so you get both more brilliant and more stupid men than you do women. Sometimes I think that there is something rather male about me: I am somewhere stranded out on a limb. It doesn't show in my body but perhaps it does in the way my mind works. This is probably a delusion: I may have no idea of how men's minds work. And if I were to be male I would want to be gay, so perhaps that puts me back in the female camp? I would be happiest, I think, as a she-male: one of those people with male genitals and female breasts you see in Brazilian porn films.

Out to dinner with the *haute bohème* of Hampstead! I wondered who the other guests might be – who would a man like Alden see as fit company for a pretty hotel receptionist/nursery school teacher called Joan from Essex? We would see. Though I had a fair suspicion that I would get to his place and find no other guests except possibly Lam, who might be needed for practical purposes.

I dressed for the occasion in Vanessa mode, which might confuse Alden, but that couldn't be helped: I dreaded to think what Joan might wear for an evening out. Anyway, should the relationship lead anywhere I would have to admit to being Vanessa soon enough. The evening was warm. Down on the canal someone was giving a party on one of the narrow-boats. I heard chatter and laughter drifting up through the summer air. I almost wished I was more like other people: had a regular boyfriend, a regular life, a proper job, a pension fund, and wasn't cursed with a mind that went round and round like a whirligig, and a body that exacted sex from the unsuitably all and sundry; that I was not a vocational girl, a priestess of the Temple Olivier, but somebody who worked in a bank. But not to the extent that I was going to let it spoil my evening.

I wore a pale green chiffony dress of little substance, by Marc Jacobs, the cream Lacroix jacket – rather more substance – and red Jimmy Choo sandals with straps winding up nearly to the knee. Some shudder at green-and-red but I'm not one of them.

I don't do matching underwear if only because I can so seldom run it to earth in the pile. I ended up with a pink lace bra, low cut with wide apart straps, and – rejecting thongs on the grounds of comfort – French knickers in red silk which fortuitously matched the shoes exactly. Really quite demure, and un-alarming to a man in a wheelchair whom I knew very little about. Rather over-decent, I thought, almost Joan-ish – but at least my pink diamond navel-stud was on display. It was a good diamond, if to my mind rather small, and had cost its original owner more than £5,000. Another investment against the rainy day I told myself, but couldn't quite believe, must surely come.

A retired admiral staying at the Olivier for the Trafalgar Day celebrations had given the diamond to me. It had belonged to his wife, recently deceased. He was going to have to sell his house to pay off the taxman: he did not want to have to sell the diamond too. Rather, he said, that a latter day Emma Hamilton had it.

I had the diamond made into a navel ring, platinum mounted. The piercing somehow became infected but I persisted, despite the temptation to pull the ring out and throw it away from suspicion that either the wife or the Inland Revenue had laid a curse on it; after two courses of antibiotics the infection subsided, and now the gem glitters magnificently, and wholesomely, when revealed – those who know no better assume it to be false. It was not a Joan Bennet kind of thing to own, but I would meet that problem when I came to it.

I felt restless as I waited. A fat oyster-shell moon was hanging low over the roofs and unlit streetlights; it seemed to want to suck me out of my dwelling, and my identities as Vanessa, Joan or any others I'd ever known, and there was a pervasive miasma of expectation lingering in the city air. It was the summer solstice, and it seemed that the world was waiting impatiently for the moonlight which it knew would barely even come before it passed, so short were the hours of darkness. Perhaps one day after all I would meet Mr Right, and fall in love, and all things would be certain and explained. But even then there might well be a bit of restlessness left on an evening like this.

The door bell rang. I closed the gaping windows, and was half way down the stairs before I remembered about getting home. I climbed back up, and fetched a £20 note from the Wittgenstein to fold into my Lacroix pocket. If people pay for your fare to them they will in all likelihood pay your fare back home again but you never know, you might not want to be further beholden.

It was a black London taxi. I saw the sky mirrored in pale-blue patches on its over-polished paintwork, and the disc of the moon on one of its unexpectedly dark-tinted windows; I noticed no license number on the back too, as if it were privately owned. I'd heard that the millionaire Gulbenkian was chauffeured around in his own taxi in the sixties, and that the Duke of Edinburgh puts on a cloth cap and drives himself around in one of his own, but the driver wasn't him. As he held the door open for me I found him to be young and handsome, with a smooth black skin which looked as if it had been French polished. On the way he told me he came from Somalia. I thought he was probably gay.

Dinner With Alden

HAMPSTEAD WAS ONCE A separate village on a hill overlooking London. It's always had arty associations since Constable lived up there a couple of hundred years ago and painted serene watercolours of the city in the distance below. There are inns near the Heath where decades before his time highway robbers would retire of an evening to count what they had plundered from their prey among the meek majority of the population who had come about their goods and cash more conventionally, by honest toil.

Alden lived in a substantial, but not the largest, house in a short leafy street that curved in a shallow crescent out of a busier thoroughfare and back to it again so sleepily that you could pass by and miss it. It was part of the late-Victorian expansion of the village when successful painters, architects, writers and industrialists more mundanely enriched from the manufacture of civilised requirements such as stained glass had built sedate red brick mansions from which to enjoy its healthy breezes and views. Nowadays you have to be hedge-fund-manager, or Russian-mafia rich to live in them, as if the ghosts of the highwaymen had come back in their benevolence towards their successors in thievery to reclaim it for them. I wondered how designing art galleries and writing scraps of minimalist music for the BBC's classical radio station could vouchsafe such luxury.

But the real shock awaited the opening of the heavy, panelled door, like the rest of the house a strange mixture of the gothic, the rustic and the Georgian. For inside was another world, all whiteness and steel and frosted glass and creamy-grey ash wood panels, like some sort of semi-organic po-mo space station. The place reeked of money. Not inherited wealth, but new wealth trying to prove its lack of vulgarity with stripped-down, unfussy but user- in the sense of owner-friendly functionalism, and as wealth will, succeeding in its goal – a seamlessly inverted form of ostentation. To gut a house like this and refit it thus would cost more than building from scratch.

How? But it was not my place to enquire. Alden would tell me in his own good time, as he might tell me about his physical impairment, or otherwise. Anyway there was neither time nor opportunity, for it was Alden himself I found opening to me. There was no sign of Lam, nor, it became quickly obvious, of any other guests.

I didn't miss Lam's attendance, creeping around

watching everything, and was not too surprised about the other guests, whose existence I had discounted as possibly notional. It was a house without switches and doorknobs: curtains opened and closed at the press of a pad, lights switched off and on as if they read somebody's desires: the lift played the almost imperceptible tinkling song of ascending larks, the bathroom the distant roar of Icelandic waterfalls; the fridge conversed softly with you, the bar told you what it had in stock in the camp voice of Hal from *2001* – but only if asked – and never tried to lock you out.

A central computer, with a console on Alden's wheelchair arm, controlled the workings of the whole house. It was a futurologist's wet dream, and Alden had somehow made it happen. I didn't actually like the house at all: it seemed to me without soul. I was accustomed to the clutter and colour of Little Venice living space. It was my own office writ large, expanded to drive out all else; too orderly, too wilfully so. But awe pushed my reservations to the periphery of vision, so I saw them without affect, small as through reversed opera glasses, like some other person's altogether. I felt the emptiness; I knew I didn't like it, and I didn't care.

As I waited for whatever was going to happen next I watched Alden's stealth wheelchair move swiftly and quietly as if it had a mind of its own, programmed to interpret Alden's will before he knew it himself. His living area was vast, multi-levelled, bleached of colour, empty, tidy and full of space-enhancing perspective tricks, designed to be photographed, filmed, not lived in. Lighting make soft, calculated patterns on walls and ceilings. There were no paintings: low sofas and chairs were hard edged: this to my mind was a temple to a stylish discomfort: inverted *Gemütlichkeit*. Other than the patch of brilliant colour on Alden's shirt, and the flood of soft evening light through the vast angular windows, I could have been back in my step-grandfather Wallace's studio. He was a disciple of Corbusier and liked nothing better than all things ugly, brutal and plain.

Trying hard, I managed to find something I rather liked: a cabinet made in bur oak, or at any rate veneered with it – a cool, poised, modern design, if perhaps too ornate for its setting. A frieze of naked wooden caryatids stretched up along the front panels as if to the skies of Mount Olympus, half in and out of the wood. It was very clever. I said so. Alden's face lit up. It had been especially made for him by Lukas – what, didn't I know the name? – a very distinguished Czech craftsman, who interpreted the inorganic through the organic – I looked puzzled – 'Wood and wires,' Alden explained, 'wood and wires and these days Bluetooth' – which didn't help much. He told me he had paid £18,000 for it two years back, and already it had increased in value by one third. I was a little disappointed in him showing himself to be so mercenary. Should not a beautiful piece be valued for its quality? But Alden could be excused: he was in a wheelchair: it was okay, surely, for him to marvel at his own successes, no doubt so dearly and nobly achieved?

He was a piece of work himself: most decorative in white chinos and a black silk shirt exploding with hand-painted scarlet roses, on leafy stalks complete with pointed thrusting thorns. I had not been wrong: he was decidedly exciting – trapped by his physical disability but also enhanced by it. He exuded energy and the erotic charisma of those who know what they want, mean to get it, and show no doubt. Of course Mrs Matilda Weiss had come down to apologise. Of course he had picked me up, fate having put me in his way to save his face; he induced opportunities as he progressed through the world.

'I like the shoes,' he said, and took my jacket, and the chair whizzed off gracefully, and without apparent instruction, so he could hang it on a peg. There was no sign of a proper clothes hanger, and I was nervous that the peg would stretch the wool fabric and leave a mark. I didn't say anything.

Now was my moment to say that I was Vanessa not Joan, but I missed it. 'O what a tangled web we weave,' as my grandmother used to quote, 'when first we practise to deceive.' But as Joan this evening I felt summery and alive and light, and free to hate his domain, and say so. Intellect, doubt and the habit of analysis can be a burden. Just to live here in the present, without relating it to past or future, is to be happy. A garment is only a garment. I would not sulk. Let it be. Let it spoil.

'It's not exactly cosy in here,' I said. He laughed and said it wasn't meant to be, it was to impress clients. I could come into the kitchen if I felt more at home in the real world, and so we went through. It looked like the Pompidou Centre but human scale. Pinky grey granite and interlacing pipes, but at least there was a pot or pan or two.

The table was laid for three. I was afraid that meant Lam, but Alden said his friend was coming by with take-out Japanese on the way home from an evening class. I wondered if the friend was male or female. Take-away Japanese seemed rather a come down but Alden was clearly a busy person and complicated food, as I had noticed when he devoured the chicken sandwich with the over sour mayo at the Bound Beast, was not high on his list of priorities.

Nor, when it came to it, was wine. He had opened a bottle of Petrus Chateau la Fleur 2004 Pomerol; three glasses stood waiting. It was expensive, but still *en primeur*, much too young for drinking. The bottle would have set him back, I reckoned, about £50. If he'd only lay that down for a couple of years it would fetch him double, triple. It was reassuring to realise he didn't know everything. I nearly said it was a pity women didn't increase in value with age as did works of art, rather the contrary – but I let that one lie.

'I thought you said dinner-party,' I said meanly.

'Sushi in the kitchen with one other doesn't quite make it.' I was pissed off that if it wasn't a dinner party, it wasn't a tête-à-tête either: three was a crowd.

'They cancelled, full of apologies,' said Alden absently. 'They had to be in Milan.'

'So who didn't have to go to Milan?'

But he'd slipped into his own thoughts, and just for a split second I saw the attention he was paying to me was not his spontaneous priority, before – almost seamlessly – he switched it back on, but raised his voice slightly, turning away from me as he spoke.

'Oh, the other friend is Ray Franchi, the painter – does that impress you? Ray's pretty famous, but he's not the kind of guy to blow his friend out when he's got a better offer. That's why I like him – you'll like him.'

I hadn't heard of him and said as much. People do not usually introduce their dinner guests as 'famous': it's just a bit insecure. But perhaps that too goes with being in a wheelchair. I was doing my best to write down Alden's faults. I did so want him to be Mr Wonderful, powerful, noble, wounded but romantic.

At least it was less worse that the third person was a man. If it was a woman it could have been La Weiss. I asked if there was anything I could do, warm plates or something? It was a very Joan thing to say. Alden laughed indulgently as though he preferred me to be a child whose ignorance he enjoyed enlightening.

'Sushi's cold,' he said.

'It may not all be sushi – some Japanese food is hot,' I said. He put up his hands in surrender.

'If that's what you want to do,' he said, 'that's all right. Make yourself at home.'

I found some square white dinner plates and put them in the oven to warm. Then I realised I didn't know how to switch it on. I asked him if he would, and he said, sure, but I didn't see him touch any controls on his wheelchair, so I guess the oven stayed off.

'This Ray,' I said, 'is he always late?'

'On the whole, yes,' he said, looking me over, with neither dispassion nor lust, but with the sort of interest with which a bookie might appraise a racehorse. He grinned, his eyes wide and full on; it was shtick, but the grin was twinkly, which gratified. And at least he was paying me attention now. 'He's a genius; that's what they do.'

Alden went on: Ray occupied the top floor of the house as a studio. He'd take me up there to see it some time. I'd like it a lot better.

'It's nice and messy,' he said, 'bless his little socks. Well cosy. Personally, I couldn't live like that. Ray sleeps, works, farts up there. He doesn't fuck up there – he doesn't fuck anywhere – quite the neurotic boy prodigy.'

I asked what Ray was famous for, and Alden said for not finishing commissioned work on time. I gathered that one of Alden's clients, Lady Daisy O, had commissioned a painting installation from Ray to be the centre piece at a gallery Arts-Intrinsick had 'newly created' in Daisy's 'palatial home'. Alden had a tendency to go into website language when he mentioned Arts-Intrinsick; I presumed because this was commercially effective in America, and that he retained his irony. The installation was supposed to be in place by September; but Ray was suffering from creative block, which was a bloody nuisance, Alden suggested, by no means least to himself.

'You know where he is then – he is coming?'

'Oh yes,' said Alden. 'He goes to evening classes twice a week.'

'How interesting,' I said questioningly. 'What humility in someone so famous.'

Alden said it wasn't what I thought. Maybe he was about to explain, but at that point the doorbell rang: a gentle cooing noise. One of Alden's touch pads winked, and a minute or two later a small, balding goat-like man sidled in; he looked like Woody Allen dressed in Columbo's clothes. He held a paper carrier bag in each hand, and the right-hand one was dripping black soya sauce onto the kitchen floor. I gestured prettily towards it, concerned.

'Shall I find a cloth?' I asked. Ray seemed to startle easily: he saw what I meant and dropped both bags.

'Stop agitating,' said Alden. 'No need. Both of you. Lam clears things up in the morning.'

Ray's looks suggested an ethnicity that was not entirely from northern Europe – I thought maybe one parent English, and the other perhaps Algerian, or Moroccan. He was attractive because he was buzzing with energy and you instinctively wanted to tidy him up and mother him. I was sorry to think he had sexual difficulties. It seemed a waste.

Ray looked at me, his tongue between his lips.

'Look at that arse,' he said. 'My God!'

And Alden reproached him, saying, 'This is Joan Bennet. She's a respectable girl. Shake hands?'

Ray came to me and kissed me on each cheek: then on the mouth, and his tongue went right in. I was a little tall for all this in my Jimmy Choo heels, but he made it, all the way up.

'You mean ripe for the plucking?' Ray wrinkled his nose at Alden. 'Another one you can use and abuse?'

Alden's smile vanished. He looked as dangerous as a man in a wheelchair can: a tiger champing the sawdust behind bars, growling and helpless to act.

'Only kidding Dilly-boy,' said Ray, a little quickly. 'Just,' he shrugged, 'kidding.'

'Joan teaches kindergarten, in Essex,' said Alden, calming down. 'The only boyfriend she's ever had just walked out on her after six years. She's a stoic; she's rising above it, aren't you? She's not only beautiful, she has a beautiful soul, unlike you – or me. I want you to be nice to her, so be kind.'

Ray looked genuinely chastened, almost puzzled, but not about anything obvious.

'Sorry,' he said to me. 'I don't meet many nice

girls nowadays. It's good there are still some in this unyielding world,' and I forgave him.

'She's Plymouth Brethren,' Alden added.

'I'm OTO,' said Ray.

'Not Plymouth,' I said. 'Just Brethren. We're allowed to wear colours. I love clothes. I borrowed these from my friend Amy. I feel very wicked. What's OTO? Why do you think the world is unyielding – do they tell you that?'

'Sweet,' said Alden.

The Japanese food was not from a wholesaler's freezer. It was sushi, and I've never been to Japan, but it was as good as London ever had on offer. I ate with chopsticks and they marvelled at my ability. I said my previous boyfriend had been half Chinese. I was impressed by my own facility for making up off-the-wall stories, and even more, by Ray's and Alden's gullibility.

A Chinese geologist!

'One day they'll find oil,' said Alden. 'Then they'll be invincible.'

Alden had sent Ray off to wherever you kept wine cool in a futurologist's dream house, and he had returned with some refreshing and incensy Chassagne-Montrachet. We ate fat pink belly-tuna in thin slices, and translucent melty halibut in thinner ones, and big shrimp with spindly thin heads I'd never seen before.

'It's flown in,' said Alden, 'this too.' I asked what

the little orange eggs were and he said, 'Flying fish roe. Tobiku.'

'To be ku or not to be ku? To be cool or not to be cool?' said Ray. 'I once had some in San Francisco with a special wasabe which nearly killed me, it was so hot. I was with these Japanese who were commissioning me. I just had to sit there and smile.'

'Smiling means you're pissed off in Japanese,' said Alden.

'Bollocks, Alden,' said Ray. 'It entirely depends on the context.'

The wine was going to his head. Was it disinhibiting some resentment baggage he had about his friend – his generous landlord?

'Whatever you say, Ray,' Alden replied, and smiled at me.

'Thank God you're not Japanese then.' I was pink and giggly. The wine wasn't just going to my head. Maybe it was the female flying fish hormones as well, but my loins were loosening; my cunt was telling me I was among friends, and I believed her.

'Shouldn't we be sitting on the floor?' I said, then felt myself blushing. But still I didn't know why Alden was in a wheelchair, or how it affected him, and it still seemed further than ever from the right moment to ask. He behaved as if it didn't register with him, so why should it with anyone else. He didn't seem offended. I withdrew into my shell, protecting my embarrassment, which despite this reasoning needed time to dissipate.

Ray was telling me what OTO stood for – the Ordo Templi Orientis: an Aleister Crowley study group, an aspect of the Golden Dawn movement. They met once a month in New Southgate: a nondescript outer suburb of little Diary-of-a-Nobody-style Edwardian semi-detached houses seemed a funny place for an Order, the Order of the Temple of the East. Maybe they were lying low, keeping their powder dry.

Ray was on the Fourth Path, he told me. And explained that the Templum Orientis was the sacred legacy of Aleister Crowley, who was born in 1875 and died just after the Second World War, voluptuary, philosopher and occultist. It was the child of his study of Eastern eroto-gnostic techniques, amongst which the Tantra.

'Eroto-gnostic is a bit of a mouthful,' I ventured.

'Hard to swallow?' said Alden, and they both burst out laughing. I laughed, but less wildly. What Ray had omitted was the nom de guerre by which Crowley was affectionately known by his followers and less so by his enemies: the Beast 666.

'The Fourth Path to what?' I asked.

'Self knowledge,' he said. 'And with it the Golden Dawn.'

'What happens when it dawns?' I asked. 'Golden showers? I don't do that sort of thing.'

I giggled again, but the men kept pointedly silent. Alden closed his eyes, as if employing a meditative exercise to keep calm. His face was a mask of frozen detachment.

Ray breathed once deeply, and as he exhaled spoke with deliberate patience, like a driving instructor with an inexperienced pupil.

'No,' he said. He wrinkled his forehead and held my gaze. Alden's eyes remained closed like a Buddha's. 'You master yourself and others,' said Ray, 'through the working of Amalantrah.'

'So if I was a girl,' I said, seriously.

'Which you are,' said Alden, opening his eyes, genial again.

'I could mistress myself?'

'Is that the last of the gunkan?' asked Ray.

'You ate all the sea urchin already,' said Alden. 'We watched you.'

'Sorry,' said Ray. They both suddenly seemed to be switched over to automatic pilot, like Alden's wheelchair. Shortly after that Ray went on upstairs. Alden and I were left alone together.

'I know what you've been wondering,' said Alden. 'Right back from when we met.'

'Do you?' I said. My voice was small, involuntarily tightened, and I heard how cute it sounded to Alden: like Marilyn Monroe.

'I know, don't I?' he said. I nodded. I felt like a little girl, and lowered my eyelids like a geisha. I was a little girl-sushi, my legs bound up in delicate tight straps, and served up on a plate: I was about to be delicately taken up and dipped in fiery wasabe and eaten.

'You want to know why I am in this wheelchair, how it happened, what use I am for sex.'

'Well,' I said. 'Yes!'

'Then shall we go into the bedroom?'

He rolled ahead. I followed. Doors opened magically to his will.

In The Bedroom

THE DOOR SLID OPEN to show a spacious room, long rather than wide. There was little bare white to be seen, which was a relief if only because the walls were almost all mirror, into one of which a plasma screen as big as a small shop window was let in as flush as a piece of giant marquetry. There were a couple of odd-shaped velvet chairs, like something out of Jules Verne had he ever set a scene in some Victorian brothel, or described a Parisian *maison close*. Otherwise there was just the ample bed.

Ample, of course, is a relative term: this one would have been more than ample for this evening even if Alden's other guests had not had to divert to Milan. What a bed! It had four posts, but no canopy or side rails; just the ceiling looked down, mirrored like everything else. The posts were again in bur oak, with more of the famous Mr Lukas's caryatids crawling up them; they didn't have to hold anything up. I daresay the bed, like its companion piece the cabinet, had increased in value by more than a third since the first day of its occupation. It was big enough to accommodate an orgy, rather higher than normal, spread with a pure white quilt, patch-worked, each white square of a different texture. I saw silks, cottons, linens, damasks, velvets – and why someone should go to all that bother I couldn't think: it was still just a plain white quilt. But there were some ten plump, silk, scarlet, startling pillows strewn across it. Alden had quite an eye for contrast.

'Relax,' he said, 'lie down. Find out.' I started to unlace my Jimmy Choos but he said he preferred me to keep them on. So I lay down on the bed, demure and obedient, legs politely together; trying to think and feel like a nice, quiet nursery school teacher whose ambition was to make a difference. I would method act this through and enjoy. I hoped he was right and the Jimmy Choos would not leave dirty marks on the pristine counterpane. It would probably be okay. I had only had to walk in them between my house and the cab and then to the house this end, the weather was dry, and it had been nothing but marble or carpeted floors ever since but all the same I had to overcome the reservation of habit.

'The pale green and the red,' he said. 'Unexpected. But it works. It's holistically connected: colour, machinery, sex. The idea is to follow the Ophidian currents and transmute sexual energy into artistic energy. And vice versa, of course.'

'Green and red are powerful together,' I said. 'The clash is good.'

I lay still compliantly on the bed. I was not sure what he meant by the Ophidian current but I had come across the sex-machinery link before, on the wilder shores of French philosophy. Phrases flitted into my head – I have an eidetic memory: that is to say I can recall large chunks of information as if I were seeing it on the page. It isn't perfect in my case, but I locate information by its place on the page, and then recall the page. It doesn't suggest one is more intelligent than other people, just better able to retrieve information. My sisters, the twins Alison and Katharine, have the same gift of photographic recall, but theirs is even more effective and accurate.

'Sex/machinery', and there I was with pages on Raymond Roussel, 1877-1933 (the latter date was his suicide), writer of the play *Out of Africa*; 'positive exploratory dreams taken to delirious extremes; seeker after the master sex machine, which will function independently of time and space and change the world.' Make a difference. We all long to make a difference. Little Joan, lying here on the bed, a fauvist picture in clashing red and green, waiting for Alden's secrets to be revealed, longing for the turmoil in her head to stop. All that ever really got it to stop was sex, and occasionally shopping.

'What is Ophidian?' I asked.

'It's lizard form stuff,' he said shortly. 'Stargaterelated.' He was barely paying attention, absorbed in rebalancing lighting at a lower level.

More pages. Roussel, forgotten now, but a powerful influence on Duchamp, painter of *The Bride Stripped Bare by her Bachelors, Even.* 'Even' what, I wondered: 'even' me? More pages scrolled by. The notion of the early avant-garde, that art is about ideas, not things. The dreamy yet hard-edged image, seductive. In literature, Roussel, Proust, Kafka, Wyndham Lewis; in art the Futurists, the Vorticists, the toppling towers of Depero, eventually Pollock and Warhol; in music the sense of prolonged orgasmic action propelled into eternity through ceaseless, fantastic repetitions; the complexities of minimalism – Reich and Riley, Phase Patterns – Steve Reich, Philip Glass, John Cage, Max Headroom. In all these forms see complexity, repetition to the point of insanity, the creation of spontaneously inventive movements, the fountain of creation spewing forth doubt as well as marvel. Mechanical discourse in language, art, music and now sex too? Now finally with the advent of the computer those early dreams of the avant-garde come true, for is this not the apogee of complexity? A world of ideas not things? The virtual world more real than reality: the computer the ultimate sex machine, bringing sex-in-the-head to the millions? Who wants the real thing any more: live sex has got too dangerous. Thus Bill Gates, the new messiah, came along and saved the world.

The notion of play on the mirrored form, sexual

procedure involving abnegation, imprisonment and liberation? I was to be the idea made flesh? The next stage? If I looked into any corner of the room I could see a thousand thousand me's: a million brides stripped bare of her bachelors. If I sat up and looked forward I could see a warp and woof of sound wave graphics on the computer screen; perhaps I was to be something to so with the composition of *Thelemy: The Silence of the Senses*?

But all the brides that were me were sure of one thing: I/we wanted fucking, soon. The intellectual context was another way – interchangeable with any on the menu – of evoking a tension that needed to be released. I feared this was to be more about Alden's artistic fantasies than actual sex. Locking my hands behind my head, I flexed my knees taut and stretched to relax, shut my eyes, and breathed peacefully and deeply as if I were in the final phase of a yoga class.

Then he pounced. The shock was elemental.

The bed tipped to the left and lowered: I rolled gently and opened my eyes again as he pulled my head towards him and into his lap, grasping my hair. His penis rose monumental like a serpentine obelisk from his lap, his belt undone and his trousers parted like the curtains of a stage. He guided my head firmly as a ballet coach might correct an angle of posture, and thrust his thing, graceful and powerful as a wild animal, into my mouth. I could not, I cannot, find a word – the common ones are banal and facetious and it was the opposite to that – but it was so alive. An animal both hunting and hunted, both pouncing and leaping to safety, both tiger and stag. My question was answered: he was right to treat his need of a wheelchair as a minor issue. There was no handicap in this central expression of his maleness.

It was very large and thick on this, the first occasion. At other times it was to seem slimmer but longer, more probing than plunging. Taken by surprise as I was, disturbed in my meditations on Roussel and the metaphysics of the avant-garde, I had to consciously remember to breathe through my nose, as the penis – the first and only one in my life – swelled in my throat, and I relaxed my muscles, opening, not defending, so that the choking next moment stayed just ahead, never reached.

When I got the chance to ease my neck for a second or two, and raised my eyes I could see past him to the huge swirling screen on the wall and I heard the sound waves as I saw them. Alden, seeing me do so, either let his penis go, or found it going limp, and pushed my mouth away, gently but deliberately. His wheelchair seemed to float back from no obvious instruction on his part, and likewise the bed slowly levelled itself. I was affronted. He had offered me no likely sexual pleasure – it was outrageous. This should not be like the Hotel Olivier: this was a proper date. I needed – oh please – the barest little token of courtship, if only an ear nibble, a kiss, a stroke of my inner thighs, a brush of lips, a tentative gesture, something, anything: not this, a penis only filling the stretched mouth, my participation limited to my endurance, no affect on either side. I needed something to respond to, with the normal female skills: to encompass, encourage and entice.

Alden meant to find 'artistic holism' at my sexual expense. I was to be the catalyst for his search for authenticity. I got up and stood in front of him, my legs astride, my hands on my hips. I was about to tell him what I felt, make a statement in reasonable terms, no criticism, just gently tell him what was real, but he was too quick for me. His chair brought him forward, and he grabbed my hair and forced my mouth back down to its slave labour. I really tried to move my head away but he would not let my hair go. I pulled, he tugged. Then, just as suddenly as it entered, the penis was withdrawn. The humming frequencies and rhythms subsided.

'You see,' he said, 'it works. That was what you wanted to know.'

'But you didn't come,' I said.

'That's a different matter,' he said. 'I like to do it properly.'

I sat back on the bed and he told me neutrally as a police report that when he was fifteen he had been making fireworks with a friend; there had been an explosion, and he was blown backwards down a flight of stone steps and hit his head. He was in a coma for four weeks, and when he woke up his legs didn't work anymore, from the knees down.

'So you've never had normal sex?' I asked.

'I don't have normal legs,' he said, with an edge in his voice he had not yet shown me till now.

'I'm really sorry,' I said. 'I meant, were you still a virgin when you – lost them?'

'I haven't lost them,' he said, his voice really hard. 'They just don't work.'

This was not to be an easy area for conversation.

'No,' he said, deciding to make things easier for me. 'I wasn't a virgin. I started pretty young. Does that make it better, or worse?' If he now had problems with his potency he hadn't started out that way.

'Perhaps it's to do with explosions?' I asked. 'You dread them?'

I had heard of men like this but had never met one: who can go on and on, but fear ejaculation.

'You're very intuitive,' he said. 'Thank you.'

'What happened to your friend – does he have the same problem?'

'He died in the explosion,' he said. 'And I lived, in a cloud of unspoken blame, from his parents and everybody else.'

'And you blamed yourself.'

'It was my fault.'

'That must make things worse,' I said, and he said yes, he thought it had. And then we were silent. I wanted to ask where all the money came from – if he came from a clerical family in Yorkshire there wasn't likely to have been much around to begin with, but I didn't ask. He would tell me that too sooner or later.

'All right,' he said. 'To business.'

He rearranged a scarlet cushion to his taste; laid my white arm along it, eyed me a little longer. Then with another of his sudden movements, sudden artistic decisions like a painter attacking a canvas with his brush, he pushed the top of my dress down and hooked the breasts out of my bra. He did not bother to undo the hooks, let alone acknowledge their mundane existence. It looked good in the mirror on the ceiling. An artistic pose, if there was a digital camera up there, hooked into the computer.

He looked at me a little longer as if considering the design I made: judging me as a painter judges and weighs up a model before he begins. He rearranged a breast and brushed both nipples with silky soft fingers – no horny manual worker he: they stood erect at once. I have nice plump and round breasts, with broad semi-circles of white around the aureoles, and the nipples, which are pink, not brown or rough; they are neither perky, nor tip-tilted, nor minimalist in any way: they are substantial.

I made a move to rise, to cover my breasts – one's instinct for privacy surfaces at the oddest times – but he shook his head reprovingly and I stayed as I was. He was the choreographer, the one who instructed: I accepted instruction. I had already accepted the rules of engagement. Let what happened, happen. Consent is consent. And I owed it to him, and to his tragedy.

'Just look at that,' he said. 'Admire yourself.' The touch pad glowed, the pattern of lights in the room changed, and I seemed to come into sharper definition in the mirror. I thought I could quite fall in love with myself. Were I a work of art I'd pay anything to own me: a Boucher come to life, exotic and erotic, breathing, sucking, fucking, lovely.

My grandmother Molly, wife of the difficult Wallace, had been something of a courtesan in her time. The paintings she left me had no doubt been earned, as his Lordship sometimes brutally put it, on her back. I could see I might well have inherited Molly's temperament.

When I tore my eyes away from myself in all my loveliness, Alden, though wheelchair-bound, was nonetheless homo erectus, asserting the fact with his cock out, manoeuvering it as much for artistic effect as for his subjective pleasure. Its fleshy solidity flung back at him, at us, via a receding infinity of mirrors, back, and back, for ever in space and time. And I was out there with it, endlessly split and detached: the baroque play of the repeated mirrored form, the infinite complexity. I started thinking of Roussel again, but squashed the inclination before it ran away with itself.

The fingers of his left hand wiggled over the touch-pad console, and the whole wall on the right of the bed slid back to reveal another of the Lukas carved pieces, this time a walnut cabinet from which he took an ordinary cheap wooden walking stick. He thrust it into the air with a flick of the wrist, like a fencer testing the weight and balance of a foil, then he reached towards me with it and hoiked my skirt deftly, if roughly, up to my waist. My diamond navel-ring caught the light and twinkled.

'That's bloody real,' he said. 'It's vast.'

'No, no it isn't,' I lied, as Max denied the cash hidden under his bed. 'They're Chinese. You can get them at any Bazaar branch.'

The under-wire of the left cup had burst its protective seam and was sticking into the flesh beneath my arm, but I rose above that. With the walking stick he splayed my legs.

'Look again,' he said, but now I did not like what I saw. I was no longer Boucher; it could have been any stupid Essex girl making an exhibition of herself in a cheap trailer-park porn film. I moved my legs together in defiance. He let me.

'You'll get used to me,' he said. 'Just tell me if I go too fast.'

So he saw a future between us. My heart leapt – it was not an intellectual reaction: I swear it was banging against my chest. I remembered our dog Vera, how she would leap up with joy and nearly knock my father over when he came into the room.

'Stay just like that,' he said; the door slid open and the wheelchair glided away and out of the room. I felt bereft. With difficulty I eased out the wandering under-wire from my bra so it stopped jabbing into me: did that count as moving? I took the other one out to make them match, and dropped the two wire semi-circles onto the white carpet. I have pretty hands: the nails varnished today in the palest pink. They looked good against the white carpet, long, but not too long, elegantly oval.

He came back, the penis still pointing upwards and outwards like a crane, his shirt removed, his white chinos halfway down his thighs. His shoulders were very well developed, which was not surprising; his flesh was tanned. A fine figure of a man from the hips up, if you left out his legs which I had not yet seen. He brought with him the bottle of champagne (Cristal – I looked) and chocolates in a green and gold Harrods box.

'It isn't spiked,' he said. 'It hasn't been opened.' He eased off the mushroom cork very slowly so that there was barely a pop, and no explosive ejaculation, and swigged some from the bottle. He handed it to me, telling me to be careful not to spill any, which struck a slightly awkward note, as a man does who folds his clothes before he gets into bed with you. But I overlooked it. It was a very, very, white untainted coverlet and a man might well want to protect it. I swigged. It was smooth and prickly.

He opened my mouth and took one of the chocolates and pressed it in between my lips, a cherry chocolate liqueur; it burst in my mouth, spilling over my lips;

but he had a tissue at the ready and wiped my mouth carefully.

'Another?' he asked, and I nodded. One chocolate does lead to another in my experience, which is why I try to avoid them altogether, so it was a relief to have no choice. This one was Cointreau. The next was kirsch. My mouth was a gooey mass of chocolate, gradually dissolving. The cherry had been the best.

'That'll do,' he said. 'You've had enough.'

From a shelf in the Lukas cabinet he took out a shiny, brown leather corset and studied it; it was designed to fit from under the breasts to the crotch, with leather thongs in front for tightening.

'I'm going to require some help here,' he said. 'Sorry.'

And before I could protest bloody Lam was in the room, with his great spooky eyes, his pointy Roswell-incident face and white polo-neck. The two of them started fussing through the items on the cabinet shelves, like matrons at a Women's Institute bring-and-buy muttering to one another sporadically as they made the right selection.

Cuffs it was now to be, and anklets. I would have liked to have sat and had some say on the choice, but was too languid. There had been something in the chocolates: of course there had. No doubt they had left Harrods innocent and innocuous, but chocolates can be easily injected with a syringe. I decided it was odds on that that had been Lam's job. There's an Agatha

Christie story where the murderer has laced the kirsch liqueurs with cyanide because the almond tastes would blend.

They took their time trussing me up, very meticulous. Alden buckled my left wrist, Lam my right. Lam lifted me up and Alden used the walking stick to push a pretty pink silk coverlet under me to protect the quilt. I was glad they were so house-proud, but I wondered what they had in mind. A sharp tug with the hook of the stick and the French knickers tore. That was okay, they'd passed muster, and the fabric was so fine they'd already frayed a bit. Time they were thrown away. I leant forward helpfully while Alden buckled on the corset, pulling the cords so tight I felt the constriction on my ribs under my breasts, and my waist being cinched firmly in. It was not unpleasant.

Alden touch-padded and the bed posts slid nearer together. Cords tumbled down, like oxygen masks in a stricken airliner; the unromantic comparison made me smile and Lam peered down at me curiously, narrowing his eyes. He was now tying the left cuff to the right post but Alden shook his head and Lam desisted. I was grateful that my arms were not to be crossed but merely stretched. I wanted Alden to get on with whatever it was he up to: I wanted to turn the next page of the script.

I was pleased by this formality, the ingenuity. This was in a different league to cheap sex-shop handcuffs, which are so flimsy and ineffective you feel they have

Health and Safety certificates attached, or the silk ties men like to use for light bondage, which are so slippery one can usually wriggle out of them.

Lukas was a different matter altogether: colleague of Alden's in creativity and superstar artisanal, with his Rousselian union of sex and ingenuity, complexity, imprisonment and liberation, his own special master machine. Alden seemed to sense that my intellect was firing up again and started pushing more liqueur chocolates into my mouth, while Lam stood by with a tissue. Every now and then Lam, gently dabbing, blinked, and the closing and opening of his eyelids seemed to take forever, they had such an area to cover. He was the mad scientist's butler in a '30s Bela Lugosi movie.

Now the right ankle to the right post, the left to the left. There was some technical trouble here. One of the posts didn't slide properly, and stuck. Alden cursed Lukas. This annoyed me a little. Sod Lukas, it was taking the attention away from me. They made do as best they could but my legs were not parted as widely as they had planned. They used what Alden spoke of in impatient terms as a spreader instead: a rigid metal bar which went from ankle to ankle and served the same purpose.

I must have been taking too much of an interest in what was going on, because Alden, who clearly preferred me somnolent, now took his time in selecting a cherry liqueur from the box and I opened my mouth to receive it but instead he pushed it up my cunt as a kind of afterthought, with his long, welcomely accommodating fingers. I needed to be fucked but Alden seemed to have no such immediate intention: it just came nearer and nearer without arriving, like Xeno's paradox. I didn't even mind if Lam stayed around. He was more like an affect-free alien than anything. He probably didn't even have a penis any more than Spock did.

Little patches of mental clarity opened and closed in the downy cumulo-nimbus clouds I floated among, pain-free and comfy as heaven. Whatever was in the chocolates was making me feel very nice.

'The rich are different from you and me,' I mumbled to myself. 'They have better drugs ...'

Lam raised an eyebrow, but his eyes stayed impassive.

'What did she say?' asked Alden, but Lam just shook his head briefly and dismissively. Alden's wheelchair took him up to the head of the bed; he took each of my hands in turn and with a pair of nail clippers, carefully, took the nails of the first and second fingers down so they were really short and smooth, almost down to the quick. Thumb, third and little fingers stayed long, pinky-silvery and oval. It would look pretty odd tomorrow but I didn't care. Alden was marking me, as a cattle dealer might brand a cow. Let him. If I changed my mind about it in the morning I could always take the other nails down to match. Time would pass, nails, like hair, always grow.

I had only known Alden for a few hours. Very nice of me to be such a trusting person. I congratulated myself. Alden, disadvantaged by a sour fate, crippled since he was a boy, was my good deed for the day, and I felt good about it like a girl-scout helping a crippled man cross a busy highway.

'I do love you!' I confided in him. 'I want to cure you and make you whole. I want to make you happy.'

'What a sweetheart you are,' he remarked. 'But sshh – you don't need to speak, Joan my pet. Best not to say a thing.' And he gave me a delicate little kiss, which was bliss: the very first time our lips had touched, and it seemed extravagantly romantic.

'Pets need collars,' Lam spoke for the first time, and Alden frowned and gave a sage nod of assent. Lam foraged a studded leather dog collar from the cupboard, which matched the wrist straps and was as wide as I'd ever seen. Alden slipped it under my neck, raised my head, and buckled the collar round my neck, fastening it at the back. Lam handed him a leash which he clipped onto the collar, letting it hang loose – or so I thought, but now I could barely turn my head to see. But there was no mistaking it: an ordinary dog lead, just like the one we used to walk Vera, our over-demonstrative, annoyingly loving golden Labrador bitch. I thought this was touching and sighed affectionately and would have laid my head on one side but I could not. It would just have to stay high, as in a deportment class at school when we walked round with books on our heads. I felt proud, and saw great symmetrical dignity in the V-patterns my stretched limbs made in the overhead mirror.

I found I was singing the '70s' Coca-Cola song: 'I'd like to teach the world to sing in perfect harmony, I'd like to buy the world a Coke and keep it company.' That didn't go down well. I had forgotten the stricture to silence. I soon found I had a rather large red plastic ball in my mouth, attached by a ribbon tied round my head, and all I could do now was gurgle.

Lam then saw to my make-up, which seemed odd, but maybe butlers are trained to do anything. I don't usually wear a great deal – my skin being lovely enough without it, and my eyelashes naturally long and dark: I mostly stick with eye-shadow, eyeliner and eyebrow tweezers. He patted foundation on with his clammy hands, ringed my eyes with brown liner, brushed on sweeps of green and brown eye-shadow. He pencilled soft dark-blue kohl along the pale inside lower rims of the eyes. You feel vulnerable around the eyes, but I had to trust him. His hand did not falter. He lipsticked heavily round such of my lips as he could get at for the red ball-gag in my mouth, though the bright red he was using was so unsubtle it would never have made the first round to my dressing table. Then he rearranged my hair to hide the straps which held the gag in place.

Alden watched.

'Now Joan perfect dream partner,' said Lam.

I looked up at myself in the mirror and saw a

bondaged Barbie doll staring back. Then like a sulky child I took offence. Not at what had been done to me, the stripping away of individuality, but because I was attached to an ordinary dog lead of the kind anyone could buy in a pet shop. They had no right to treat a nursery school teacher like this. Alden obviously had all the money in the world. Wasn't I worth better than that? How could he skimp on the dungeon paraphernalia? I struggled, but with legs and arms held fast and the corset only comfortable if I lay still, my leeway was only an inch or two in any direction. 'That's enough!' I tried to say, but what came out was mewing. The ball gag muffled language. And I had lost interest in sex: anticipation can devour itself and be reborn as boredom. I felt very, very cross with Alden.

A sudden unexpected sensation up my cunt: another chocolate, I assumed, my mouth being too much hassle to get at or into. And then two more, pushing the others higher: my interest in sex returned. Whatever was in the chocolates was quick acting, and lasted I estimated about ten minutes, but time was hard to assess, as if it wasn't conforming to type but doing something that would interest Einstein.

The pattern of lights changed: I focused on the mirror above, vaulted with repeated me dolls. I was alone in the room. The door was open. Anyone could see in. There was no sign of Alden or Lam. Perhaps Ray might come down and see. I wouldn't want that. On the other hand he might rescue me. I was conscious suddenly of a tingling at the pulse point in my wrists, my ankles, under my breasts, which intensified and fell away at the same time as a pulsing humming sound began, rising and falling in volume – the hertz waves again, I thought, translated into sound. If I struggled the pitch changed. I tested it out a little. I had a vision of myself as part of some atrocious mechanised disharmony devised by avant-garde composer of evil genius: in other words, from first principles, Alden. It occurred to me that the tingling sensations came from areas where they place the pads if you get your electrocardiogram done. All this had been an elaborate feint, a cover for nothing more than wiring me up for hospital monitoring: I was nothing but raw recording fodder, to be subsumed into *Thelemy: The Silence of the Senses*.

Turn the page of the eidetic memory: here's the digest. Whatever's in the chocolates has worn off. I am beginning to feel stiff. The ball in my mouth is making my lips sore. I take refuge in thought. The Abbey of Thélème, Rabelais' creation, around 1530. 'How the Thelemites were governed: and of their manner of living.' The one governance: Do what thou wilt shall be the whole of the law – Fay ce que vouldras. A rule asking to be taken in vain by its adherents, for Rabelais' folk of the Thelemite community were 'free, well-born, well-bred and conversant in honest companies, and have naturally an instinct and spur that prompteth them to virtuous actions, and withdraws them from vice.' Ironically, it became the motto of Sir Francis Dashwood's Hellfire Club in the caves under his High Wycombe estate two hundred years later, where all kinds of sinister doings went on. Another century or so and 'Do what thou wilt shall be the whole of the law' became the call to arms of voluptuary and black magician Aleister Crowley, the self-styled Beast 666, born 1875, died 1947, who claimed that the Golden Dawn could be won through the focused attention of the base and depraved into their own voluptuary satisfactions. The thoughts become dangerous. I switch my mind to more immediate considerations.

How long am I to lie here? Supposing they never come back? Of course they will. My whereabouts are known, I came in a black cab. I can be traced back. Just to loosen the corset would be a comfort. It is crushingly tight. How did the Victorians live with these things? A twenty-one-inch waist was nothing to them. The lady's maid would put her foot in the small of your back and she'd pull the strings tight with all her strength. I have Lam for a lady's maid, unasked. My waist is 24 in normal times and from the feel of it it's squeezed down to 21. Alden has strong arms, understandably. I am sure I am dribbling, though I can't see any sign of it in the mirror above. The pattern of lights re-constellate around me. I am spotlighted. I can't turn my head to shade my eyes. I shut them, but it's so glaringly bright my eyelids can't keep it out, so I open them again and squint. Yes, it's true, I am dribbling. That's horrid, humiliating. Think of other things. This is own fault, you stupid cow. You should never be sorry for people. While I agitate the background drone rises in pitch. It seems to be picking up my heartbeat now.

I flee again into the world of facts.

The search for the dream-partner? Where had I come across that? More Crowley? Yes. 'First raise the sexual energies before sleep by constant sexual stimulation without orgasm, then concentrate onto a talisman bearing a requisite symbol, and in dreams the aroused libido will copulate with the dream-partner. The talisman will thus become magically charged, and would make a particular wish come true.'

My great-grandmother visited Aleister Crowley in his house in Primrose Hill Road, down the hill from Alden's place, up the road from mine. It was 1929: she went along in terrified anticipation, seeking a spell that would release her from love, but found a scene of shockingly inane domestic decorum: the Beast holding a skein for his mother while she rolled wool from it into a ball, the better to knit his winter jumper.

But her friend, Nina Hammet the sculptor, found him otherwise three years later in his apartment at Ninety-Three, Jermyn Street. Tales of Satanic masses, witchcraft, sacrifice of virgins and sexual excess of every kind at his Abbey of Thélème in Cefalu in Sicily had been titivating newspaper readers for years. Nina recorded the overwhelming smell of incense, mysterious fires which would burst into flame around the room, burn vigorously and then just as suddenly douse themselves, and quite horrid portraits on the walls of the mysterious entities which came to Crowley in visions. She left as soon as politeness permitted. When he subsequently sued her for describing him in print as a 'black magician', he lost. The collapse of an unwise libel case, as so often, rubbished his position in society. He was shunned and excoriated. Nevertheless the cult of Crowley lingers on. Think about it, Joan. Knights of Thelemy resurrected in Southgate. Ray a student. Alden with his atonal symphonics, the thelemic silence of the senses. Higher powers. Control over others. The Will, for good or bad. This is bad. With a shiver of recognition, I fear that on the Day of Reckoning I might be caught on the wrong side.

The music drones on at a pitch which is now like a soft breathing purr, and it's sending vibrations through my body which seem to have anaesthetic powers. None of me is hurting. And it's sending me to sleep. I am broadcasting back to myself my own soporific narcosis. A feedback loop of sleep. I have the brainwave that you could market this drone and make piles of money. But no other thoughts succeed. I sleep.

My awakening is shocking. I am almost without restraints, lying on my side, though my right leg is up by my left shoulder, pushed up and held there by one of Alden's strong hands. The lights are dim; the ceiling mirror is blacked out. The gag-ball is still fixed in my mouth; other than the fact that Alden, naked, is driving his penis into my vagina from behind, I am relatively free. It is a patient rhythm, a regular, mechanical piston. In – thump, out – thump, in – thump, out – thump, goes the pile driver. His resolution and determination, just not his impetuosity, is most impressive. For me, the wished-for consummation has come, and it's pretty good. Remembering it now I think of the William Blake line: 'What is it women do in men require? The lineaments of gratified desire'! With every steam-hammer drive of his, my inner answering self responds. I can hear my own cries, and his gasps. I feel ecstasy welling up gradually, to the unbearable and beyond, the culmination, the after shocks, only slowly fading … the best kind. Thank you, Alden.

Perhaps for Alden the dream partner indeed approaches. It isn't me. He grinds and pumps on. He could stop now so far as I am concerned. The evening must surely soon be over. Rationality must return. Now he has both my hands in one of his, together in front of me: the angle has changed, but the beat continues remorseless. The other hand releases the tie round my head so I'm able to force the gag-ball out with my tongue. I cry out, because the ache when my mouth muscles revert to their normal form is extreme, yet exciting: if this goes on will I become a full-blown masochist? Suddenly I want more. My arse arches towards him of its own account.

And then he stops, and withdraws, and says, 'I'm sorry, Joan. I still can't.'

Or won't, or won't! How men will punish women by failure to complete sex. It is strange to be called by my name, even though it is not the right one. I have quite forgotten I had an identity. I try to ignore the hollow feeling in my cunt, now there is nothing in it, and become quite maternal, and when I have recovered some self-control I say: 'It's all right, there, there,' and so on.

To which he says, 'No, actually, Joanie, it is not all right,' and I feel I have let him down, I have failed as a woman. I have failed to neutralise the trauma of the past. The explosion that haunts him still. I see the eager, handsome youth, the chemicals stolen from the school lab, the boy playing with fire: the mistake, the shock of realisation, the roar, the pain, the dark, the waking to the reality of the half-life of the future, then the triumph of great difficulties heroically overcome, of fortune achieved – but the trauma remains. He still can't trust the world. Fulfilment can't be reached. The body triumphs but the soul fails. Tears of compassion fill my eyes.

My earlier paranoiac fantasies, that I was part of some musical composition, have vanished, only to be replaced by maudlin sentiment, which I wish to disown even as I feel it. I hope it is something to do with the drugs I have been given. I dash away the tears, glad that my hands are free to do such a thing, before Alden notices.

I have been fucked, and not fucked. I am confused.

I am more Vanessa than Joan again. I want to get home, if only in order to re-establish some kind of sanity. My mouth is recovering, but my arms have been pulled in their sockets and I am beginning to feel it. My knees ache: the spreader-bar kept my legs unnaturally straight and my ankles apart for too long, and my cunt is sticky from sodding chocolate of all things. I need a bath and I want a rest, and I am not sure what I feel about Alden, except now I can see his poor helpless legs, and they are too thin for the rest of him.

'I'll come back tomorrow,' I hear myself saying. 'Maybe you'll be used to me by then. I'm sure we'll do better. Only – please – could we somehow do without Lam?'

He thought about it. His prick had subsided, and lay, a great long lobcock thing, red from exercise and abrasion against over-narrow loins. He pulled the pink silk over himself, modestly, as I sat up. He did not like to be looked at. I wondered at my own confidence in expecting he would want to see me so soon, even at all. And I would like three or four days to recover from this.

I was off the bed, piecing together the rags of my dress, abandoning the French knickers, running my fingers through my hair to put some sense back into it, rubbing my neck to help the marks from the collar buckles go away. His eyes follow me.

'I'll send a taxi at 7.30 tomorrow,' he said, eventually.

'We'll try and do without Lam if that's what you want. But I really think I need an assistant.'

I refrained from saying that once he had managed a complete sex act the elaborate foreplay – for so I had decided to think of it – we had gone through that evening would be unnecessary. It might even begin to seem absurd. But I had to let him come to that conclusion in his own good time.

Going Home

LAM APPEARED FROM NOWHERE, as was his talent, perhaps training, certainly his inclination, and said my car home was on its way. He followed me to the peg where Alden had left my Lacroix jacket stretching – cover myself with that and I could be moderately decent, at least to the superficial glance – and counted off a hundred fifty-pound notes, new and stiff, glowing in that relaxingly distinctive and agreeable rusty-orangey colour. Five thousand pounds. He took his time. He wanted to show me that I was nothing but a hired hand like him, just less permanent. I sat down while I watched him, the better to relieve the rubbing of my Jimmy Choo straps against a patch of chafed skin left by the the spreader-bar's metal anklets. Anklets should be stainless steel, but lined with at least leather, or better still sheepskin. The ball-gag had been simply plastic: at the very least it should have been silicon or leather. I didn't think Alden would have chosen them. I bet it was Lam.

He waited after he had given me the money. I couldn't believe this – now he wanted me to bloody sign for it.

I protested, just to wrong-foot him, to puncture his unctuous implied contempt, that I couldn't possibly take the money, that I did not want it, did not need it. Maybe I was an idiot. But I also told myself that if putting myself on Alden's staff at this stage of the relationship would collapse it, or if not, at any rate greatly weaken my hand, I might seem replaceable: another nursery teacher Joan would lie on the bachelor bondage bed. The world was no doubt full of them: impressionable and more or less occasionally unsatisfied girls who would put up with anything for a bit of attention. What you pay for up front can always be replaced. I was playing for greater stakes: I wanted him to want to share his life with me. Oh the fantasy! I was a girl from a good family, more than well educated, socially secure, his equal. He would surely recognise the Vanessa beneath my Joan disguise? He needed me. I could make his house into a home. I would cook – we would never have to get take-outs, however high class. I would teach him about wine: what age to drink what. He would teach me about everything else, and how happily I would learn from him. I would encourage him in his music: if he were happy with me it might even get better. With me he would soon be sexually rehabilitated: stem cell research might even lead to re-growth in his spinal cord so that he could walk again.

Christopher Reeve had died too soon but science might yet be in time to mend Alden. We would live happily ever after.

I knew as soon as I had these thoughts that they were absurd. These were the fantasies of the seventeen-year-old who believes that a kiss means love and marriage. Whatever was in the Harrod's chocolates had left me unhinged. The bundle of notes was tempting, even though taking them would tip me over the edge into unqualified, undeniable whoredom.

'You take,' said Lam, annoyed and impatient. He really did not like me. 'Taxi get you tomorrow same time. Mr Alden say: buy clothes, bring receipts. Model shoot here tomorrow. Mr Alden say your taste better than me: buy top quality; buy colour. No cheat Mr Alden.'

The long speech seemed to have exhausted him. I could hear the taxi outside. I shrugged; I took the money. My jacket had, as I feared, a nasty mark in it where it had been ruthlessly jammed over the designer peg: the beads and sequins made it quite heavy. Before I came back here I'd better sew on a ribbon tag so that at least it could get hung up properly, if I could find a needle and thread.

'Lam,' I said as I went, 'if there's to be any repeat of what happened this evening I want good quality gear in properly lined metal, preferably padded with real sheepskin or calf leather, Japanese silk bonds and definitely no plastic. Mr Alden deserves better.'

He just looked at me blankly. I don't think he knew what I was talking about. Perhaps Alden was just phenomenally mean; or perhaps Lam was deaf. Maybe I still wasn't speaking clearly because of being previously gagged.

It was the same cab, with a discreet, custom-made wheelchair hoist and no public hire license number on the back. The driver was the same sleek, beautiful young African who had delivered me. I asked him what his name was, and he said Loki. My voice really was a little blurry: my lips were swelling. Normally I would have asked how a taxi driver from Somalia happened to have the name of the Norse trickster god, but I was not sure he would make sense of what I was saying, and I didn't have the energy to enter into any protracted conversation with anyone at the moment.

Loki opened the door for me when we got to my house in Warwick Road, where the water of the canal reflected the moon and stars, and helped me out: looking at my sleepy eyes, my swollen lips, my mussed hair and torn dress, the thongs of my Jimmy Choos wrongly laced, he must have seen I was scarcely fit to be out.

He behaved as impeccably, courteously as if I were a lady of the land, which indeed I just about am, though not by bloodline: my mother's sister's husband's eldest brother is a baronet, and of course there is a connection with the dreadful Lord Wallace F.

Getting to Know You

I WOKE THE NEXT MORNING refreshed and none the worse for my experience. A good bath, some essential oils in it – camomile and a touch of angelica root – for aromatherapy; after a sound night's sleep whatever it was that had made me feel poorly was already cleansing out of my metabolism. Also, of course, sex always has a tonic after-effect.

The fact that I had £5,000 in cash and instructions to spend it on clothes made my step all the lighter. I called through to Max and said I had a migraine. I knew he would square it with the management: he owed me for the tennis champion, an incident that now seemed to me half a lifetime ago. His wife would be checking in this morning after an early arrival at Heathrow around nine and I wished them every happiness. Because of my ministrations he would be feeling less tense and have got a better night's sleep than otherwise: it is best to be in mental, physical and emotional nick for any kind of power games. Clinton may have been right when he maintained that blow jobs didn't count, in spite of the uproar from the feminists. It is a here-and-now kind of thing, and affection does not necessarily flow between sucker and sucked: nor should it, because it won't necessarily give rise to any sense of emotional obligation. 'But you and I made love last night, don't you love me?' is at least a reasonable kind of question, as requiring the Latin prefix 'nonne': the 'yes' of the yes? neither-or-both? no? trio: nonne? ne? num? 'I gave you a blow job last night – don't you love me?' if asked, must surely require the prefix 'num' if it's to be a sensible question at all.

Mouths and arses are not the most numinous receptacles of love in the longer term, though connecting at the time to the pleasure centres. Vaginas are obviously the more profoundly connected to the mixing and loving of male with female; new life is thus created, though that particular sacramental function these days gets overlooked.

I would have thought if I hadn't known better that Alden was gay. The houses of people who have had children, or even mean to have them, are different from those of people who live without the expectation; these are cleaner and more self-conscious than the dwellings of the breeding kind, more post-modern, metro-centric, reflecting a culture with a declining birth rate, where appearance is valued above function.

Personally I had what I wanted: a top floor in a house built a century and a half ago, and showing it, looking out over the Canal at one of the prettier topographies in London, with a shabby old kitchen and an ergonomic office stripped for intellectual action.

I decided, thinking about Alden, that what he needed was social approval, acceptance. Why else the Radio 3 music? He wanted to be taken seriously. He designed environments for people who wanted to display art, but there wasn't a single painting in his own place. The reason might well be that he doubted his own taste. The painting you buy is such a giveaway. At least mine were inherited so I wasn't responsible for them. Maybe he could make a living from the art and design business, but his lifestyle suggested that there was nothing ordinarily sumptuary about its funding. But what? Something he was ashamed of, perhaps. Was he an arms dealer, or manufacturing portable toilets, or importing false teeth, or diluting antibiotics like Harry Lime in *The Third Man*? Something that would douse conversation at dinner parties?

My mind was over-active again: a doctor once claimed I had Bipolar Two syndrome, the liveable-with, workably acceptable, up-and-down kind of manic depression, and when I was a student the university head-shrinks put me on lithium – but the side-effects were worse than the BP2: I just couldn't bear the way it slowed my mind up and it made my hands tremble, so I stopped. I learned instead to let my mind race, and enjoy the skill of controlling it like a rally driver does the gears of a car on the winding corniche roads of a mountain range.

Woo-hoo! I sang aloud. I tossed the soggy new July *Vogue* I was reading into the air, and watched it tumble into the loo like a shot bird. £5,000 cash! Hey! 'Nothing cheap, a lot of colour.' I leapt out of the bath, dried myself, and put £2,000 of it straight away between the pages of Jung, vol.13, *Alchemical Studies*. I slung on some Matalan jeans and a yellow T-shirt with the word 'So?', skipped my way to the taxi rank and headed for Knightsbridge with the rest.

Shop assistants can be very helpful, especially in SW1, where black-burkaed Arab wives and girlfriends wield their store cards in the designer boutiques, never given cash in case they use it to run away. They buy the fanciest clothes to wear beneath the shrouds, present their man the receipts, model the clothes for him, and their girl friends at the odd tea-party: then run round to the up-market thrift shops and exchange their purchases for cash. I would get Alden £5,000 worth of clothes: but I reckoned I had only to spend £3,000 doing it by deft recycling. £2,000 was what one of the more expensive professional girls would have charged for an evening's bondage and full sex at the end of it. If the money shot was missing it wasn't this girl's fault.

The small shops are not above changing a receipt for the sake of a sale, and some of the clothes you find are gorgeous, from A-list designers, only one or two wearers from the catwalk, and lingerie to die for.

You have to pay full price for shoes, though: I like the shoe departments in Harvey Nicks, so I went there and bought four pairs which set me back £1200, the most expensive an absurd pair of winter ankle boots by Stuart Weitzman in silver with a ruff of leopard fur and rather dangerous looking chrome heels, in a sale for only £320. Response to the butch-fey contrast of winter boots with a flimsy dress never fails. If I was to buy clothes to 'model' for Alden, who was paying, the least I could do was coincide my taste with what he liked – which I inferred was tasteful-and-expensive nuanced with a little vulgarity: good girl plays the tart.

I left all my packages to date with the girl in the shoe department, and took the escalators to the sunny Fifth Floor Bar and drank a glass of chilly Pouilly Fuissé, refusing the eyes of all the men who were trying to meet mine.

Instead I meditated upon Alden, his long strong cock, blushed and seasoned from use, lolling across the poor puny leg, and exulted in the feelings of my body, aching here, sore there, which are the reward of good sex and keep the memory of it alive. I wondered what Alden had meant about 'modelling', and had a fit of nerves that it might be just that: literally, and without the sex. But I took a grip on myself: I didn't quite think it would be. Some girls don't mind it: being hung in slings and bonds and left to dangle and twist, get whipped a bit, but just be observed, and not get any penetrative sex – but that seems totally pointless to me.

And I wanted to know more about Alden; one side of him seemed so open and friendly, honest and frank, with his bright eyes and floppy hair, traumatised, wounded, secretly vulnerable. He needs me. But he needs me – helpless. And, if he keeps an artist in the attic, what does he keep in the basement? Is he the new Bluebeard – or Bluetooth – seeing sex as technology: one half man, one half sexual pleasure by remote control ...?

He longs for acknowledgement as a creative genius, to be known as a great musician, respected not by the vulgar mass, not as a sing-along celebrity but up there in the ethereal zone of the avant-garde, ahead of the game with a fusion of the aleatory and techno-minimalism. His tastes and influences were catholic, from Webern to Satie, Ives to Varèse, Cage to Reich and Terry Riley, Brian Eno to Iggy Pop, all coming into full frontal and final flood in Alden, worshipper at the shrine of the Golden Dawn.

My brain is running hares again. I've been staring into space, but I notice a man across the circular bar from me who supposes my attention is fixed on him. Shit! He's an Arab in a very good suit and rather too much gold jewellery. He will have a very fast car and a tasteless flat somewhere behind Harrods, with a drinks bar and a water bed. He will have a long penis, will take Cialis every day for breakfast and be determined to get his money's worth before it wears off. The ghost of a smile, and he nods towards the door: I must say I am a little tempted. It would be so excellent to be free of thought, just for a time.

But I move my head from side to side, and look down at my glass. No. No one else in the bar will have noticed the exchange, it is so fast, but certain. I look around the bar, finishing my wine, and catch his little shrug – her loss, not mine – and he turns his attention elsewhere. It's a near thing, though. Fucking bipolarity: my doctor says if I won't take lithium, Valium is the next best thing in emergencies, and after that sex, and after that shopping.

I've left the Valium at home, declined the sex, and spent all I was going to part with of my allocated money. On my way out of the store to the Lowndes Square side where the taxis wait at the round hotel I see a little last year's Marc Jacobs purse, orange with buckles, knocked down to nothing – £103 – and use my one working credit card. That takes it up to its limit. I'll pay some of the Jung money into the account tomorrow, I promise myself. It's there for emergencies, but this sort of was one. A kind assistant from the Trish McEvoy counter helps me with my bags to the taxi – one shopaholic recognises another, I suspect, or maybe she wanted to get out in the sunlight for a minute – and I go home to prepare myself in tranquility for the evening. It was the right thing to do: the Jacobs bag had got my head back into gear, so I even managed half an hour on my thesis.

The doorbell rings at ten past seven, and I trit-trot down with all my bags and carriers, and there's Loki at my door with the black cab waiting behind. I'm wearing the Weitzman boots with the leopard-fur trim and five-inch heels, which is about as high as you can go and still walk. I'm wearing jeans and a sleeveless Miguelina goddess top in a diaphanous orangey-pink which you wear with a soft beigey-pink floating tie at the waist – jeans are fairly indestructible and the gauze tie could at a pinch be used as a top. My stockings were black mesh hold-ups almost to the groin and with a wide pink band across the top, but they would not be seen, of course, until I took my jeans off. I had the little Marc Jacobs bag, with the receipts in it as well as lipstick, comb and stuff. None of this was exactly Joan, but I'd had my instructions.

And then Loki says, 'I've got a message for you, Miss Bennet. Mr Alden says he's sorry, he can't make it to-night, and so can it be tomorrow instead? He's had to fly to Scotland unexpectedly.'

I sighed sweetly and said: 'Oh, what a relief. I've so much marking to do. Tomorrow's just great!' I smiled, nodded then closed the door on him. It was a close one: I nearly said 'Tell Mr X to go fuck himself,' but I didn't. I could I suppose have said to Loki, 'How about going down the pub then?' – but I didn't seem to have done that either.

I had some unfinished business with Alden. I've

had the odd hard physical slap in my time – we won't go there though – and once I was sworn at for a slut, which hurt a bit. But I am not accustomed to being stood up. The walking out, the letting down – if it's got to happen, I do that.

When I got upstairs I took today's choice off and put the clothes aside for tomorrow, to save myself the trouble of going through all that freedom of choice again, then called a few girlfriends but they were all busy, or had just had babies, or wanted to moan about baby-sitters. So I took two Temazepams, went to bed, and slept right through until eight next morning.

I was calm about it in the morning. It was probably for the best, I decided: there were still marks on my wrists and ankles. I was dwelling in a kind of erotic haze. I could feel the ball-gag still in my mouth.

I had breakfast in the staff canteen. Spare food from the guests' breakfast menu – best organic bacon, crisp and delicate, not too salty, poached eggs on toast, a couple of chipolatas made from Gloucester Old Spot pigs, and a roll and apricot preserve. And the coffee was divine. I hadn't realised I was so hungry. If you're prepared to eat the surplus from the restaurant you get the very best quality food but slightly congealing and crusty and not necessarily hot where hot is expected. If you eat what they cook in the staff kitchen, it's a quarter the quality and cost: that is to say tough, fatty bacon, stale eggs, heavy rolls, plain apricot jam rather than preserve, instant coffee not real, and so on, but often straight from the stove. Those less secure than me turn up their noses at the restaurant leftovers; that's their choice.

Max came down to find me as I was dabbing the last butter and confiture off my lips.

He said he was so glad I'd come in this morning, and not taken yet another day off. He'd hoped I would because he had a job for me. A really civilised young gent from Saudi, asking for a nice girl to take to lunch and spend an hour or two with him in 404, one of the posher suites. Not a cash job; his father kept him on a tight rein, but he had a diamond ring to offer.

'Where'd he get it – nick it from his mum?' I asked.

'Probably.' Max gave a little laugh to humour me.

'How old is he?'

'Sixteen.'

And I said, he'd better be, because not only is age of consent a can of worms in this country – paid sex it's eighteen, unpaid sex it's sixteen – but in Saudi you have to be married to have sex with anyone, male or female. In theory. Max said he didn't think there'd be a problem: he was a pleasant and civilised youngster staying overnight before flying back to Saudi with leave from his English public school to attend an important family celebration. The father was a frequent guest at the hotel, and always booked 404 for himself and family members – the worldly-wise Max was curiously calmed, reassured and impressed by consistency.

But I demurred. I'd just eaten breakfast so the

thought of lunch a couple of hours on didn't tempt me: my young brother Robert is sixteen – they're no conversationalists. I could envision tedious awkwardnesses. Also, I tried to keep these jobs down to two a week, and there had been the tennis player a couple of days back; and the evening with Alden had counted as five in one – now full sex with a teenager who might not be as old as he claimed? I decided to say definitely: no.

And then I thought about Alden who'd stood me up. I really needed to wash that man right out of my hair for form's sake, somehow, temporarily, otherwise my resentment might fester and threaten the relationship in the longer term, and this was probably the way karma, or God, had provided. I needed defragmenting like a computer, grounding, settling, and this was the way to do it. Alden couldn't possibly know: how could he? Loki was to collect me at half past seven: nine hours to wait, and it would pass some of that time. So I said: 'Okay, Max, let's go for it.'

I don't usually go with Arabs, especially not young ones, untamed by wives. They desire, yet despise western women, not without reason. The whole world knows about our binge-drinking sluts. They've seen every porn film on the net including the rape ones and are neurotic about sex to begin with. Their religion and culture persuades them that sex outside marriage is a sin, that if it were not for women there would be no lust: the West beams its porn screens at them and they resent it. But it also gives them copycat ideas. They tend to like blonde, fragile-looking girls, and then take their bafflement out on them. The really nasty ones make you perform for them in some way that humiliates you – animals seem a favourite, though hard to organise in an hotel – before engaging with you, and hand you over to the bodyguards when they've had enough. A girl limps moaning away.

But a lad of sixteen with a family connection vouched for by Max, offering his mother's ring in payment is a different matter, and one should not prejudge individuals, certainly not on grounds of race. Max said he'd had a word with management and they were okay with my being at lunch in the main restaurant, even though I was staff. They, too, were rather nervous at having the young man in the suite on his own: they could depend on me to sound him out and make sure he was the kind who would behave, and wouldn't ask his friends round for some noisy all-night party.

Max would get the ring to his friendly fence, and I'd get a quarter of its proper value, no doubt. Somewhere around £1500, he reckoned. He'd take a 20% cut: I'd get the rest. It is always safer if goods in lieu change hands, certainly than cheques or credit cards: all transactions are so closely monitored these days, so barter comes into its own.

I keep emergency clothes in Max's office – vocational girls can find themselves in need of a quick change of appearance at short notice. I put on a prim little white blouse and a pink suit: very fresh and young looking. I felt rather good. I had slept more than I had for years the night before, had had an excellent breakfast, and had mysterious adventures with Alden to look forward to. I don't think you could quite describe me as being 'in love' but something was making my eyes glittery and my skin peachy. I thought the lad in 404 was rather lucky.

The table was booked for one o'clock. Max took me up to the boy's suite at half past twelve. He was tall, coltish, good-looking, pleasant, half-deferential, half-conceited – a typical product of those more expensive schools. He had big hands: the one wrapped round his champagne glass looked as if it might break it. He spoke in perfect English with the accent of the jet-setting classes: English upper class with an American drawl flecked with occasional slang from the black inner cities. He shook my hand formally, said he was grateful to meet me. He'd thought we should meet briefly before lunch so that if either of us changed our minds we could take leave of one another straight away. He was immensely courteous and condescending.

I said for my part that I thought he lived up to his name – Hasan – which means handsome. He asked me what Vanessa meant and I said 'butterfly', and he said he liked that; I was colourful and charming. So it seemed fairly certain that the afternoon would go as planned.

He confessed that he had not made love to a woman

before and that it was not in his culture to do so. He nevertheless did not wish to have to go back home a virgin and ignorant of the ways of the world. He did not want to have to be dependent on his father and the gossip of boys for knowledge. He had seen a few porn sites at school but they seemed to him crude and disagreeable, and they turned him off. He preferred to do things properly or not at all. He had seen the body of one of the house matrons at school: she would display herself naked before a window at night for the benefit of the boys, but she had been fired.

I thought if this was the pattern of the new Arab princeling, peace on earth might yet be achieved. He hesitatingly asked me if I could just quickly take my clothes off so he knew better who he was talking to over lunch, so I did. Not a strip tease – we were short of time, after all – but clinically, as if I were at the doctors. He studied me from back and front, and touched my breasts.

'I had not realised quite how different a woman is from a man,' he said. 'In this country they try to be the same thing, but I don't think they will have much luck: it's not the will of God.'

His religion was right: he could understand the need to keep a woman well covered. The naked female body was quite definitely an incitement to lust. He delicately and reverently put a finger into my clit, just half an inch, and then withdrew it.

'Paradise is at the feet of the mother,' he said, and

asked me if I had children and when I said no, said he was glad because soon he would be dishonouring me, but sorry, because someone as beautiful as me should be busy reproducing from an early age. He then excused himself rather hastily and went into the bathroom for five minutes and I put my clothes on again.

He tripped over his adolescent feet on the way down, thus spoiling the illusion of total competence, but even then he just smiled benignly and said he was afraid his age made him clumsy. He hoped to grow out of it and had been assured that he would.

What did we talk about? We agreed to only have one course, the sooner to get back to 404. He had a posh version of fish and chips and mushy peas and I had a salad. I drank champagne: he, mindful of his religion, drank Sprite from a champagne flute. He moaned a little about this and that, as teenagers do, mostly about his parents. Once he got home tomorrow he would have to spend a lot of time sitting next to his mother while she tried to push nuts and sweetmeats between his lips. She wept if he objected. It was moral blackmail. He had essays to write; it wasn't as if they were all sitting under some date palm in the desert, and he wasn't a girl. He wished she would not do it. His father would try and take him to a whorehouse, but he thought that would be unspeakably vulgar. His father had three other wives, apparently, and I asked if this upset his mother but he shook his head firmly, and said no: his father was very respectful of women and always careful to serve all three equally. We drank our black coffee quickly and left.

Picture the next scene. Young Hasan lies naked on the bed, his cock reaching almost to his navel. It is as big as it is clumsy, awkward as it is hopeful, coltish as his feet and hands. The bodies of adolescent youths are a strange mixture of soft and bony, protuberances and concavities. He has his hands clasped behind his head while he watches me strip, until I walk about the room with only my heels on.

'How your breasts bounce!' he says, amused. 'How strange and uncomfortable it must be for women!' The cock twitched and jerked of its own accord. He looked at it as if it was some over-importunate stranger whose language he failed to understand. He tried to hold it down, and asked how a man could tell false boobs from real ones, so I explained it was a mixture of texture, appearance and likelihood. If a woman has a bean-pole body and very round big breasts they're not likely to be her own. Likewise if they are formulaically circular. If a woman wears flat heels her breasts will usually be her own. I had no time to elaborate because he unexpectedly leapt from the bed with the energy of a jack-in-the-box and bore me down beneath him, pushing my thighs apart. He entered me at once, thrust thrice and immediately groaned in orgasm.

'That was too quick,' he said, blushing apologetically. I had to agree. I told him it took practice and in a little while we would try again. He lay on his back on the bed and I gave him a lesson in theory. I explained that there was a thing called foreplay which made women receptive. I explained a man could ignore it but to do so limited his own long-term pleasure. The woman would put up with him, no doubt, but it was always better to have her full-hearted enjoyment. By and large where the cock went the finger should go before. I explained about the alleged difference between the vaginal and the clitoral orgasm. His hand moved into my cunt, and he found the clitoris and made me squeal involuntarily. Some women's are more hidden than others, I said, but it's always there somewhere. His cock was already swelling again. Another minute and he was in me again, and I was breathless and pounded: he realised he had to support himself on his elbows and took the weight off me.

That lasted a full five minutes. Then it was back to instruction, 'I bet your teachers like you at school,' I said. 'You listen, and learn.' He said his favourite subject was physics. He would like to be a nuclear scientist, but he needed extra tuition with the maths.

If he was looking for holes, I went on, he must go very gently until he got the angle right. Bottoms needed lubricating. Rough sex, domination, was fine by consent but must be worked up to gradually; although sudden changes of mood and attack could be welcome. Breasts must be treated equally: if the left was nibbled then the right should be equally so, otherwise it made women feel oddly uneasy. Condoms? A requirement, especially in gay circles or the black community. He said in Saudi you didn't run into that too often. I said actually if you stuck to heterosexual, well-heeled partners, as I did, then you could proceed pretty much as women had in the old days, worrying about pregnancy rather than disease: relying on coitus interruptus to get by. I referred to the 'please cum all over my face' phenomenum in the porn films, a play-safe device which did instead of condoms.

By now his cock was standing impudently up again, and he turned me over, and entered me from behind as I crouched. I explained that you didn't have to do it in the same position till you'd finished, but could swap and change, so he took the point at once: now I was on my back with my legs over my head, but that excited him so much his timing went haywire again: at six minutes, though, it was still an improvement.

I explained about the necessity of lubrication for anal sex, the idea of which had at first rather appalled him. I had neglected to bring any but he found the free organic hand cream from the hotel bathroom which I didn't reckon would do me much harm. But I said first there really had to be some foreplay: he couldn't think only about himself for ever: we had to now go into the whole business of oral sex. He seemed rather surprised to find this so high on the sexual menu but I demonstrated the art of the blow job, which is patient attention to the man's pleasure but not necessarily always your own. He came in my mouth, neck stretched to heaven in marvel. I swallowed. I said not all women would do that but personally I thought a dose of young male testosterone did me good. He recovered from sudden shyness to lick into my cunt, blowing and fingering. And the next time we went on for twenty minutes; properly, foreplay to oral sex to full sex to anal sex. I tried not to cry out too loud, because 406 was occupied: the walls at the Olivier are not all that thick.

He asked me how he could tell when a woman was faking, and I said if he was wondering she probably was faking, but it was rude to enquire. Some women got very spiteful and bad-tempered if a man had an orgasm while she did not: but this was a very frequent occurrence and most women would fake out of consideration to the man, or if she had other things to do and wanted to get it over with.

One more time, or was it two? We had a little siesta side by side, then some more. He was inexhaustible. The thing rose and collapsed and rose again as if he was making up for years of lost time which I supposed he was.

'Nine times,' he said, happily. 'Is that good?'

'That's very good,' I assured him. 'And like riding a bicycle; once learned you never lose the knack.'

Concerned that I was tired, and thanking me for my instruction, which he generously said would stand him in good stead for the rest of his life, he told me it was time to bring the session to an end. He was courteous but firm. He had a flight to catch at eight o'clock; he supposed I couldn't help him with his packing? I said, actually no to that, and had a bath in 511 which was empty, checked in with Max to touch base, then went home to recover. I washed my hair, and put it in curlers.

I felt quite noble and content: my day had been well spent. I had made a worthwhile contribution to the well-being of society. I was like Joan, I thought, 'wanting to make a difference.' It is gratifying, anyway, when one is good at something, to pass one's knowledge on.

I put on a CD of Mozart's K421 quartet in D minor and I waited for Loki to arrive. The delicate music sounded like dance and conversation in shifts, sometimes both at once and seemed to grow naturally out of the stillness of the evening.

Clothes Mare

SEVEN TWENTY, AND THE bell went and there was Loki once again. No, there was no cancellation. I said in that case Mr X. would have to wait for me to change. I was not going to all that trouble again only to be told the date was off. Loki seemed rather nervous and said Mr Lam, the pale, scary one, had told him I was not to be late. So I admit I hurried and didn't change my mind about anything other than the Jacobs handbag which I decanted into my cheap but cheerful silver Fiorelli – and then had to decant back again when I changed my mind. I asked Loki if he thought it was nice when I finally made it downstairs, and out of the door, and he said, 'I expect he will like it, but shall we go now?' and smiled with all his white, perfect teeth: meaning to reassure me, but clearly nervous. We raced through the streets, so far as anyone can race through London at seven in the evening. I tried to find out more about Loki's background with deliberately casual questions, but Loki would not be drawn further; he was of course having to concentrate on the traffic.

I also brought along the big yellow Selfridges bag into which, yesterday, I'd stuffed all sorts of odds and ends: shoes, furs, velvet skirts, chokers, earrings, a selection of thirties flapper gear: I'd nearly added a white embroidered Victorian nightie, in lawn, but it took up too much room. Everything else squashed down into almost nothing.

Lam let me in.

'You late,' he said.

'Oh, the traffic!' I said. 'Where does it all come from?'

There was no sign of Alden. Lam went through my bags, checking each item against the receipt and adding up the total. He was grudging in his satisfaction. He didn't exactly smile but his wide thin mouth turned up slightly at the edges and his eyes looked less alarmingly suspicious than they had yesterday – well, a bit. He was wearing a white polo neck sweater again, which made his head look too big for his body. He was a bit of a cross, I decided, between the *Close Encounters of the Third Kind* aliens and Gollom in *Lord of the Rings*.

I didn't sit down because it's easier to stand in five-inch heels. The leverage on them as you get up from a chair can be extreme, and they seem about to snap if you don't get the angle right. Alden glided in, looking particularly cheerful and positive: almost serene.

'Joanie my sweetheart,' he said, 'I hear you got the shopping exactly right, I thought you would. There's a bad girl hiding inside your good girl skin, isn't there? Maybe it's the other way round.'

I didn't really care what he said: I was just so happy he was pleased with me. I found myself chattering on, about how my friend Amy had helped me choose, and made me over, and done my hair. She had spent almost an hour on it, getting it into curls which she heaped up on my head ancient-Greece style, with a few falling, and dangling green ribbons. I listened to myself with awe: who the fuck was 'Amy'?

We exchanged a few disarming pleasantries about the day before, he thanked me for my patience and apologised if he had gone too far too fast, but as I probably realised he did have a few sexual hang-ups he needed to do serious work on, and he'd worried all day in case I'd not wanted to see him again. He'd called the hotel yesterday, the concierge had said I was off sick and that he didn't have my mobile number – thank you, wise, cautious Max, I thought: you always cover the exits – so I must give it to him now in case we forgot later.

So I gave it to him, but with four of the digits wrong. Alden as a stalker was a terrifying prospect: unlimited money, Lam to do his bidding – no thanks. If the worst came to the worst I could leave my job. There were other hotels. But then, of course, he did know where I lived. I killed my paranoia. I didn't want to spoil a beautiful evening.

He said tonight would be completely without erotic interest for me: he hoped I wouldn't mind too much. I said I would be glad of the rest. He was taking measurements of light frequencies and colour subtraction in the visible spectrum, he told me – or something like that – collating them against the typical sound frequencies of erotic activity and allied agitations in the thalamus. Physics was not my strong subject at school and he would certainly assume Joanie wouldn't understand a word he was saying. So I just said that was really interesting and he must be very clever. He got very serious, took my wrists gently, and turned me round to look straight into his eyes.

'I am,' he said simply, like a Pope speaking *ex cathedra*.

He was obviously serious, so I took him seriously. I reckoned he was trying to work out some link between combinations of colour and form and sexual desire, and also represent them in sound, the better vehicle to provide listeners to Radio 3 with a piece of music they'd love, and make love to without having any choice, and without knowing why. Alden, I thought, was trying to invent an aphrodisiac music which was compulsive. Sound can summon up in the listener all kinds of emotions – nostalgia, grief, elation, happiness – why not lust as well? The first day's work with me as subject – ending up pitched at around 111 hertz and pulsed at the rate of a heart's beat – had acted as a tranquillizer and pain killer and sent me to sleep but that was probably not what he'd hoped for.

I was kind of with him conceptually up to a point:

up to the point where tonight he was going to conduct experiments on the colour aspect of his theory, but using as his raw material – and this was where I lost him, it was so beyond out to lunch, or even dinner – the clothes I happened to have chosen to wear. It was possible, I acknowledged, to be both clever, and serious, but mad. It was also possible to be harmlessly mad. I was in a little too deep now to be comfortable with the speculation that his madness was other than harmless.

There was no sign of food or drink, which was a pity, because I was hungry again – I hadn't had a great deal of lunch, and the afternoon had involved a lot of aerobic exercise – though had he offered me chocolates I would have refused.

Alden asked me to walk up and down the room as if I were on a catwalk, which I did. Why not? Eventually he said the boots were wrong, and I had to agree. Can things bought in sales guarantee one the confidence that they would at full price? At some stage or other along the way they must have been rejected by quite a few people. I was rather relieved to take them off.

'Never look as if you try too hard,' he said. My calves ached as the soles of my feet descended to ground level: the muscles cramped. I said so and jumped about a bit and Alden said Lam knew all about aching calves and gave an excellent massage, and I wished I had said nothing. We should go in to the bedroom, said Alden, and I should lie on the bed. I must have looked nervous because he laughed and said, 'Don't worry, the only props today are clothes.'

So I limped and hopped to the bed, squealing. Joan would squeal: Vanessa, properly brought up, would suffer in silence. I was back in Joan mode. I took off my jeans and lay on my front. Alden said he thought the stockings were fantastic. That was nice. They were rather striking. Lam sat on the bed and massaged the backs of my legs with his clammy hands while Alden went through the clothes which had now been hung neatly in the wardrobe. There were racks of clothes and shoes behind the ones I had brought: so I guessed I was probably one of a succession – but how many girls are ever not – and he used the walking stick to move the hangers along the rails.

'I suspect female colour sense is different from the male,' he reflected, 'though there's no body of research that shows it up. I'd never have come up with anything like this.'

The muscles in my legs relaxed: the cramps dispersed; but I think that was as much the passage of time as any skill of Lam's, but how can one tell? There was no body of research that showed it up, but it was rather like receiving a massage from the creature in ET.

'ET, go home,' I muttered under my breath, for I sensed both his helplessness and his power.

'You get paid,' Lam said. He thought I was grumbling, but hadn't heard what I said. 'No worries. Good girl!' There didn't seem to be the threat of an 'if', so I thought maybe at last I'd won him round. He was an ally? That could be useful. I was pleased. There was no point in engaging with him on the complexities of financial transactions between me and Alden so I gave him a lovely smile. His massage was technically correct and his hands were warming up quite nicely. He asked me to keep still, and with a surgical plaster stuck a metal device the same shape and size as a 50p piece, in the small of my back.

'For science,' he said. 'No worries.' And I didn't.

Alden the while laid out various combinations of clothes in neat piles. I was glad to see many of them, if not all, were the choices I had made. Each pile had shoes to go with it, mostly Manolos, though there are far sexier kinds, if few less expensive, on the market. Stuart Weitzman once made a pair of glass Cinderella slippers, with diamond studs and spun-platinum soles, for some star to wear to the Oscars. They cost two million dollars. She didn't win anything, and I guess she didn't actually pay for the shoes, though she did go on to marry Count Von Bismarck. My point is, that's why the boots at three-hundred-odd quid had seemed such a bargain.

It turned out he wasn't going to have me catwalk, but kind of catsprawl – simply lie upon the bed variously dressed: I got to choose the pose as I fancied, but in outfits he had chosen, and in his sequence. He could trust me on the poses because I was, he said, 'a natural model'. I was flattered. I suppose he meant it, but I'll let fine words butter my crumpet if I feel like it. I was to watch myself in the mirror above. I'm as narcissistic as anybody, so that was fine – but how was I to win his interest and affection, if I went on being Joan? I just engaged his lust as it was, and today there was little evidence even of that. He and Lam left the room.

Yellow cushions had replaced the scarlet. The 111 cycle hum started up: it sounded like the second A below middle C – not soporific, simply all there, meta-here, filling all the spaces in the room from invisible sources of imponderable number. It was continuous this time – no heartbeat pulse, so maybe he thought that was the element that had sent me to sleep. Lights shone down on me, their closely related, constantly changing colours swirling like Rudolf Steiner wet-paper paintings, though less primary and more like those in Turner's oil paintings. If I turned my head I could see the computer screen: all Steiner swirls today, nothing linear.

I liked what I saw, I realised, in varying degrees. All pleased, but some variations in colour and style turned me on more than others, even made my breath come shorter and my heart beat faster, and the patterns on the screen intensified by firming up and focusing into the sharp edged, infinitely receding into the microscopic, fractal geometry of an expensive kaleidoscope on acid. Had he mickey-finned me with acid, I wondered – but how and when? I had neither eaten nor drunk anything since I'd walked through the door, not on this visit, no

Alice-Through-The-Looking-Glass I. But it only took micrograms: could you absorb it though the flesh with the right solvent? Was that what was on the small of my back under the tape? But my memory of the couple of times I took LSD recalled certain physical sensations that I wasn't experiencing: I thought I was pretty sure of that.

What was under scrutiny, I could see, were those responses you get when you dress for work or for a special occasion: when you look at yourself in the mirror and like what you see – or take the lot off and start again. The 'real me' changes every day, which no doubt is why a girl has to have so many clothes, flounder in a sea of garments. I thought Alden must be preternaturally clever indeed, and was proud to have been selected for his research. He should of course have confided more in me in the first place; he didn't have to do all that surreptitious druggy stuff – I would have cooperated without, had he come clean.

I admired the confidence and speed with which he had made his decisions, selecting, discarding, reselecting. There was even an historical pattern to his choices; as I went through the outfits I changed from '50s garage pinup to Pirelli calendar to incipient modern porn from the '60s and so forth: increasingly indecent. The sets of clothes would be short of a skirt, or panties, or both, no bra, no top – then down to the Weitzman boots alone, finally nothing but a hair ribbon. Nudity, oddly, did nothing for me: the buzzing hum, which I had worked out depended upon my erotic reaction to myself, faded almost to nothing. Remove the hair ribbon: and it was nothing. But wind a scarf round my neck, or put on earrings or high heels, and it returned.

There was still no sign of food or drink. I was getting tired and bored. Jumping up and down and changing clothes all the time is exhausting. I pulled the electrode off my back, and started searching vainly in the tumble of clothes for what I had arrived in. Lam was in the room almost at once, fiddling with the bed posts.

'He said no sex,' I said. 'I'm tired.'

'No sex. All this science,' said Lam.

I laughed.

'Not funny, Joan,' he insisted. 'Laugh bad.'

'Tell Alden I'm bloody hungry,' I said, 'and that I've had enough.'

'Sure, sure,' he agreed. 'I tell Mr Alden. Sit on bed.'

So I did. He was my friend and ally – wasn't he?

'Now you talk dirty,' he said.

'I will not,' I said.

'Mr Alden not be pleased. Work wasted.'

'Mr Alden can go and play with himself,' I said and giggled, but Lam's brow clouded and I bit my lower lip to stop. I shivered, and not because it was cold. I seemed to have forgotten what the joke had been.

Lam took my left forefinger and slipped a rubber cuff around it, then the same to my left toe. Before I could work out what was happening he had clipped finger and toe together. Two tapes led from cuffs to bedpost. This was old fashioned non-wireless technology: pathetic. This whole bed was pathetic, was out of date already: it would be losing value daily. The cuffs on finger and toe tightened and relaxed. They were monitoring blood pressure, which was rising by the minute. Lam pushed me on to my side; in my folded position this was not difficult for him. He re-stuck the device onto my back: it was just out of the reach of my right hand. Now I was down and I could not get up. I was bent double, toe to thumb. I could have rolled off the bed but that would leave me in the same predicament, only bruised as well.

Then he went away. I was wearing only the leopard ruff boots but they had good heels and I did what I could to rip the patchwork quilt with my right foot, but the yellow cushions were in the way and offered such yielding, fluffy resistance I could do no damage at first. But I kicked again and again, and again, until one tore and a cloud of feathers rose and gently fell all over me. I was very angry. I was being used as an experimental animal. I would tear Alden's throat out, I would have him banned from the Olivier, I would go to the police and cry rape.

'Lam,' I shouted. 'I'll call Immigration. Get you deported as an undesirable alien – back to the Planet Uranus. Up. Your. Anus. Lam.' It didn't come out very clearly though, because of the unnatural position I was in. But at least I wasn't frightened: I was too angry for that.

The buzz grew louder, and cranked up outrage further still. Waves raced across the screen. I looked away, and there was nowhere to look but mirrors and see a furious, red-faced, naked, trapped and struggling thing, hair frizzy from heated tongs, straggly and all over the place. The sight so appalled me it shocked me back into sense, conjured up Vanessa from the real world. She composed myself quickly. Vanessa had more sense than Joan. If this was being filmed for the delectation of others, which Vanessa suspected and Joan would rather not think about, the film makers would not have the satisfaction of what they wanted, which would be unsimulated scenes with erotic content. Even if it was not, if all this was genuinely for the sake of science, where were the consent forms?

This was outrageous. Composure abandoned me again: my posture didn't encourage it. Fear seeped in: why had I got myself into this? It was terrifying, satanic. The noise level was rising so much I worried for my eardrums: the computer screen was a mass of static lines: rage rose in me again, but this time it didn't kill the fear; I would have a stroke, a heart attack, I would die – and then Alden was beside me, in his chair, unclipping finger from toe, helping me to stretch my poor limbs, profusely apologising: saying Lam had no right, he was out of order, *ultra vires*. He, Alden, had been delayed on an important phone call from California; if Lam ever did anything like that again, contrary to his explicit instructions, he would pay the price. But please try and understand – I must do this – that Lam had only one motive in his mind and that was to look after Alden's interests: and Lam was not from round these parts, not from our world, and sometimes got it wrong.

His voice was persuasive because it was soft, it was kind. Besides, he had stopped the hum: he covered me with a blanket, he told me how wonderfully I had succeeded, how proud of me he was: he was the doctor, all bedside manner and I was the patient, and he was healing me. I believed him. You will be rewarded, he told me.

'I don't need paying,' I said. 'This isn't about money.'

'You mean you're doing it for love?' he asked, and Joan actually blushed.

'I'll be rewarded in Heaven,' I said.

He seemed embarrassed; his glance shifted away.

'You're very sweet,' he said, still not looking at me. 'I'm so touched.'

'You're Prospero, aren't you?'

'Prospero was lucky enough to be shipwrecked on a desert island,' he said. 'These days you have to have enough money to build your own.'

'Do you love me?' I asked. He just raised his eyebrows and pursed his lips, as if to say he'd like to explain, but it would take more time than was possible: or some such bullshit.

It's an odd thing, the declaration of love business.

Get in with it too early, and the man backs off. Too late and he's wandered off. But if you blush you show your hand. I couldn't remember when Vanessa had last blushed. It came so simply and naturally to Joan. I blushed.

I had simmered down. It was quite cathartic – like the après-sex feeling: all passion spent – to recover from fear and rage.

'Tell you what,' he said. 'Let's go up to Ray's and see if he'll rustle up some dinner – you must be hungry.'

'Yes,' I said, 'I am.' But I felt vaguely disturbed, insulted by the suggestion: the evening was suddenly moving fast away from the intimate, the seductive, into social banality.

'But I'm not sure I trust the food anywhere in this house,' I added. 'What was in those chocolates the other day?'

'Something new,' he said, 'a shamanic, gateway psychotropic from the rain forest. It's perfectly safe. It's organic. It's not an artificial pharmaceutical.'

'How d'you get it?'

'I have friends, connections. Some are chemists.'

Bet you do, I thought. That's where the money comes from. Drug dealing. All the private art galleries in the world wouldn't bring about this wealth. But buying and selling paintings is a good way of laundering money, especially if you pretend to do it ineptly: write-down. The art world is probably full of noble, etiolated aesthetes who have friends who are 'chemists'.

No wonder he is socially insecure – and sees himself as a great musician.

'Don't worry, Joan,' he said. Shit. I loved it when he used my name. 'There'll be nothing like that again. Now I know you better I value you too much.'

Nice to hear but easy enough to say. I said thank you, but, if he didn't mind, could he call a taxi and I'd be off home. He seemed taken aback. Perhaps he had seen the evening as drifting towards sex: another – maybe successful – attempt to free himself from the trauma of sudden explosion. And so indeed had I, funnily enough. But since he was now suggesting we went up to Ray's, then by the time we got round to making love it would be well after midnight, and all I really wanted to do now was get back home. I'd had a long day. Forget sex, I felt fidgety and irritable.

'I have to wash my hair before I go to work,' I said. 'I have to be up early.'

'Your hair looks absolutely delightful,' he said. 'Dishevelled. A demonic sprite. I love it to death.'

He looked at me all little-boy, and wistful. He smiled the big broad, charming smile of a George Clooney, except the gums showed – but the teeth were perfect.

'I wish you'd stay,' he said. 'That first night, you know – I so much wanted it to end differently.'

I remembered the piston-drive, perfect rhythm, but leading nowhere. I had to close my eyes. My body remembered too: sensation shot down from brain to crotch, the expectation of fulfilment taking physical form, demanding satisfaction.

'It would make so much difference to me,' he said. 'It's so rarely I have the nerve to approach a woman sexually. Who would want a half man like me? I feel safe with you.'

'Well if you put it like that,' I said, grudgingly, like Joan in a bad mood.

He hooked out clothes from the jumble with his walking stick hook – French knickers, a sturdy bra, black knee-highs, a Zandra Rhodes tweed ankle-length tartan skirt, Prada black long-sleeved polo neck – my mother couldn't have made a less seductive choice. I was to wear these for supper with Ray?

'They're very plain,' I said. 'Rather dull.'

'Ray likes very plain rather dull women,' said Alden. 'You don't qualify but you might make an effort for his sake? Do your best. Ray has problems, but he's a great cook.'

'What sort of problems?' I asked.

'Where to start?' he said. 'Artist's block? Premature ejaculation?'

I laughed, because between them Alden and Ray made quite a pair: their problems neatly complementing each other. He looked haughty and continued:

'Death by a thousand principles? Hermetic Order of the Golden Dawn? Little trips to Southgate for weekly meetings: coming back with the "Secret of Power"? Then moaning about constipation or cumming too soon. You name it. I put up with it because he's a genius. You could put up with it because he can cook and is a nice guy and a warm human being and you like him.'

'I didn't think anyone did premature ejaculation any more,' I said. 'I thought they just took Viagra, or something.'

'It's against his principles,' said Alden.

'That's daft,' I said.

'It's not organic,' he said, which I could see was true.

I still had no shoes, but Alden hooked out a pair of pink ballet pumps with blocked toes, and thongs which wound up round the leg. I gave them a disparaging look.

'They're the only ones with flat heels,' he said, which either implied compassion, pity for my calves, or else that he seriously preferred me to look dowdy. I put the whole bloody ensemble on as instructed, too tired to bother to fight, and slouching with anomie I followed him like a dog up to the attic floor in the open lift, which had arrived at his imperceptible command. There was a mirror here as well. Amazingly I looked even more than plausible: I looked good. He saw me looking and said, 'What a little narcissist you are,' and Joan asked what a narcissist was and he told me it was someone who was erotically turned on by themselves: in other words in love with themselves.

Now I know it is more complicated than this. If anyone was the narcissist it was Alden. It was the pot calling the kettle black. The Neurotic Personality of our Time. Karen Horney – the psychoanalyst: what page? Somewhere near the beginning: towards the end, third paragraph? – Yes, got it. 'Narcissism, the "N" type. The striving for glory in the environment – conceit, exhibitionism, vanity and messianism. An associated innate facial expression' – yes – 'a broad smile, showing lots of gum.' That was Alden's smile. Me, I have perfect teeth and pretty lips. 'Narcissistic rage, going red in the face' – 'mass discharge of the parasympathetic nervous system' – me on the bed just now: how true. Awful. I could see I had some of the N-type traits, but Alden had the full scorecard.

I was having quite a relapse, I could see that. Something might have been triggered by the something new and strange and perfectly safe from the rain forests in the Harrods chocolates. Perhaps it was long-lasting, intermittently so. Perhaps I should go back to the doctor and get some lithium. But I didn't think so. Better to stick to the road more travelled of sex and shopping.

After this brief lull of self-awareness the mental storm blew in with a second wind. Alden, the 'N for Narcissism' type mixed up with the 'P for Perfectionism': 'obsessiveness, compulsiveness, repetition, and the maintenance of neatness, order, symmetry.' His annoyance when he and Lam had to use the spreader bar for my ankles instead of the matching cuffs. Or was that A.M. Benis, and the NPA Personality Theory, which I'd come across on line? The three major types,

Narcissism, Perfectionism, and Aggression. Ah yes, the latter. Also applies to Alden. 'In a pejorative connotation the trait may reveal itself in the context of sadism or sadomasochism.' One thing you could say about Alden, his pathologies were well balanced out – N, A, and P in the middle: all three.

For me, you could add a touch of Bipolar Two to the 'N': sexual recklessness, impulse-shopping, urge to sudden travel. But really we're all of us a little off balance, it's healthier that way, more human. Mine was a perfectly tolerable mix of symptoms. At least we Bipolar Twos are happy (mostly: when not acutely depressed), attractive to others, and like to have a good time. Better being that than the Bipolar One, who is morose and solitary but tends to genius. More like Ray, in fact.

My mind was going ape again; how was I ever going to get it back in its box – call it back from the remembered printed page and into real-time me's: who were ascending in a lift specially fitted out for wheelchairs with a man I – quite intolerably – wanted to fuck?

I nearly fell to my knees before Alden's wheelchair and offered to service him – tranquilliser sex – but restrained myself. Joan would never do such a thing. There was safety in Joan. Vanessa was going through a quite severe episode of whatever it was that afflicted her, and had produced Joan as a safety measure. So just be Joan, and prim, and virtuous, and all will be well. Just be Joanie.

Being Joan

RAY'S STUDIO WAS A vast room at the top of Alden's house. Joan loved it the moment she set eyes on it. You know how it is, you get used to the places you frequent. Your world narrows: mine had lately, down to my flat, the view of Little Venice, the Olivier Hotel and the Bound Beast, the Rectory for occasional weekend visits, and the shops of SW 1 and 3. Alden's house, with its formal, creeping bleakness, I could live without – though I could see how a woman could improve it. But here was a sensual richness Joan found most congenial, just when I had come to believe that Vanessa's world was all there was. For suddenly here was a different, sensual, novel one, alive with the smell of turpentine and garlic, where the eros was not confined and organised, but was bouncing around the clutter in healthy chaos. Except that Ray himself, self-oppressed and twisted by his neurosis, seemed so disconnected from this garden of delights of which he was both centre and progenitor that he was not rejoicing in it at all.

The studio took up most of the top floor. The kitchen was a stove and a sink in an alcove, the bathroom a shower behind a screen, the rest was space: paintings stacked against the walls, oriental wall hangings, vases, glass jars, tins of anchovies bought for their labels, piles of vinyl records and a bicycle with a flat tyre; an easel, crowded surfaces, an old deal table, jam jars with dried out brushes in them; an old blue sofa, squishy with use and age, button back chairs in a dilapidated state, rugs everywhere, Kelims – including a nice Heriz and what might be a Kazan; a wide low bed, unmade, in the far corner into whither Ray presumably crawled at night or in the early morning when work was done.

'You look better than the last time I saw you,' said Ray. 'You were rather éclatante for my taste.'

'Told you so,' said Alden, amiably. 'You'll have to learn to trust me, Joan.' He said he'd brought up a CD of *Thelemy: The Silence of the Senses* for us to hear. After supper we could all listen to it? He thought he might re-title it *Thelemy – The Murmur of Eternity?* He was nervous, as people are when they first offer their creative work to scrutiny by the outside world, and Joan found this endearing: he was brave, but he was vulnerable.

She wandered about the studio, uttering little cries of delight, while Ray sliced red onions and grated garlic. Alden whinged that the wooden chopping board was unhygienic and needed to be plastic or marble, and Ray said Alden was more likely to die from over-cleanliness than he was from dirt.

'Because you won't have any antibodies to protect you,' he added.

Alden looked around the room, and his tone lost its geniality: why had nothing been done to the painting? What had Ray being doing with his time?

Ray turned around from the onions, rubbing his eyes with the back of his right hand from which a large square cleaver dangled.

'Block,' he said. 'I've got creative block – hello? Ring a bell?'

'Been down to Southgate lately, by any chance?' asked Alden. Ray rolled his eyes, and turned back to his cooking.

The 'painting' Ray was working on – or not working on – was executed on traditional canvas, but the shape was anything but traditional. The background was painted a ghostly blue and had then been divided into dozens of little squares, each rimmed with a slim wooden frame, and into each of the four sides of every frame was fixed a little mirror, at an angle: so what was painted in each square was thrown back myriad times from one side to the others. It was rather like the bedroom downstairs, in concept, but the execution was jumbled, organic, full of nooks: an attempt to reproduce the infinite, as if by the observation of perpetually regenerated form some magic goal, as impossible as perpetual motion, could be reached.

In each of the completed squares Ray had, with the finest of calligraphy brushes, painted a complex thicket of tiny contorted strokes, which to him no doubt held profound meaning, but to me presented none. Perhaps half of the squares had been filled. Ray's promise to Alden, now thwarted by his artist's block, had been to fill up the rest so it could be finished and delivered to Alden's client Lady O by mid-September. The task didn't seem impossible to me, nor too hard: you would just take up your brush and make little lines, steadily, one after another, and eventually it would be done. But it didn't seem that way to Ray. He asked me what I thought.

'It looks slightly skew-whiff to me,' I said, before I could stop myself. I ought to have bowed down and worshipped, as artists expect you to, in the face of their hard-won creativity.

'It's meant to be,' he said proudly, not seeming to mind. 'You have a good eye.'

'I told you she had, Ray,' said Alden, and I felt wanted and needed: couldn't help it.

Ray said the eccentricity was achieved by the uneven number of squares; there were ninety-three of them.

'Why ninety-three?' asked Vanessa, her mind racing off again. Ninety-three is the holy number of Thelema, the Outer Order of the Ancient Mysteries, founded as a religious system by Aleister Crowley in 1903, after much astral attack and infighting amongst its advocates. The number is obtained by the combining of the geomantic value of the word thelema – Greek for will – and agape – Greek for love. Geomantic value is a term used in numerology, the occult science of numbers. 'Ninety-Three' is a sign of greeting and recognition between Thelemites. Even Vanessa gives up on Crowley's greatest work, the Commentaries of Al – arguably a crock of ponderous tosh replete with cutely-used language tendentiously self-bootstrapped to convey substance where none belongs. The eidetic memory is not performing to concert standard: there are dark patches, lacunae; though I do recall Section 20 being headed: 'Beauty and strength, leaping laughter and delicious languor, force and fire, are of us.' And further down the page, 'Compassion is the vice of kings. Stamp down the wretched of the earth; this is the law of the strong. This is the law and the joy of the world.' Not exactly politically correct.

So Ray is a Thelemite and I suspect Alden may be too. Alden's probably aiming to employ ninety-three hertz in his messianic, 'N'-for-narcissist bid to take over the world through BBC Radio 3. At Joan's expense. Joan is Plymouth Brethren. Actually so was Crowley – there's a coincidence: or at least his parents were, particularly rigid and disciplinarian they were too, which some commentators claim may have driven young Aleister to react by choosing a path of voluptuary excess.

If this evening does not end in some kind of fulfilled voluptuary excess on Alden's part, I think I will go mad.

Fortunately Ray produced some pasta to help subdue my bipolar anxieties. There clearly wasn't going to be much sexual excess from his direction, despite his ninety-three fixation. Sex, shopping – and food: all tranquillizers to still the restless mind, which may be why 57% of bipolars are classified as obese.

The table being too cluttered to use, we ate from plates on our laps. Ray and I sat on the edge of the big blue sofa which was pulled up in front of one of those kitsch electric fires with false flames, Alden opposite us in a chair, behind it. Ray had used lots of garlic, good lean mince and plum tomatoes – not purée which can give everything a rather metallic taste. A good Chilean wine: 1997 Almeviva with a Rothschild label. Nothing *en primeur* about this one. I had the feeling Ray was not short of money: he just didn't have any interest in spending it for the sake of it. Alden, on the contrary, though having all the outer show of wealth, agonised endlessly, though sporadically, about what he spent.

All through supper Alden wouldn't let it go. What would happen if Ray's painting, which they called *The Blue Box*, was not ready in time? Lady O might be disinclined to pay what she had promised. She would argue about breach of contract. Ray had to get his fucking finger out of his backside, get on with it. Ray winced at the language, but I think that was for my benefit. Arts-Intrinsick's lease was coming to an end. Alden would in all likelihood have to pay out even more, either on renewal or for somewhere else, and turnover was up by only 5% over last year. There were some good new commissions in view but nothing was finalised. 'The other business', whatever that was, was more cut-throat and competitive than ever. As readily accessible communication technology improved, the margin between what Alden could produce and others did was diminishing. The easy days were over.

But whatever Alden thought he was really talking about, to me his words seemed to refer to his problems completing the act of sex: the initial débâcle with me, no doubt a reprise of many, many times since the accident, was still very much with him.

I suggested that Ray try hypnosis for his block: so long as he actually wanted to get over it, hypnosis would work. Ray said he didn't approve of it: it was too facile a solution, like magic. Alden laughed and said Ray was a fine one to talk – easy solutions were just practical ones, except for those who were perverse enough to be attached to their problems, players of Wooden Leg and Ain't It Awful out of *Games People Play*. Why did he hesitate? Especially since power and domination were apparently now at Ray's fingertips, he being on the Fourth Path. If, that is, you were to put your trust in the Southgate people, which he, Alden, frankly didn't. Southgate were renegades. They didn't know what they were doing, and why belong to what was a mere Outer Order anyway?

'It's the real OTO for me, or bust,' said Alden. They were talking over my head, rudely, but then Joan could expect no better. Man's talk. The Ordo Templi Orientis, the Inner Order. Founded by Kellner and Reuss, Rosicrucians, 33rd Degree Masons, in 1910, only to be taken over by the egregious Crowley. Southgate OTO: it was as though Alden and Ray were talking about competing Boy Scout troops. My brother Robert went to one for a time and it was all in-fighting, noble talk and, I suspected, child molestation. I helped myself to more spaghetti.

'I have the powers,' said Ray, stubbornly. 'I just don't mean to use them selfishly, or lightly.' Alden said that since so much was at stake and it was obvious to everyone that all Ray needed to shake off his artist's block was a good shag, surely there were enough girls down there in Southgate struggling with Paths One and Two, who'd be only too grateful for a bit of domination?

'Don't even think of it—' said Ray, evidently shocked.

'Not follow in the footsteps of the master?' Alden continued. 'Mind you I wouldn't fancy it myself – bad skin and flat hair are the mark of the dedicated female Thelemite. Excuses. There're plenty of other seas to fish in, girls anywhere you look.'

And they both looked at my rather wild and plentiful hair, totally loose by now from its Greek curls. I wished I had a comb.

'No Thelemite she,' said Alden.

'She has tomato sauce round her mouth,' said Ray,

as if this was rather a wonderful thing. It is nice to be appreciated.

Supper over, Alden played his CD to us, or rather Lam did. Alden pressed his touchpad and lo, enter Lam. It seemed he was never off duty. Surely Alden could have used his touch pad to play it himself? He made the usual propitiatory cries of the nervous creative: only a first attempt, the next would be more complete, it was only a relatively wild, rough mix, he needed a couple more sessions with Joan – my heart leapt: it was not going to end here: there was time for me yet to solve his problems and firm-in my status.

And Ray said, 'Sod this Alden, stop sucking your thumb and let us hear it – if you want us to?'

Touché, Alden, I thought. You asked for that. But he'd already signalled to Lam: out of the sound system came a new configuration of the hum which had sent me to sleep: presumably what Alden had managed to wring out of today's session. It was in a lower range and the heartbeats were more variable. I felt sleepy. I put my head on the sofa arm.

'She go sleep,' Lam observed. 'Very good. Languor delicious.'

'I told you so,' said Alden. 'This is marketable.'

Ray said, 'Yes, if you want a soporific, but I thought you were after an aphrodisiac.'

'I reckon it's that as well,' said Alden.

'What's the point if you sleep through your own excitement?' asked Ray.

The next thing I remember is waking with my nose pushed deep into the faded blue cord-cloth of the sofa and, as before, banging away from behind, the end of the penis right up in me as far as it would go, to the edge of where pleasure almost becomes pain, and it's clearly noticeable that the orifice is designed for functions other than sex. I was slightly on my side, Lam had one of my legs hooked over the back of the sofa with one clammy hand on my ankle to enhance Alden's comfortable access, and the pounding was as rhythmical and insistent as was consistent with Alden's courting technique. I moved to get more air and protect my nose but Lam had my hair round his other fist and pushed my head back down; but not before I had a glimpse of Ray at his easel – and Ray had a brush in his hand and was actually painting.

I had no idea how long I had been sleeping: for all I knew Ray had taken Alden's advice and shagged me already, to the instant dissolution of his artist's block, and now it was Alden's turn. But I thought probably not. Ray seemed too intent on his canvas, and rather stiff-jawed and disapproving of what was happening on the sofa. Can one come in one's sleep? I imagined I had. There seemed no desperate need in me to reach orgasm, as if the initial one was some way behind, and my body was gathering up its resources for the next burst of interest – when without warning Alden simply stopped, withdrew, and wailed, 'It's still no good. I can't!' He sounded petulant and spoilt, and it occurred to me that his emotional development had stopped with the explosion. Hasan, at a nominal sixteen, conducted himself with more dignity than Alden.

Lam let my hair go, after a quite unnecessary final tug, and lifted Alden, who was twice his bulk and twice his weight, effortlessly, and put him back in his chair – Lam was spindly, but he was strong.

I restored myself to my proper state – like a computer being restored to a previous date and time, the better to bypass any current problems – and went to the bathroom to wash, as much to save Alden's face as anything, for there was nothing to wash away. By the time I returned Lam was dabbing Alden's brow and hands with a cloth and Ray, standing over them, was remonstrating.

'I don't want you doing this sort of thing in my studio.' Ray's voice rose with indignation. 'It is not a sex den. You have ruined the atmosphere, just scuppered it.'

'Sorry, mate,' said Alden, 'I created the atmosphere. And were you not painting? Can that be a brush in your hand – of course not! Just a trick of the light.'

'I painted for five minutes,' said Ray. 'It's outrageous. I do not want to be part of your sexual activities. Getting your pound of fucking flesh, first from her, then from me.'

'Why don't you get yours then?'

And so on. It was like my twin sisters, Alison and Katharine, when they occasionally had a spat.

'No one asked you to join in. Perhaps that's your problem?' said Alden.

Ray danced about with rage.

'And that poor girl, she was asleep.'

'What about me?' demanded Alden. 'What do you think it's like for me? To be dependent on Lam, to have to be lifted onto a bed, a position arranged for me?'

'Bring out the violins,' mocked Ray. 'Do what you want on your own bed but leave my sofa alone.' It was a real row.

'She slept, I fucked, what's the matter with that?'

'The matter,' said Ray, 'is that you're a fucking cripple. All you can ever get is someone who's sick in the head or else sorry for you like Joanie. You can't do without your special effects. Spiked chocolates and a bloody hum farting away all the time.'

'If you'd just have a proper shag,' said Alden, 'you'd stop being so neurotic.'

'I'm the neurotic one?' said Ray. 'You haven't had a proper shag since the day you had your legs blown up.'

'You haven't had a proper shag since the day you were born,' said Alden – his voice had lost its weight: he actually sounded lame – 'Mr Premature Ejaculation...' They believed in hard truths, these two.

'Ninety-three,' said Lam, suddenly talkative. 'Ninety-three. Love under will. Compassion: vice of kings.' And then, warningly, 'She listen. Girl think too hard, pretend not.'

But they were too incensed now to take much notice of Lam, or me.

'Better not to come at all,' jeered Alden, 'than to come too soon.'

'You don't know the half of it,' said Ray. 'One false brushstroke and the whole web shatters. I am never going to paint again!' And at that he flung the paint brush into the electric fire, where the handle flared and melted, wrinkling, accompanied by a ferocious metallic smell. I think it must have been made of old fashioned bakelite. Lam leapt to retrieve it.

'No fire,' he said. 'No fire.' And I may have imagined it but it seemed to me Lam simply took the burning bakelite and smothered the flames with his hands. They were damp enough, God knows, to douse most fires.

'Can someone get me a taxi?' I asked.

They turned and stared at me.

'She not go yet,' Lam said. 'She not finished. Ray shag. Ray paint.'

'You must be joking,' I said.

Ray, his gesture made, seemed to be rethinking.

'Joanie,' said Ray, contemplatively, 'Lam's on the Seventh Path. He has a fine intuition. He's come all the way from Tibet to Southgate for the course. He's half way to being a master.'

'Lam's a freak,' I said. 'I am sure he's very useful about the house but he's a weird freak. Now get me a taxi. Joanie cross.'

'Joanie,' said Alden, 'sit down and relax. Look into

137

Ray's eyes. Now we've found you, we don't want to let you go.'

Well, I didn't want to be let go, either, frankly. I liked it up here in the attic. It was a friendly place, and Alden and Ray were already feeling like family. They quarrelled, they made up, they struggled with problems to do with their creativity and sexuality, and it was just great to have a home-cooked meal for once, instead of microwave in the flat or the staff canteen at the Olivier. Which reminded me I really had to get home some time and see my own family. But they were so dull.

'You sit, Joanie,' said Lam. And I did. You get to have a certain intimacy and camaraderie with your persecutors, and oddly enough, they with you. Besides, if Lam could put out flames with his bare hands, if he could make Loki go through yellow-to-red lights, if he could lift Alden like a doll, if he came from Tibet like the *Book Of The Dead*, Lam deserved respect. He said sit, so I sat. As far as I knew if I turned to go his hand would simply extend into a tentacle and pull me back. Besides, I was sure enough I couldn't be hypnotised. My Uncle Matt had proved it to me.

I looked into Ray's slightly squinty Woody-Allen eyes. The idea that he could control me was absurd. If it was Alden it would be different, even though Alden, who I presumed to have had some troublesome earlier dealings with the Thelemites of Southgate, made no overt claim to occult powers. Alden relied on perfectly ordinary ways of manipulating women: that is to say by being inconsistent in his response to them. Sometimes passionate, sometimes indifferent: a touch of sadism, a show of acute vulnerability. The emotional weather always changing. The way to train a dog, my father once told me, was never to be entirely and predictably consistent. Sometimes you gave them the reward: then when they most expected it, you refused it. I thought of our poor slobbery bitch Vera: it had worked with her.

But Ray? Ray couldn't even train a dog, let alone Joan, a girl with a nursery-teaching diploma who held down a good job, albeit part-time, in the Olivier Hotel, with an upright Brethren background to stiffen her moral sinews. Never!

'I'll only do this with your consent, Joan,' Ray said, holding my chin, tilting my head towards his. His eyes weren't so bad; not wide, like Lam's, but deep.

'Fire away,' I said. 'No swinging pendants?' I was trying to lighten the moment, lessen an intensity which was getting quite embarrassing.

'This isn't hypnotism,' he said rather crossly. 'It is Love Under Will. Enjoy. You are a very special person. You are feeling sleepy.'

'I've done that already this evening,' I said. 'And see where it got me.'

'But you liked it.'

'Oh yes,' I said. I was feeling nice and responsive, quite woozy and deliciously loose-limbed.

'And you wouldn't mind doing it with me?' he

asked. 'I need your consent before I put you under domination.'

'For God's sake, Ray, you've made your point: get on with it,' said Alden who was fidgeting around, moving his chair from place to place, and trying to catch my eye all the time, so it was hard for me to concentrate. 'Fuck your ethics. We need the painting finished.'

I deliberately locked my eyes with Ray's. His face was in exact focus, as if every angle and line was delineated with a fine calligraphy brush, while Alden was only a moving blur that shifted in and out of the background.

'Sure,' I said – to Ray. 'I'd like that.'

It occurred to me that there might have been something in the spaghetti bolognaise, or I had been fed with substances while asleep, but there didn't seem any call to drum up any paranoia about it: Alden and Ray were friends and family now. Alden could get his scientific results without having to resort to drugs; with my help Ray would enter into a new creative phase – after Hasan I quite saw myself as an accomplished sex therapist. I saw the logic in my vocation developing a socially useful role for me. Vanessa could always work through problems that presented, drawing on her memory's copious access to the wisdom of Jung: Joan could afford to take time off. This was going to be quality time for me, as the 'girl who wanted to make a difference.' I sighed happily. Lam leaned into view, and nodded briefly, as if he could read my mind.

'Whoa,' said Alden. 'Not so fast. What are our goals here? Our targets?'

'Love is the Law, Love under Will,' said Ray. 'Joan is to become subject to my will. She's got none of her own. She will be safer like that. She's all over the place – it's the stuff you give her. You were in a hurry just now. What's changed?'

'I need to be included,' said Alden.

'Too true,' said Lam. 'Only then Ray paint.'

He sat peaceably in a corner listening, sweet faced, as a man might who knows things are going well for him.

'Joan,' said Ray, 'you are feeling very happy, aren't you, and drowsy as can be.'

'Oh? – yes,' said Joan, but she felt a prickle of doubt: slight but insistent. Vanessa was still somewhere inside, the vocational girl, the one with the First in philosophy, sharp as a needle.

'And you trust me, don't you,' said Ray. As an afterthought, after a glance towards Lam, he added, 'and Alden too?'

'That's better,' said Alden.

'I am so safe,' said Joan. 'So safe with both of you.'

Now it was Alden's turn to get cold feet.

'This is just plain front parlour hypnotism,' said Alden. 'You only make people do under suggestion what they'd do anyway. What's the point?'

'It's a question of narrative,' said Ray. 'Wait and see.'

'You wait, see,' said Lam to his master, though I was beginning to wonder quite who was mastering whom.

'Choose a word, Joan. A nice word but one which won't be used too often. We don't want it turning up by mistake in casual conversation.'

'Theleme,' said Joan, or was it Vanessa, knowing on which side her bread was buttered? 'That's a nice word,' she went on. 'Like Thelma, but softer.'

'Good, good,' said Lam. 'Most propitious.'

'When I say the word Theleme, Joan,' said Ray, 'my will is your will. And Alden's.'

'Thank you,' I said. 'You're so kind.'

'To release my control over you, I say the second word – what will it be?'

'Sirius,' said Lam. 'Sirius – suitable word.'

'Joan must choose it,' said Ray.

'Sirius,' I said.

Wherever Lam was from, I decided hazily, it wasn't from Tibet. Vanessa remembered reading that in the States a higher proportion of adults in therapy discovered hidden memories of abuse and abduction by aliens than by fellow humans such as their male relatives. But I was floating out of my body now, looking down on myself, knowing that though Joan might be convinced she was 'under will', Vanessa was invincible.

'When you hear the word Sirius you forget what happened when you were under will.'

'Can I go home now?' I whispered.

'No – Theleme – you can't,' said Ray. 'We want you to clear the table now, and wash the dishes.'

So, I got up and I started to clear the dishes from the table. I was quite sure that I was in my right mind, not hypnotised nor under the will of anyone. I have to admit I got up and did it. I had left home because of my mother's insistence on me doing exactly this.

Alden and Ray had been drinking: two thirds of a bottle of whisky had gone. They bickered on while I worked.

'Supposing we override the forgetting bit,' said Alden. 'Supposing I want her to remember? The more physiological reaction I can get out of her the better. Lam toe-to-thumbed her: she lost her temper. That was really useful.'

'We're not concerned with your needs,' said Ray. 'This is about me.'

'Besides,' said Alden, 'this under-will business is all claptrap. She'd have done the dishes before she went anyway. She's a good girl.'

'Sirius,' said Ray. 'Joanie, come back and sit with us.'

I shook myself free – I was not quite sure what of, but it was like a leech falling off the skin when a flame is put to it. I was me. Whoever that was. I went to sit down and helped myself to some whisky.

'No drink,' said Lam, crossly. I ignored him.

'Oh, Joanie,' said Ray, in a studiedly casual voice, 'will you be a good girl and finish doing the dishes?'

I gave him an old fashioned look.

'You must be joking,' I said. 'Do them yourself. Why can't Lam? Isn't that the kind of thing he does?'

'Theleme,' said Ray. 'Lam is on the Seventh Path and has been sent from the Dog Star to help us, and when you think back that is how you will remember him. You will respect and obey him.'

'You can't do that,' said Alden. 'Retrospectively.'

'You've skipped some homework,' said Ray. 'The bit that says you can. Joan...you are being a bad girl. You don't want to be a bad girl, so you want to finish the dishes and scrub the floor.'

'Yes,' I said. 'Sorry.' And I got up and went back to the sink.

'See?' said Ray.

'She's playing with you,' said Alden. 'She's just yanking your dick and pulling your leg.'

I don't know if I was pretending or if I wasn't. It was entertaining to act the part of the will-less Joan, but once the part was assumed then perhaps Joan was indeed will-less. Every movement I made felt so exquisitely, sensuously right. I got their dishes done, then decided to look for a bowl, but settled for a saucepan. I searched out a mouldy scrubbing-brush beneath the sink. I found the greatest pleasure of my life scrubbing the floor. Had anybody told me to do that?

I daresay I was meant to forget and in theory should have, but Vanessa heard, saw, remembered as she moved across the room scrubbing – and the floor

144

certainly needed it – what Joan did not. Joan was under will, Vanessa was not. It was Vanessa who heard scraps of phrases: 'the secret whore of Babylon' from Ray: 'constant copulation, the build up of transforming powers' from Alden: 'she the one, she the one' from Lam. Joan just went on scrubbing and wiping and changing the water in the saucepan, without even wearing gloves. She broke a nail. She might as well clip the whole lot: two nails on each hand had already been taken down. She felt she had better stick up for herself.

I came over to Ray and said, 'I'm a bit tired. Can I stop now?'

'Joan, you are not in the least tired. You have all the energy in the world. Back down on your knees. There is a whole area underneath my easel which must be finished.'

I went back for more water.

'No, that's beyond the call of duty, Ray,' said Alden. 'Sit down, Joan.'

I felt uneasy. What was I to do when instructions conflicted?

'Alden prevails,' said Lam: I think he did. I know I sat down. Alden wheeled over to me, caught my hand and said, 'Joan, listen to me. You have called the taxi and you've decided to go home. It was a wonderful evening: spent with your new friends and new family, and you're looking forward to seeing them again soon. You know what a valuable contribution you are making to their artistic integrity. You are so very proud of that.'

'So very proud,' I said.

'Now, Joan,' he said, 'you are finally safely home. Isn't it nice to be back? What wonderful adventures you've had! Now you can just lie down, put your head on the pillow and go to sleep. But where's your bed? Oh yes, there is it. Looks very like Ray's bed, but we know it's yours. So off to the bathroom, sleepy head, and wash your hands and face.' So I went. I was so comforted by Alden's caring attention to detail. It would never have occurred to Ray that I might need to go to the bathroom.

I returned to find the three of them were conferring.

'Off you go,' said Ray, 'off you go, sleepy-head, off with your clothes – just drop them on the floor, you can pick them up in the morning: curl up and snuggle down.'

And I took off my clothes, dropping them on the floor, went over and got into Ray's bed, and crawled beneath the heavy quilt, and fell asleep from exhaustion.

In retrospect, what seemed to happen was that from time to time they'd forget to release me with the word Sirius and I'd remember things they assumed I'd forget. Or else Alden, wanting me to be in a state of intense emotion and reaction all the time, defied Ray into making sure I was. There was a good cop/ bad cop routine: Ray 'gave me the cigarettes', Alden 'hit me'. Or vice versa. And meanwhile, all the time, I was intimidated by Lam. What a ménage! And I under training as the Scarlet Whore of Babylon, with her constant sexual copulation! (The other kind was spiritual, I was given to understand, not for the likes of me, not being a Thelemite. I was just the talismanic one, the dream lover, to be reached out for.) And all I did, unfeeling, was sleep and dream about nothing at all. Sleep under Ray's will was notable for its dreamlessness.

Ray's bed was delightfully frowsty and warm; though the mattress was rather thin and nobbly, with ancient lumped-up kapok, like the guest bed in the spare room back home at the Rectory. My eyes opened to Ray throwing back the bedclothes: a surprise, because I believed myself to be in my own bed, and so could not work out how he had got to be in my room. He was very drunk: he was trying to get his ratty old sweater off over his head and somehow got caught up in the arms. Alden and Lam stood behind him. I thought Lam had been drinking too – his eyes seemed unfocused, which gave his whole head a fuzzy outline as on TV, when they pixillate-out faces to protect the innocent or the guilty from being recognised. Alden's smile was just idiotic. I pulled the bedclothes back up to cover me but Lam immediately whipped them off with a tiny movement of his forefinger. I cannot believe myself as a credible witness to Lam's behaviour any more. The heavy quilt seemed to leap across the room.

Dawn was breaking outside the skylight. I sat up. There didn't seem much point in worrying about being naked. A small bird peeked down at me from the skylight, before flying off. The room had the look and feel of the early morning after a night before, when resumption of unforgiving day shines its bleak truth over the evidence.

But it wasn't all bad. The floor looked so clean, and over in the kitchen area everything gleamed. On the easel Ray's *Blue Box*, which had shimmered and glittered so yesterday evening, this morning looked wan and unimpressive. A few hours sleep and I was all Vanessa again, glad to find myself free of Joan. I did not want to be messing about with this bunch of freaks: I wanted a bath, I wanted to get home, I wanted breakfast and to get to work. Feeling sorry for Alden had simply got me into trouble. Something I was trying to remember: what was it? Yes, Crowley's 'compassion is the vice of kings.' How true, but how horrible to say so. Something else my brain was working at: a printed page, an old catalogue, Marcel Duchamp's famous avant-garde painting of 1914, *The Green Box*. Ninety-three little squares. That number again.

'Always ninety-three?' I said aloud.

'Nothing to do with you,' said Alden. They were all seated at the table, staring at me as I woke. 'That is priestly knowledge.'

'You only 156,' said Lam.

'Scarlet Whore,' said Ray, 'of Babylon. Number 156

in the Kabala.'

Good God, the Kabala strikes me as page after page of uninterrupted tosh. It is hard for the eidetic mind to forget anything: it doesn't automatically erase what its owner discriminates against, or judges worthless. I needed to be Joan again, nice Joan, whose mind worked normally if slowly, if only to blot out all those tedious pages: the Kabala, the Judaic book of secret knowledge, like the Apocalypse a hundred times over, wild, drug-induced fantasy, interpreted by people who never saw a drug in their lives. The Bible's Apocalypse is mercifully brief. And then the mind was off again – the flawless red heifer of Jerusalem, who must be sacrificed before the Third Temple can be built. Where could I find a reference to that – of course, Gershom Gorenberg in *The End of Days*, 2,000 pages on the apocalyptic struggle over the Temple Mount, between Jew, Muslim and Christian. Vanessa's poor mind was searching pages, feverishly – 'I'm getting up,' I said but Ray now had one scrawny leg over me and his clothes off so it was difficult, but I tried. He had a thin wiry body and a long thin questing penis, standing, waving. It had a kink in the middle of it, as President Clinton's was reputed to do, but Clinton was a fleshy man and Ray was almost painfully thin, so it was the more noticeable.

'Theleme,' said Alden, and I stopped struggling. Best just to get it over, and then get out of here. I hoped it wouldn't take too long.

'Poor Ray,' said Alden. But I was annoyed and hurt, even as Joan. Joan never expected this kind of thing, though Vanessa might well have. Why did he want to give me away? Share me? Did I mean so little to him? Upset must have showed in my face because Alden said, 'Do it for my sake, Joan. Be kind to him.'

His chair was sideways to the bed and he stretched out a hand and touched my shoulder, and smiled sweetly. He wanted a ring-side seat, I could see. But for once I wasn't an experimental object, just a straight fuck.

'Ray fucks, he paint,' said Lam, who always got to the point.

And it was Ray's bed, after all.

Ray had few sexual graces. Nor was he the kind you could instruct, like young Hasan, nor would you want to. I lay up against the pillows: he wormed his way into me, and burrowed away. I could feel the kink, and that was exciting, and before I knew it I took myself by surprise by coming, a kind of early morning elation, and Alden was leaning forward, interested, which in itself was stimulating because he usually went away and watched from a distance. There was no suggestion of an incipient threesome – other than Alden's voyeurism, let alone, mercifully, a foursome. Lam seemed to have fallen asleep on his chair. His mighty eyes were closed. I daresay he was in truth just an ordinary rather pale, rather clammy young man with mild thyroidism from a dingy suburb, of the kind who might flourish as servants, and any other impression was a retrospective suggestion from Ray.

And now Ray had my attention because he was coming and coming, and shouting – it is nice to elicit such a noisy response from a man, pleasant to have such power over another person – but then, without warning, he was weeping. Hot tears fell on me and I felt such indulgence towards him and wanted to comfort him, and glad to be able to offer this service.

'It worked,' Ray whimpered, 'it worked. She is the promised 156.'

'Bloody crap,' said Alden. 'It worked because you're so drunk you forgot you couldn't do it.'

'I am a master of the universe,' said Ray, and fell off me and fell asleep. Alden and Lam departed and I got up and had a bath and made breakfast. The sun shone in, the work on the easel had come back to life, I found some very good coffee, and as good an apricot comfiture as even the Olivier could provide. I was in no particular hurry to go elsewhere.

I listened to Radio 4, the magaziney trivialities washing comfortably over me, the announcers' voices trained to emphasise meaningless words and raise and lower their inflections in any way as long as it has nothing to do with what they were saying. They could call this anodyne logozac, or wordzac: a comforting muzak of thought and language for people who like me at the moment craved cerebral downtime; unlike me, though, a lot of people out there must want that twenty-four seven. I was in no particular hurry to go anywhere. The Scarlet Whore of Babylon is at home everywhere. She has no fight with her circumstances.

Domesticity

FOR THE NEXT WEEK I cleaned by day and fucked by night, like any traditional housewife. They had discovered another use for me, if only by accident. Having found their Whore of Babylon it was not enough: she could clean the house, iron the shirts, buy the food, make the dinner and run errands too. Let her find the envelopes, lick the stamps, and run to the post.

'You can't just sit about here idle all day,' as Alden put it. 'You'd be bored.'

They preferred me to live in. Loki drove me over to Little Venice and we came back with a couple of suitcases.

'I don't want too much of your female stuff cluttering up the place,' said Alden. I called Max and told him my mother was ill and I'd be away for a few weeks. Management was so pleased with me – Hasan's family had apparently made a booking for the entire winter season – Max said he reckoned I could come and go as

I liked. But he'd miss me: what had really happened? Had I fallen in love? He was quite a romantic, Max. I told him I thought perhaps I had.

I could think of no other reason for my behaviour – transformation of proud independent woman into placid cow – other than that perhaps I really was 'under will', or else that being Joan kept the clatter and torment of wild thoughts at bay, and the sheets of print in my mind safely sealed in their files. My mother always complained that I went to extremes, and I could see that it was true. I either thought too much or too little.

I was given a little room off the master bedroom with the Lukas multi-sensory bed and the white patchwork quilt. It had no windows but it had a vast television screen, a computer, access to the Internet, and an iPod to keep me happy. Not that I was able to spend much time in here. Alden, attended by Lam, would have to be got out of the house to his Arts-Intrinsick meetings: he would have mislaid papers, decided he was wearing the wrong tie, and then he couldn't find the day's entry code that served instead of a house key, and so on. I would have to do the running to and fro.

Ray would be upstairs in the studio painting like a man with a sentence of death hanging over him. Some half of the little squares were finished now, filled in with their manic, fiddly little hairlines, each single one of which seemed to fill Ray with trauma. The mirrors spat back their reflections, bouncing from surface to surface, back and back into apparent infinity. I was fascinated. He seemed to be constructing a new universe, a new virtual reality which would inform, reify itself in the real world. He was the Intelligent Designer: this was the beginning of some new metaphysical dispensation not of parochial import, but eternal, cosmological in scale, and in which I had my humble, but crucial part to play. Ray sang as he worked, a tuneless dirge, or sometimes listened to Alden's CD, but not when I was in the room because then I just curled up and went to sleep, and neither fucked nor worked.

Alden was working on ways of making the hum music not person-specific, and though he worried that there might be a technical contradiction in this, refused to give up. Joan had responded to the sound of her own heart beats, alas no-one else had. This was for Alden an unwelcome development.

Sometimes they had people to lunch, or for pre-supper drinks, and then I was sent to my room. This increasingly irked me. I did not mind being the cleaner and the whore but I did not see why I should not be treated as a social equal. On a couple of occasions I was sent back to spend the night at Little Venice. I picked up my thesis and stared at it and couldn't make head or tail of it, but my mind started its churning again and I thought my head would split, so I sorted drawers and hung up clothes instead. I had quite got into the habit.

Whether it was Alden or Ray who had decided I

would be the useful and passive kind of person who puts things in order and made things possible for others I don't know. I do know I cleaned Alden's house and Ray's attic as they had never been cleaned before. I moved furniture and sculptures and swept beneath them: I cleaned round light switches and the loos were spotless – it was a big house; there were four bathrooms and two washrooms. I removed heat rings on tables, I polished, I stacked plates properly, arranged pans in height order, handles parallel. I washed paint. I wore gloves, and was sharply spoken to if I forgot.

Lam shook out the rugs for me in the little yard at the back of the house. He had strong wrists: one whack and dust flew obediently. The brass fittings on the lift shone. The buzzer would sound from the studio and I'd whiz up to hand Ray a paintbrush, or find him a better one, or change his turps, or he'd up my skirts – I wore a kind of Victorian maid's outfit, a real one, vintage, not fancy dress, a tough black drill with a little white lace apron and frilly cap – for a quick shag on the sofa. Ray could last for a good half hour now, having agreed to abandon his principles and take Viagra or Cialis, but didn't want to lose good painting time so I could be on and off the sofa in fifteen minutes.

And then he'd have to be packed off to Southgate – socks found, cigarettes, lighter – the more useful I got, the more hopeless he became – he was going to daily Golden Dawn classes. He confided in me that he hoped one day to become the foretold SDA or Sapiens

Dominabitur Astris – Latin for 'the wise one who will be ruled by the stars.' Lam would often go along too. They were all nuts but it was none of my business.

In the afternoons there was time for me to go to the hairdresser and the beauty salons, where I would be coloured, depilated, smoothed, oiled and generally toned up. The gym was disapproved of – muscles might develop: a soft helplessness was more attractive – and physical energy should be preserved for better things.

After supper I would take a bath, go to my room and Lam would come in and do my make-up. With practice he was getting quite good at it. He could cover the range from healthy pony girl down on the farm, freckles and blue eye-shadow, to kohled Cleopatra, mysterious and sulky, and all stages in-between: secretary, bride, whore, factory lass, leather freak, hitch-hiking student, *Sex and the City* professional. It could be disconcerting because I would see a tentacle rather than a hand reach out for mascara or eye-shadow, and it was hard to keep in mind that this was an illusion, a post hoc suggestion from Ray, not a reality.

Then it was time for the bed, for experiments, for cuffs, manacles, gag-balls, collars, lace corsets: incessant changes of clothes, a horrible metallic dental gadget which kept the mouth propped open wide, ever-changing music, or active non-music ('the hum'), hypodermics, breast clamps, jabbing needles – Lam took blood from time to time, which would be sent off by messenger for analysis of my hormone levels and God knows what else, the results being fed into his computer. Lam would heave Alden onto the bed, I would bend over the side of it to take him in my mouth, and Ray, emboldened and excited by new opportunities, with new and widened horizons, would enter my cunt and my butt with promiscuous caprice.

Or Ray would be in my mouth while I rode astride Alden: and the cuffs on my wrists and no doubt the seams in my corsets, tight under my heart, would be feeding back to the oscilloscopes, pulse generators, frequency counters, logic and spectrum analysers, plotter loggers, signal generators and all other necessary equipment, the complete story of my sex life, video to be translated into audio, to be incorporated into *Thelemy: The Silence of the Senses*, designed to send Radio 3 listeners aroused to their beds. It was a noble task or an absurd one; I could never be sure which. Joan thought the first, Vanessa the second.

And Lam would photograph and film: cameras round the room, darting here and there. And still Alden never came. Perpetual sexual arousal without end leading to a greater spirituality, the wisdom of Tantrism – perforce – added to Crowleyism, every desire gratified, every impulse expressed, through free experimentation in drugs, sex and physical excess: that tragic explosion in the school lab, once upon a time, creating the second coming of the Beast 666: Alden X.

My unavoidable readings had led me to the conclusion that all those annoying early avant-garde painters, Vorticists, Futurists, Cubists, Surrealists and so forth were trying to create a new reality through the 'infinite complexity' they kept on about. Their friends the musicians were after the same thing. And lo, it had all born terrible fruit, in the form of the computer. And now Alden and Ray were trying to move the whole thing on a stage or two: I, the living me, sex, beauty, warts and all, was being sucked into their audio and visual machinery and being computerised. I was muse to the new computer age; I was hertz instead of music, I and all humanity were reduced to tiny lines upon a canvas, mouse clickers, nothing else. I didn't like it, of course I didn't. No wonder I was bipolaring along like mad.

So far as Joan knew I was in my right mind, and this was not even a variant of normal life, just normal life. This was how I spent my days. But then most people think that of their lives. When I watch people on *I'm a Celebrity* or reality shows, my life as the Whore of Babylon seemed no stranger than theirs.

And then things entered another phase.

I am not quite sure what happened. Some gadgets on the Lukas bed failed: both mechanical – one of the poles wedged and could not be moved – and something to do with his having to put up with incompatibilities between the primitive midi configuration Lukas had used and that which Alden was using in his other apparatus. There was also a failure of 'granular synthesis' to cope with the required intensity of orgasmic sound.

Lam clucked and whickered sympathy. Alden swore and cursed all technology, damned the bed as cheap and out-dated, and Lukas for ripping him off, got his wheels tangled in wires, and cursed Lucifer.

'You Hertz 111 girl,' said Lam, giving me a severe pinch as I lay there bound and helpless. 'You trouble. You not 93.'

Thelemy was overdue by three weeks and still Alden was nowhere near completion. Which you could see as the story of his life, but that was not a joke I was prepared to make. The bad mood went on for days: I was getting the blame now for failing to produce the required category of sound. My experiences were intense but not intense enough. Ray rashly said but only 1% of people could tell the difference between the excellent and the adequate, and that sent Alden into a sulk – a hissy fit, as Ray described it.

As if this was not bad enough, depression – which I know to be catching – moved in on Ray, like a weather front on a satellite chart. You feel it approaching. It was no more romps on the sofa for me but straight back to the intensity of work: he moaned on again about his erection problems – for which he blamed potency pills; they had 'disturbed his energy harmonics' – and was back to the old humiliating premature ejaculate days. He could contribute nothing to Alden's sex sessions; he did not have the heart to pick up a paint brush. *The Blue Box* stood on its easel untouched. Ray took to his bed and would not have me near it. It occurred to me that he was Bipolar One, a sorrier state to be in than mine. Bipolar Two can find its own resolution in everyday life – though this remedy could be drastic, as I had found out – but Bipolar One can do nothing when depression sweeps in. Ray had just to sit it out, and especially avoid answering the phone to Lady Daisy O, who kept wanting to come round and inspect *The Blue Box*, which, as she accurately pointed out, she had put up a down payment for. Snotty bourgeoise bitch, I thought. Joan was on Ray's side.

Two Women

ALDEN, NEVER ONE TO stand idly by for long, took matters in hand, not so much the bull by the horns, as the cow by the udders. He took the initiative and invited Lady O round. Better for Ray to face her than to hide. If the worst came to the worst Daisy O would just have to change the date of the exhibition, though this would do nothing for Alden's cash flow problems at Arts-Intrinsick. The important thing was that pressure was taken off Ray.

I heard him confide in Lam that he did not think much of the Southgate crew.

They were amateurs. Renegades. They had advanced Ray too fast along the paths. Now Ray was suffering. He was using 'the Will' when he had not necessarily built up the proper resources of power, and he was paying the price. As a result *The Blue Box* was suffering too. It was a disaster. I had the feeling I was somehow being blamed for this, too. But then men did that. When things go wrong they turn to the nearest woman and blame her. My father would do it to my mother. He'd poke his nose out the door and say 'it's cold', as if it were her fault and she would automatically say 'I'm sorry.' So I took not too much notice.

'You bad girl,' Lam said, poking me with his finger. 'You 111 hertz girl. You try be 93.' He might or might not be an alien, might not have private parts like Barbie's friend Ken or Action Man, but his insensitivity was entirely male.

Alden wanted me to dress and act the secretary for his meeting with Daisy O. He did not want Ray upset any more than he was already. He wanted me to stand by and take notes. He supposed I could do that? He suddenly sounded doubtful. I said of course: I was secretary to the parent-teacher association at my nursery school and no-one had so far complained. With me present, Alden went on, Lady Daisy would be less likely to be abusive or nasty.

Loki whizzed me back to Little Venice, which seemed by now a strange and humdrum dwelling, piled high with frothy and thoughtless tat, ungraced by artistic aspiration, or any of the things which give meaning to life, and was the natural territory of someone far, far sillier than me.

I came back in the clothes I wore for the Olivier – navy knee-length skirt, court shoes, white blouse and a string of pearls – looking very much the secretary. A raised female voice came from Ray's studio, brisk, stern and displeased, but resigned, like a nanny talking to a

163

naughty child. Lady O had arrived early. Ray's voice in reply had an edge of whinging self-pity: Alden's, which interrupted and replaced it, was fluent, reassuring and phony.

'You brought me here to show me this?' Daisy O exclaimed. 'He's barely started it!'

Daisy O was an heiress from a Silicon Valley family. She had married an English peer and now entertained herself shooting grouse and buying art, in which she was genuinely interested. She was a connoisseur, unlike Matilda Weiss, who, as Alden explained to me, saw art as way of buying influence and showing off. I had Googled Daisy and found 182,000 references. (Alden clocked up 98,000, Ray 726,000, having lately gone on the syllabus of a leading art school.) Daisy was certainly not interested in her appearance, any more than is the Queen of England. She was very tall, around 6ft, and slouched, and her fair hair was scraped back savagely from her face and held by a rubber band. She had no time for frivolities. Her shoes were flat, her elasticised skirt did nothing for her figure, bunching round her waist as it did. She wore a white shirt splodged with great yellow chrysanthemums. I thought she had buttoned it up wrongly until I realised it was purposefully asymmetrical. I had seen one like it in Liberty's recently – by a Japanese designer – and thought I had never seen anything so hideous, and wondered who on earth would spend £3,750 on such grotesquerie. Now I knew.

Yet Lady Daisy was not without allure, in her natural, healthy, big-boned, energetic way. I always knew when someone who came into the Olivier was from California. They brought sunshine and confidence with them, even though as now, they might be in a fury.

I found a newspaper article on Google which told me more. That Lady O was opening up the lower half of her London residence – one of those huge dull houses near Belgrave Square near where Lady Thatcher lived – as a non profit-making gallery. It was to be called the En Garde, and be open to the public from mid-September. The design firm Arts-Intrinsick had won the commission to refurbish in a highly competitive market. 'Arts Patronage Devolves To Private Hands As Government Provision Fails', went the headlines. 'The New Face Of The Arts: Saatchi Mark Two – But All Proceeds To Charity' ran below. Centre piece of the opening exhibition was to be a commissioned piece, *The Blue Box*, by up-and-coming artist Ray Franchi. Another feature of the opening would be a first performance of *Thelemy – The Murmur of Eternity* by noted composer Alden X. Readers who were listeners to Radio 3 might already have heard his striking piece in the Minimalist Maelstrom. I had been promoted to an eternal murmur, I was happy to discover, rescued from the *Silence of the Senses*.

Lady Daisy was busy counting squares. She told Ray there were twenty-nine left undone.

She had to have his guarantee that the work would be completed in the next three to four weeks. Let him not try telling her this timing was intentional, she knew perfectly well it was not.

'Of course it's not intentional,' said Ray. 'My brain just won't currently do the translations.'

Lady O said she had been working with artists too long not to know when they were having her on, screw the translations, Ray had her over a barrel and wanted more money, was that it?

Alden said he bitterly resented her attitude and not to use that language, please. It upset Ray.

Daisy said Alden was another one, she supposed she'd find now the music had run into a creative block and magically wouldn't be ready unless she handed out some more funds. He'd played the disability card once too often.

'Disability real,' said Lam. 'Disability no card.'

'Tell that creep of yours to shut the fuck up. Get him out of here. And her too,' she said, looking at me. 'What is said in here is confidential. I don't want her taking notes.'

Lam stayed where he was. I took my cue from him and went on busily writing. Alden attended to his touch pad and barely audible music came out of the walls. Daisy didn't seem to notice at first.

'Just get on with it,' she said, literally stamping her big flat foot at Ray, 'and hurry the fuck up.' I've stamped my foot in my time, but it makes an impatient little tapping sound with heels: Lady O's just made a dull thud.

'My integrity?' he pleaded.

'I won't tell you where you can put it,' she said. 'Fuck integrity. What about my gallery? What about my fucking integrity?' Which was more or less what Alden had said to Ray many a time, but it was different when a woman said it.

'Bad language,' said Lam. 'Bad.'

Daisy told Lam that if he had issues with direct language, she had no objection to him stuffing himself right up his own arse if he had one, and told Alden that since the parquet floor was rising she had already arranged for it to be re-laid by someone competent, and that she hoped he was looking forward to getting the bill. Alden's music was louder now. It seemed to confuse her. She looked this way and that.

Daisy said she had half a mind to ship *The Blue Box* out then and there as she was perfectly entitled to do, and hire some hack art restorer just to fill in the squares. But even as she spoke in her flat, nasal tones, her voice faltered. The midday sun shone straight down from the skylight and for once the whole ensemble was without shadows. Seen like this it had what I can only describe as a kind of thickened density: it stared straight out, not just reflecting back from the universe into itself, but inwards, down and down into its own soul: a gateway of sympathetic magic between macrocosm and microcosm. Awesome.

'What's that noise?' she asked. 'Are there insects in this room?'

She seemed really distressed. I wished Alden would turn the hum off. It had been added to and enhanced in complexity since last I heard it. Now I knew it was so personal to me, I didn't want it shared amongst strangers. Ray crossed over to her and took her hand, which was brave of him. He was half her scale: puny. I felt defensive of him. It was the sheer force of creativity which denatured him: carried some of his strength away as it washed through him. He sacrificed himself for us.

'Look in to my eyes,' he said, 'I so want you to be pleased with me.'

I saw Daisy's face soften, and grow trusting. He told her how much she had done for the Arts in this country and the corners of her mouth turned up a little and she actually looked pleased.

'We in the avant-garde have so much to be grateful to you for,' Ray said. 'We in the Thelemic movement are so proud to have you with us. Be sure your support is important to us.'

Your call is important to us – the voice was artificially soothing, ingenuous: Daisy might as well be through to a call-centre. I started to giggle, out of sheer nervousness, but Alden darted me such a look I shut up. I was not forgotten: I was part of a plan.

'Let yourself be guided by me,' Ray said. 'And Alden too. We are part of the way, the truth, and the light.

Come with us on that path. Trust us. You can close your eyes now.'

And Daisy actually did, and stood there swaying, a great big beautiful puppet, and half of me wanted to shake her awake and save her and half didn't, because I wanted her to get what she deserved.

I knew who she reminded me of now – my best friend Jude, who fucked my father in the greenhouse when I was off being interviewed to get into Oxford. Was that person me? Wasn't I now Joan, the girl with the body but no brain? The music was louder and confusing me too. Ray turned to me and said, 'Isn't she lovely, Joan. Don't you think so?' And I nodded. I did.

Alden gave Lady Daisy a little pinch as she stood there, looking bemused but kindly in her asymmetrical blouse with its ugly flowers, and I thought if only she took it off she'd look much better. She was smiling at me now as if I wasn't a bug to be trodden on, after all. Alden could pinch her all he liked; it was me she took notice of. I appreciated that.

'We're all going downstairs now,' said Alden, and we all trooped down to the mirror room and sat in a semi circle on our Philip Starck chairs. I noticed I had no clothes on, though everyone else was wearing theirs. It was like one of those anxiety dreams, when you suddenly find yourself naked and exposed in the street, only I knew wasn't going to wake up for quite a while. The music was louder down here. Lam had an ordinary digital camcorder out, a hand-held thing, because problems with the Lukas bed had temporarily crashed the whole computer recording system, and he 'wanted to get on with it'.

'Don't get too fond of Daisy, Joan,' said Alden, 'because she's been very, very bad. She needs to be punished.' And I thought of my friend Jude, and I thought yes, indeed Daisy does. And poor Ray was looking quite pale and exhausted and I knew Daisy had drained the strength out of him, which was very bad, for the Arts, for the world, for everyone. And I knew it was up to me to right the balance.

'Daisy very rude,' said Lam. 'Not good girl.'

'Daisy,' said Alden. 'Something very bad has happened.' And he went into a long spiel about how Daisy's brother had been kidnapped by terrorists in Argentina and the only way for Daisy to save his life was to have sex with the colonel. Daisy was no fool and asked many questions but Alden had an answer to everything. Even when he told her the colonel was a woman she accepted that. Indeed, she seemed rather relieved. I hadn't realised, either, that I had joined the terrorists and was now their colonel. But it all made perfect sense.

Daisy whimpered in a corner, semi-clothed. I had ripped off her chrysanthemum blouse and tugged off her hair-band and she now looked a great deal better: she had really nice big breasts which was why I reckoned she stooped: it wasn't her height. She was a beautifully-proportioned bronzed giantess with big pink nipples from California who didn't know how to behave: who had looked at me as if I was an insect and reminded me of Jude and had to be taught a lesson. I chose from a selection of whips, rubber-thonged, designed to redden but leave few marks. Or so they said. I had not been a dominatrix before. I could see you could get a taste for it. I put aside the rubber whip and chose one with plaited leather tassels.

I dressed for the occasion in red leather thigh boots with impossibly clunky heels, and a black corset, taking my time. I knew it was all true and I knew none of it was true at the same time. That is to say Joan knew it was, and Vanessa knew it wasn't. Whatever. Both of me was angry with Jude, and one of me was extremely angry with Daisy, who was a central source of the evil of global capitalism, and a persecutor of free expression and the arts, part of the über-conspiracy, destroying from within the very thing it purports to support.

'It's all far too crude,' said Ray. 'Some kind of sense will break through.'

'Neither of them want it to break through,' said Alden. 'That's obvious. They're both lesbians.'

I heard that; they should be so lucky. I would make her dance about a bit with the whip: this was between me and her.

She whimpered like a great big baby. I made her stand up and turn with her back to me and bend over. Her buttock cheeks were round and full. They would take the lash nicely. She was shivering. 'Party headquarters' was cold. It was midwinter in Argentina, as Alden reminded me. He loved to instruct.

I took the whip and swished it through the air, once or twice. It made a good, final kind of sound. I advanced upon her. I raised my hand—

'No Joan,' said Alden patiently. 'The whip is just set-dressing, it's a prop, for God's sake. The dildo's fine, but we mustn't mark her.'

So I made her lean against the bed – how that came to be at 'party headquarters' I don't know, but there it was – and spread her legs with the tip of the whip while she stood passive and terrified. I knelt in front of her and tickled her clitoris – it was quite large, like another nipple – with my tongue, getting it exactly in the right place as so many men in their ignorance fail to do. There's nothing like a woman's touch; we know from first hand what a woman responds to. I went on circling until she shuddered and cried out, and came; and then, my own pleasure deferred, and hers sated – but she wasn't allowed to stop: she had to 'remember her brother' and put up with it, and she couldn't do anything about it anyway, because her hands were tied together behind her: I've no idea how that happened – I drove the green soft plastic dildo up inside her, it was a monstrous, ugly, vulgar, cheap-looking thing, not at all fit for the aristocracy, if well-suited to bringing a global capitalist down a peg or two: and turned it on to full speed. I felt it buck about inside her and had to cling on the end for fear of losing it: while she begged me to stop, but I knew better.

'See how you like that,' I said, 'you little whore!' I'd been called that myself from time to time, and now I could see the attraction: it passed the responsibility from the perpetrator to the victim. Now I could do whatever I liked with her. I was justified. I grabbed her hair and slapped her.

'Please let my brother go,' she said, forlornly, as if remembering the narrative she was meant to be in. But I knew she was playing a part just as much as I was. You can't get people to do things under hypnosis they wouldn't do of their own accord – it's just surprising how much 'their own accord' includes.

'But why does this have to be a dominatrix scene,' I heard Ray protest. 'Why can't they just have cheerful sex?'

'Because cheerful sex no longer turns you on,' said Alden. 'And she's an impertinent, foul-mouthed bitch and deserves a lesson.'

But Ray must have prevailed because I soon found myself aged fifteen lying in long grasses amidst wild flowers in a summer field with a gentle breeze and the birds and the bees, and we were young and lovely. And Daisy was lying close to me, and we were happy as the day was long because we loved each other. Youthful, supple bodies, mine white and soft, hers bronzed and strong: how different and yet the same. Now lips against lips, tongue searching tongue, breast comparing breast.

Her little finger searching my small, pink, unused holes for entrance, mine hers: now two fingers, now three – we were quiet, that strange still silence as the god of love descends and all things are in abeyance – and then a sharp warning voice, Alden's:

'Teacher's coming!' And we sprang apart and grabbed for our clothes, and tried to hide our nakedness.

And I'll swear I did see the teacher there clear as daylight, outlined against sunlight, the one who spoils all pleasures, grudges all joy, who make natural things seem sinful, and drains the fun out of life. She was real: she wasn't in the head. The square shaped body, the scraped back hair, the full black skirt, tight high bodice and button boots, the very opposite of our easy, idle nakedness. She was not in Ray's scenario, or Alden's: I don't know where I found her, but there she was, when we least expected her. She had an objective reality of her own. She's the one who circles the outer limits of the universe, like a kind of evil Mary Poppins, spreading neurotic guilt, casting doubt and alarm, detecting impropriety, stopping fun. Teacher's coming! She always is, one way or another. Mrs Do-What-You-Ought, Not-What-You-Want. Standing there in button boots, stalking the Garden of Eden, spoiling everything. Mrs Do-As-I-Say-Or-Else-You'll-Be-Done-By-As-You-Did. Nasty old women in a high-necked collar and button boots, too old and mean to have fun. Wilting the spirit and sapping the energies. What chance did Rabelais and Crowley ever have, with their hopeful

Do-As-Thou-Wilt-Shall-Be-The-Whole-Of-The-Law
with Teacher forever sneaking up from behind. Teacher's
on the warpath – so Alden can't come, and Ray too
soon, and all manner of wretchednesses abounds.

Now the four of us are on the bed, and Ray is
actually managing to mount Lady O, telling her that
he is the Lady Colonel's superior officer, and soon she
will be free to go. The joyful lesbian scene has had
its effect, and Daisy, under will, is in no position to
complain of any inadequacy in performance she may
detect. Alden is out of his chair and inside me, from
the back as ever, and I really think, as his breath comes
shorter and quicker, that the spell is broken and he will
climax – but no. He sighs, he stops; the Gods of Tantra
claim him yet again.

All finally quieted down, Alden told Lady Daisy
that she had been stunningly brave, sacrificed herself
for love and her brother's safety, that the incident was
now closed, that she would cease to hassle Ray about
finishing the work, which she would happily rely on
him to finish in good time – and (my suggestion, this)
would not ever wear the asymmetrical blouse again.
She would give it to the poor. She would play *Thelemy
– The Murmur of Eternity* at the En Garde opening, and
not ask Jimmy Page to play live as she had planned.

Alden told Daisy she was very pleased indeed with the
work done by Arts-Intrinsick, and would recommend
the firm at all times appropriate. She was to assure
Ray on her returning to normal, which would be when

he clicked his fingers, that the suggestion about the restorer 'finishing' the *Box* was a bad joke, for which she would apologise. She would remember nothing of the afternoon except that she had said 'Fuck integrity', for which she would also say sorry.

Ray clicked his fingers and Lady Daisy said, 'I'm sorry, everyone. The stuff about the restorers was a bad joke, and I was being ironic about integrity.' Then she went down smiling to her waiting limo. I was not angry with her any more. We had both given each other pleasure. I could see that women could be friends. I thought I might even ring up Jude; I missed her. And I could see that my father might have been more responsible for what happened in the summer house than Jude was. I did still blame the twins, though, who had run to tell our mother what they had seen. They might be a pair of child prodigies, but that didn't stop them being spiteful snitches.

And Ray, re-invigorated, went to his canvas and took up his brush and painted another square. And I remembered just how it had all happened, with only a few patches missing. They had wiped Daisy's memory but had quite forgotten to wipe Joan's; and Vanessa's was fairly hard to wipe, since she was never addressed by name. Their mistake.

A Weekend in the Country

I WAS SENT HOME FOR a few days to the country. Ray managed a final major exercise in will control before the spirit drained out of him. I had my orders. No parties while away, no sex with strangers. No eating of junk food. No sexual fantasies. No masturbation. Alden piled in with his own instructions: no drinking, no smoking, no bitching, and no losing of the temper. Just life as a good Essex girl waiting to take up a post at an infant school after Christmas, going home for the week to enjoy the innocent pleasures of a Plymouth Brethren household.

Loki would meet me at Liverpool Street Station at five o'clock on the Friday afternoon, ready for an evening's work, by which time the Lukas bed should have been repaired and some breakthrough achievable in *Thelemy – The Murmur of Eternity*. It was quite a privilege to be seen as responsible for the music of the spheres.

But a bore too. I would have to traipse all the way

by tube between Paddington and Liverpool Street, at opposite ends of London, twice. I didn't dare ask Loki to drop me off and pick me up at Paddington; to do so would mean confessing that home was in Wiltshire not in Essex, that I was Vanessa not Joan. I knew neither Alden nor Ray would tolerate Vanessa, who knew too much, thought too hard, and would laugh out loud at their faith in the Golden Dawn, Thelemy, OTO and all the ponderous self-importance of aspiring necromancers.

But it was good to be going home. I hadn't been back to see Mum, Dad, the twins and my little brother for some four months. I may have as many mixed feelings about my family as the next person, but I love my home. It's a rectory, next door to St Michael's, a small, rustic, hilltop church: 12th century, restored in 1845 and again in 1875, the year Mrs Blavatsky formed the Theosophical Society, forerunner of the Golden Dawn, the Thelemites and the OTO. They say there was once a pagan temple here where they worshipped the sun.

There is a mention of our house in the Domesday Book, the 1086 register of larger dwellings. The Norman doorway with its dog-toothed arch must date back to that time. Beams twist, floors undulate, the plumbing is noisy, the roof creaks on still nights; but there are roses in the garden, and hollyhocks against old stone walls, and clematis, honeysuckle and jasmine festoon the mullioned windows. We have a ghost, a desultory poltergeist who moves papers from room to room, and occasionally makes plates fall off the dresser. But that may be the twins' unconscious fault: kinetic spookery is often connected with the presence of neurotic, teenage girls.

My mother drifts around, sometimes in her vestments of office, sometimes not, always kind, vaguely anxious, trying to tempt the young in to her services with guitars, bongo drums, conjurers and prayers she makes up herself. She used to be a counsellor and conducts her feel-good services as if they were a group therapy. Her congregation, elderly and dwindling, put up with her because she is a nice person and tries hard. She is always in the right, which is sometimes difficult for a family to take. My father is a stern Church of England traditionalist, and what he sees as my mother's 'soppiness' drives him to quiet apoplexy. He doesn't believe in women priests. 'A woman preaching is like a dog standing on its hind legs,' he quotes from Dr Johnson. He once said she had herself ordained to annoy him.

Alison and Katharine accuse her of passive-aggression, but she just smiles and says they're entitled to their opinion, and understands their anger. She forgives them which they say proves their point. Little Robert is her favourite, and she discourages any display of anger or violence from him, thus, my father says, threatening to make him turn out gay. Which to my father would be a terrible and disgraceful thing. To Mum, though she would deny it, it could be an

179

outcome greatly to be desired, for then he might never leave her. Easier to lose a son to another man than to a woman.

So we have our family tensions, not least between Mum and myself, but she loves me and I love her. And my parents love each other, in spite of my father's astonishing behaviour with Jude, which my Mum has forgiven according to her lights, though I'm not sure I quite have.

All the same, I am her least favourite child. She thinks I live a secretive life, which I do, and that I lie to her, which I do. But I took the job at the Olivier in part to save my family's face; so my parents could have something to say to their friends – 'oh, Vanessa? She's gone into hotel management – yes! – a training scheme at the Olivier in London, she could have stuck it out in academia, but she does like to work with people.'

What my mother really wants, of course, are grandchildren. I've failed her so far, and the twins are so backward sexually and so advanced intellectually, she's resigned to not holding her breath. They communicate with each other rather than the outside word; for sport they throw Latin tenses and Greek conjugations around like tennis balls. Babies would terrify them.

I don't know whether Robert is gay or not, and I don't suppose it is anything to do with Mother either way. I'm pretty sure he won't turn out like Hasan, who I hope by now is spreading happiness amongst my sisters all over the planet, whenever he can dodge his father.

My brother currently slouches round in slacker mode, sneery, arch, spotty and reluctant, driving everyone mad: last winter he exasperated and embarrassed my father by getting suspended from Eton for a week for shaving his head. Even my mother acknowledges that currently he is being very 'trying' but says it's his anxiety about his sexual orientation that makes him like this. My father snorts and goes back to his books.

My grandmother pays Robert's school fees by covenant from beyond the grave. I got left the paintings, and the twins will have a small flat in Oxford in a couple of years. All these goodies were earned by my grandmother on her back, as Lord F, her one-time husband loved to say. She was beautiful, charming and greedy, a courtesan, and no doubt it's all somewhere in the genes, having by-passed my mother. My grandmother by all accounts flirted, seduced, and married for money and titles. She left angry men wherever she went – and I daresay once or twice heard herself described as the Scarlet Whore of Babylon – but not, I reckon, as often as I have in the last few weeks. When I was a girl I used to wonder what went on in the pagan temple where now St Michael's stands. Sex and human sacrifice, I supposed. It's all rather tame now and getting tamer every day my mother is in charge.

I love all my family, of course I do. We're a clever lot: we all enjoy the life of the mind. The conversation over the dinner table is lively and instructive. My mother relates the news of the parish – always a source of diversion and amazement; my father instructs us – like Alden he has a tendency to instruct rather than to converse – upon the fragile state of Western civilisation. So it was a great relief to be out of London, and to be Vanessa not Joan any more, allowed to have an intellect. It is as difficult to appear stupid when one is not as vice versa. In London I always had to remember to leave repartee to Alden and Ray, and the effort of not delivering a smart line over dinner could be almost as tiring as being a mixture of experimental animal, sex slave and sex toy all night. And it was so good to be amongst books again: I realised how few there were in Alden's house. This is what gave it its desolate air. Ray at least had a few old paperbacks about and some old Phaidon art books on which he perched and spilt his coffee mugs.

The week off was also an opportunity for various rather bruised, abused and battered parts of my anatomy to rest and heal, and for my heightened state of arousal to be calmed down by the kind of familiar, comforting boredom that sets in whenever a girl visits home.

But even after a couple of days' quiescence I still seemed to be emitting a field of orgone energy. My mother had asked a theology professor friend and his wife round to dinner, and he played one-sided footsie with me under the table, with the calm confidence that suggested he realised the kind of girl I was. That shook me. I'd given him not the slightest encouragement that I was aware of. One likes to be seen as a good girl until revealing the bad girl, not the other way round. Sex begets sex, I suppose. It gets into the air. He was at least sixty five. They were old family friends, and came to dinner every few weeks. I respected him for his book – *The Decline of Western Religion*. I liked his wife very much. I jabbed his foot with a stiletto heel and he didn't try again. My mother didn't like me wearing heels around the Rectory: she was convinced they were bad for the floors and would cripple my feet and give me bunions – but then she didn't know how useful heels can be as a weapon in defence of one's virtue. She'd never had to do much to protect hers.

I took the opportunity during the week of going to see Dr Philip Bardsey, our family physician. He was very busy but found space for me after hours on the Thursday evening. He was a fleshy, jowly man, now on the edge of retirement, a smoker and overweight, with stubby, not always very clean, fingers and blurry eyes – but a good diagnostician. He had been my doctor since I was twelve; he'd been giving me thorough internal examinations since that age, too.

On the very first occasion indeed he broke my hymen, by mistake, but told me it was just as well. Blood could build up in the uterus and that would not help my mental state; which was an issue at the time, since my mother had taken me in to him complaining that I was over-excitable and hysterical. He told her he preferred to see me alone. She'd made a scene, and admittedly so had I, but eventually he convinced her and she went on home and left me with him. He asked a list of questions, and then told me to lie down on his couch and face the wall with my knees up. In went his hand, latex-gloved; which was a mixture of the horrible, the strange and the delightful. A sudden sharp pain for me and a small cry of surprise from him – and when I was back on my chair, after a little spurt of blood had been mopped, he suggested that since my mother, of the two of us, seemed marginally the more hysterical, it might be better if I kept quiet about the matter of the hymen. I could see he was right.

I trusted him enough at the time to ask him if there was anything the matter with me, and he said actually he thought I might be Bipolar Two – I was a bright girl: I could look it up sometime – but it would be to my advantage not to get an official diagnosis. He was not going to write anything in my notes. Keep up the sex once you get to it, he said, keep up the shopping, take a tranquillizer if inside the head gets really bad, steer clear of psychiatrists and you'll have a good life. It was really good advice, if not what my mother would have liked to hear.

Since then we had been in a kind of collusion. He knew something about me – that I was Bipolar Two and wouldn't grow out of it, but he would save me from a damaging diagnosis if he could. I knew he had taken my virginity and the internal examinations weren't strictly necessary, but I would shut up about it.

Later when I was at college the diagnosis was

confirmed by the shrinks at the student health centre. I'd been sent to them as a result of my involvement in a gang-bang scandal: but what the authorities saw as sexual excess, I saw as the perfectly normal pursuit of pleasure and excitement. They told me at the centre that lithium might help stabilise my moods: I took it for a little and then stopped. I liked my moods as they were. My problems were more to do with my studies interfering with my sex life than the other way round.

Now I thought I should report in to Dr Bardsey about the sudden surges of mental over-activity I was experiencing and see if he had any more suggestions.

I stayed in the waiting room until the last limping old lady and wheezing old man had left and then Dr Bardsey opened the door and asked me into his consulting room. I stripped off to my bra and pants and lay on the couch. Why hang about?

'Straight to the point,' said Dr Bardsey. 'How have you been, Vanessa?'

I said I was fine, other than that my brain was firing on too many cylinders and he asked if I'd taken any unusual drugs lately and I said perhaps, but they came from the tropical rainforest and were perfectly safe.

He asked if I had ever been to a rainforest and I said no. He said he had, and they were foul, dripping, mouldy, sinister places and that with a few notable exceptions such as curare, anything that came out of them was likely to be baneful, fungoid and evil. Never take anything, he said, except substances that are formally banned: they're safer. I was probably suffering from rainforest medication: now a new health food store had opened in the area he was getting all kinds of cases of unexplained toxicity. It would probably wear off. He'd prescribe a higher dosage of tranquillizer if I liked. I said yes but I assumed I'd have to earn it, so I wriggled out of my pants, turned to the wall and pulled my knees up and in went the cold gloved hand in the familiar way.

'You're quite swollen in there,' he said.

'Over-use,' I said.

'Better that way than the other,' he said. A finger from the other hand, ungloved and warm, now circled my clitoris. I shuddered and came.

'It's so nice in there, Vanessa,' he said. 'You really are my favourite patient. You're so uncomplicated.'

'What do you like about doing that?' I asked.

'It's the source of everything,' he said. 'I never get over the marvel of it.' And he was such a greasy, unhealthy, flabby, crude kind of person from the outside, too. Reluctantly, the hand withdrew.

'Thanks,' he said. 'I hope one day you have babies.' He was such a dear, romantic old softy.

I asked him if I could have a good supply of morning-after pills. For Alden had come to the conclusion that the birth pill I was on was impairing my libido and not helping *Thelemy – The Murmur of Eternity*, and that since sexual energy was strongest when a woman was fertile, the best thing to do was avoid any contraceptive precautions other than *ex post facto* ones; which made sense. Dr Bardsey said he'd thought I was on the pill: and why did I think I needed them? I explained and his hairy eyebrows shot up and he asked had I gone mad? What was the matter with me? My hormonal balance would go to hell; and that was the last thing an undiagnosed Bipolar Two needed.

I wondered why I hadn't thought of it myself. Being 'under will' – and you never knew when you were and when you weren't – was rather like living in an advertisement. All looked normal, but you had to detect the truth in what was missing, in the gaps between sentences. I knew quite definitely I had to bring home morning-after pills and that was that. Obliging Alden was more important than any hormonal cycle of mine.

'I'll have full sex with you if you give me the prescription,' I said, and he looked bewildered and upset and said perhaps he was wrong about all this; perhaps I should see a psychiatrist after all.

I backed off quickly and apologised. He had his own way of doing things and I must respect it. I would tell Alden I had the morning-after pills and actually just go on taking the contraceptive pill. There was nothing wrong with my libido, I was sure of that. If it was damped down it was probably just as well. Otherwise I would explode.

I took off my bra and sat on the chair so he could palpate my breasts, as was his custom. I am shyer about exposing my breasts than my cunt. I suppose by the time you get to your cunt, it's too late. While it's breasts choices can still be made. Breasts seem so personal, so individual; cunts seem much of a muchness if you are a woman, though I suppose for men they do come over as more individual.

Good breasts – and I am proud of mine, though I tend to like to keep them to myself – are a family tradition, though it has by-passed Katharine and Alison. The twins once came giggling in to show me a naughty postcard they'd found in the family papers. It showed this lovely thirties-ish girl with a bare bosom, a delicate hand hiding one and the other proudly open to public gaze. It was my grandmother. The twins – they must have been about twelve themselves at the time – asked if I thought they would look like that one day, and I said no. They were flat as pancakes, and of a less robust build than the rest of the family, almost as if they shared one physical being between the two of them. They were not pleased by what I told them, but it was true. Just as I was not pleased to be told I was Bipolar Two, but it was true.

Dr Bardsey came round behind me and felt my breasts carefully and lovingly. I was glad I hadn't frightened him away. I should not have been so head-on: that was bloody Alden's doing.

'You don't ever have to worry,' he said. 'These breasts will never get cancer. There's too much pleasure in them.' He took his time. One hand felt; I don't know what the other hand attended to, but it was no part of me, and I didn't strain my imagination. When I was dressed we parted formally, shaking hands.

I left with prescriptions for tranquillizers, sleeping pills, birth control pills, a blood test done, but no morning-after pills. Well, I would manage.

Families are complicated. Return to the safety of home, and find you can't say 'please pass the salt' without it being a loaded statement. It will be heard to mean 'the food is under salted' or 'you're neglecting me,' or 'why didn't you notice I needed it?' Because all the other unanswered questions are lying festering behind every simple pass-the-salt request: the important ones like, 'Mother, why did you leave me standing at the school gate for hours when I was seven?' Or 'why was I sent to a state school when Robert went private?' Or the really big one for me, 'why did you have an affair with my best friend, Daddy?'

Such subtext infests every passing inanity; though the past is more or less forgiven, it's never forgotten. Families are too complicated for comfort. So when I went back to London I was sad to miss them, and yet glad to be gone. One orgasm, and that clitoral, in one week, was just not enough. If my mother suspected what was going on she didn't say, and it would never occur to my father that it could.

I got back to Paddington at 4.15, caught the tube to Liverpool Street Station, and was there on the dot of five for Loki to pick me up and take me back to the bosom of my real life with Alden and Ray.

In the Name of Art

LOKI TOOK ME STRAIGHT back, not to Little Venice, but to my new, virtual home in Hampstead, but when I got there things were in chaos. The house, usually so quiet, rang to the noise of shouts and ill temper. There were builders in the bedroom dismantling the bed. The whole great structure had to be moved to the Lukas showrooms to be renovated and repaired, and the electronics modernised. It would take two weeks. Alden raced about in his chair getting in the way, insisting that no-one knew what they were doing except him, and fretting. When he excoriated the builders they reacted badly, put down their tools and said a job which would have taken three hours without his interference had taken six. They would be back in the morning to see if he'd calmed down.

Lam had backed into a corner and stared out with haunted, astonished and confused eyes, like a frightened dog on Fireworks Day: he hated noise from the outside world. At least Ray had got his head out from under the bedclothes and had found the energy and spirit to come down and play the diplomat with the builders, who agreed to stay if Alden would just let them get on with it in their own way. Alden sulked and went upstairs to his Bluebeard studio.

I made a move to come too but he said, 'No. I need to think,' and then as a cursory afterthought, 'Glad to have you back.'

I picked my way through workmen and sections of bed back to my room and sat down. I had no desire to be banished to Little Venice, which felt as if it belonged to someone else. I was still needed here, even though the place of employment, my tool of trade, the bed, was apparently no longer usable. I think sex has this rooting effect on women. That's why when it's with guests at the Olivier it seems okay. You leave the room but you don't leave home.

But the presence of other people in the house was unsettling for me, as it was for Lam; it made it seem far less special and extraordinary: the real vibrations of the builders banging about rubbished Alden's more 'cosmic' vibes. At last the builders left, which was a great relief, even if they had taken the bed; I helped Lam fold the patchwork quilt which had been left in a pile on the floor. I gave the room a good sweep and the floor a polish. I was a dog marking its territory. I was Joan again.

'Floor clean,' said Lam. 'You good girl.'

I was half way through the polishing when Lam

came in with a pile of clothes, handed them over, and said, 'Club time now. You work.'

Tight red satin blouse, tight red satin skirt, black net stockings and suspenders, black patent shoes with very long toes, no knickers, red plastic bag, hoop ear-rings. Traditional tarts' wear, except no tart I know would ever wear it.

Also what looked like a white mink coat, which I certainly would not wear.

'Wear coat,' said Lam.

'Not wear dead animals,' I said. 'Won't.'

My heart beat faster at this display of defiance. I half expected him to roll me up in the coat and throw me effortlessly against the wall, but he just looked at me impassively as if computing something and then said 'upstairs now,' and so we went up to the attic, leaving the coat behind. *The Blue Box* had not been touched since I left. The easel was looking positively dusty. But Ray sat bolt upright on the sofa looking purposeful and Alden was looking brisk and positive in his chair. The fire's faux flames flickered.

I felt I was attending an interview, and it wasn't necessarily going to go well for me.

'Well Joan,' said Alden. 'I've probably lost a client, Ray's bloody paintbrush won't stick up. Here we are, up shit creek without a canoe. We're going to plan B: we start tonight. I hope you're feeling fresh and rested after your holiday.'

I said, 'Yes thank you, I am.' I almost said 'sir.' If

you scrub and polish floors you start thinking and behaving like the maid. And I was in this ridiculous outfit. And I was – I assume that my American readers know that we English are masters, and mistresses of understatement – rather hoping to get laid.

'Look into my eyes,' said Ray. I did. He seemed very decisive today, which was nice; shame he hadn't done any painting. 'There are going to be no mistakes this time.'

After that it's not exactly memory, it's snapshots or flashbacks. They come to me unasked, like pop-ups on a computer: not necessarily in date order, stubbornly clinging to the screen long after the command to go. Vanessa observes the activities of Joan, and marvels: disassociates herself from them but is intrigued, even fascinated by what goes on. Sometimes Joan knows she is Joan: sometimes she thinks she is whatever Alden or Ray tell her she is. Sometimes Joan play-acts panic and distress: sometimes Joan and Vanessa are as one and I know then that one day we will leave all this behind.

Joan is happily shopping at the farmer's market for organic food for Alden's and Ray's – and of course her own – dinner, and has a sudden vision of herself suspended naked by an intricate mesh of knots, swinging to and fro at the eye level of observers, while a master of Japanese rope bondage demonstrates his technique to an audience of middle-aged men. She can stare closer at the snapshot, and see that it's been taken with a flash, that it's night, the background is the Divan Club in Soho: Alden and his wheelchair are there, also Ray is leaning against the bar, but there is no sign of Lam. She remembers odd details: the gathering was called a 'munch', the tutor comes from Portland, Oregon, that someone's mobile rang and there was murmur of discontent. That her neck fell elegantly back as she swung: that it was not painful so long as she submitted to the ropes and did not struggle, but that her hair swept the ground and she worried about it gathering dust and dirt. Beyond that, nothing. She remembers the postcard but not the context of the incident.

She has pieced together quite a lot from postcards, and from bits of information let slip by Alden and Ray when she is not under will, when she goes about her menial business in the house: an ordinary girl who just happens to be living and sleeping with two guys and doing their housework and shopping because she loves them. She is so adept at this performance – it is a performance? Surely so – that Alden and Ray are quite taken in by it, and forget she's there and talk without inhibition. Thus she is able to build up a picture of what happened in the weeks of her lovers' and masters' contingency arrangements while they waited for the technology to be restored which would allow their main game to resume.

Joan is to work nightly at the Divan Club. Film, with soundtrack, can be shot here on conventional digital equipment, of saleable quality, and endlessly editable. There are hidden cameras, and not so hidden ones. Alden has taken a financial interest in the establishment. He has lost several Arts-Intrinsick commissions: the reward for spreading his talents too widely, concentrating too much on his music, and not enough on his design skills, or stroking rich matrons. If Lady Daisy O does not get *The Blue Box* installed in time there will be hell to pay, and he will get the invoice. But now his cash-flow problems are already on the way to being solved.

Ray needs his erotic responses stimulated further to help him get on with the work. Simple threesomes and a modicum of bondage are no longer enough to keep him from tossing his brush into the electric fire. He is impressed by the drama of his own desperation. He has persuaded himself that any scruples he has about what Alden might make me do under will are of no weight when set against his sacred and imperative duty to paint. He has persuaded himself thus that the decisions about what I am to get up to are Alden's, 'Art's', mine, whoever's, but not his any more.

Lam will be Joan's bodyguard. Alden will have to make do somehow without him. Financial survival is worth a bit of slumming. My inhibitions about remembering Lam's involvement during the two weeks are strong. He is not in the Japanese Bondage snapshot though he is to be seen in the Violated Bride clip, hauling me out of a bath before I drowned. Suffocation fetishists tread a fine line, and can get carried away.

The trauma from that *mise en scène* is one that has not been wiped from my mind: I guess their excitement must have just made them forget to say the exit word. So I must have made an impression, I must have been pretty good. The body remembers what the mind does not. I would find myself trembling during the day, or crying for no reason.

A Weekly Routine

THE DIVAN CLUB, IN Greek Street, Soho was in a basement which stretched under the whole block all the way through to Frith Street and, with a further emergency exit into an alley which led into Old Compton Street between where they each intersected with it. It was members-only, and security was efficient and professional. The interior was made over in a mixture of Ottoman Empire and Arabian Nights, all marble and mosaics, lanterns and feather plumes, jewel colours, reclining sofas and subdued lights. The barman wore a white turban and silk balloon trousers. The bar was glass: the stools traditional, the glasses you drank from were Venetian ware and elaborate to the point of folly. But the clients liked them, and they were paying. You could bring your wife here, but by no means everybody did.

A man and a woman managed the place: an unpleasant couple called Clive and Audrey, about whom I have nothing nice to say. At all. Clive had a bouncer's build, a bald head and a red moustache and looked very perverse to me when I first saw him – he wore an embroidered green silk blouson, golden slippers with curling points, yellow bejewelled turban and pantaloons and a scimitar tucked into the sash. Audrey had a big-jawed face, hard eyes, and dried-out blonde hair with split ends. She wore heavy silk caftans embroidered with gold thread, in a different colour every day. It didn't matter what she wore: if she'd dressed like Mother Teresa she'd still look like the Madame she was, a dealer in flesh. She did not like me, I did not like her and we both knew what the score was. She had not wanted to take me on, saying I trouble, too well-spoken, it would put the clients off. But Alden insisted. He had more insight than her, for I was to prove so popular with the clients that she was able to jack the prices they paid for me, for my various services up, and up: and up. She hated me the more for proving her wrong.

So who got the money? Not me: I didn't, because Alden and Ray insisted that I worked for the simple love of sex. Under will, I was happy to participate.

There was a lesbian night on Wednesdays, and every night was topless night. Loki would deliver me to the Divan, and collect me afterwards. Sometimes Alden and Ray would come with me and sit beside me until a client asked me to dance or go with him to the Joy Room, otherwise known as the Dungeon. This was badly lit with optional glaring spotlights, painted in black and scarlet, and kitted out with every variety of bondage and fetish accessory.

Sunday I was allowed off. Alden and Ray liked to have roast beef and Yorkshire pudding, roast potatoes and peas for Sunday lunch, and they liked me home to prepare it. I was happy to. They took its excellence for granted and I longed for them to ask someone else to lunch who would at least enthuse a bit, but they never did. Lam was a vegan and didn't eat meat and wanted roast potatoes but not done in the beef drippings so these had to be done separately in oil.

Roast dinners create a lot of dirty dishes, but none of them ever offered to help. They'd watch football or a film while I cleared up. After that I could get away and catch up on some sleep. In the evening I would go up to the studio and try and assist Alden and Ray with their sexual problems – as I often did when I got back from the Divan – but Alden remained in Tantric mode and couldn't find a way out of it. Ray's brush stayed in the turpentine.

I slept in most mornings except Mondays, when I'd go to Harrods for hair treatment, facial, manicure, pedicure, eyebrow plucking and so forth. Before I set off for the Divan, at around eight, Lam would give me a massage. I grew to like them. His fingers were damp but strong; they seemed to feed strength into me. I told Ray once how restorative the massages were, and he just laughed and said he wasn't surprised. I must remember Lam was a 'multi-dimensional of the lighted realms.'

Being 'under will' at the time, I took that on board, if only I daresay because the 'lighted realms' sounded so much more cheerful than the dark shadows and guttering candles of the Divan's dungeon. After that Lam seemed less alarming, less likely to be hiding tentacles, or to have one of those lizard faces people like David Icke believe many important personages who walk this earth hide beneath their human masks.

Monday evenings and all day Tuesdays we would normally go out filming on location, though occasionally sets were built in one of the many spare rooms behind the Club. The place was a warren, and for years had been used to store imported foodstuffs from Italy. Still, from time to time, as you lay spread-eagled and tied with the red ball in your mouth and your eyes wide in alarm, or stood tied and cuffed to your cross in the Dungeon, you'd get the whiff of basil, oregano, marjoram, rosemary and so on, and the dusty smell of ancient pastas – but perhaps the place was haunted. I would not be surprised.

For some scenarios, simple 'under will' was not enough and I would be given a new persona. Alden had more narrative talent than Ray, though he was less good at the 'under will' bit. Alden would explain to me that I was a naïve country girl on my wedding day, eagerly expecting her new husband – only to find he'd brought the best man with him to share her: or that I was the young student walking home when the bad boys leapt out of the bushes and set about gangbanging her – and I would believe I was whoever I was told I was. And then I'd be told I'd liked it, and I'd believe that also.

Their theory was that if I believed the event was real and reacted spontaneously, the resulting film footage would have twice the impact of a simulated scene. You could of course claim that any real scene had been simulated, and prove it by the final shot of the participants all smiling cheerfully together: then the footage could be sold legally and distributed on the open market. And since I was under will for the purpose of the closing all's-well-that-ends-well smiley shot (which would be filmed out of sequence) I would look happy enough.

And then the memory would be removed, so what harm would be done?

I would have asked Alden or Ray to remove the memory of my father's affair with my best friend Jude, and I'm sure they would have obliged, but to do so would have been to disclose the existence of Vanessa. I was in far too deep for that by now, and nothing Alden or Ray had said suggested to me that they would easily accept the idea that they had been deceived. They had cast me as the one deceived: they were the designated deceivers. Vanessa was better educated than they were. They would not want to admit that in many ways their slave girl knew more and better than they did, nor that she was more confident in her sexuality than they were, and socially more at ease.

Vanessa could tell a bad wine from a good one, a viable piece of contemporary music from one that was not. She could put *The Blue Box* in its historical context. She had probably read more around the Golden Dawn than Ray ever would. As for Lam, she doubted that he was even literate. Lam's head sloped away so sharply at the back and sides there hardly seemed room for the left frontal cortex, or Borka's area, where the reading and writing functions of the brain are located – any more than there was for the parahippocampal gyrus, which governs laughter and mirth. Oh mind of Vanessa, mind, mind, be still!

A Family Episode

S OMETIMES WHEN LOKI WAS driving me to the club
I would look out from the dark of the cab at the
bright streets of London at ordinary couples, at single
people hurrying from jobs or to normal dates, and I
would wonder how, why, I had fallen into this most
questionable and exotic way of living. Did I fall or was
I pushed? I was pushed, but then I must have wanted
to have been. Was there some buried incident in my
life, or underlying hypocrisy in my family? To do with
my father deceiving my mother, my mother for putting
up with it? I despised her more than I blamed him.

Mind you, it wasn't easy for her. Lust my mother
could have coped with easily enough: she had her
early training as a counsellor, she understood its
passing nature. The Church had taught her about the
sacramental aspect of sex. Life amongst the parishioners
enabled her to keep her own problems in perspective.
She had the great privilege and strength of knowing
she was good – which I think was one of the reasons

my father ended up in Jude's arms: Jude being so bad in a sloppy kind of way, and thus needing no living up to.

But love was a different thing. I think my dear, patient, peaceful father would have sat the unwelcome emotion out, but Jude went in for the kill, and seduced him in our summer house one Sunday afternoon: just to stop him looking at her with those awful, soppy eyes. That was the explanation she gave to the twins after they burst in and found Dad and their big sister's best friend rolling about together on dusty rush matting: 'Just to stop him staring at me, with those awful, soppy eyes.'

My mother was upstairs nursing bronchitis. I was away in Oxford at an interview for a college – Brasenose. I had got four starred A's at A level, Jude had got three ordinary A's and a B. It was nothing to do with my father or his eyes: she was just envious and taking it out on me. And instead of having the sense to just shut up and forget about it, the twins, unforgivably, went running to tell Mum.

She screamed, she wept. When I got home I scarcely recognised my calm, beautiful mother, raving and with her face mottled and swollen. Mind you, I'd had a glimpse of it, just a hint, the day she didn't want to leave me alone with Dr Barky: the day he told me about Bipolar Two and broke my hymen by mistake. She'd wept and shouted and he had told her she just didn't want to let me grow up: she was a clingy mother and ought to know better, and I'd screamed at her that I wanted her just to go away: then she just seemed to deflate, and walked off. Perhaps she should have stayed. She gives in too easily, turns the other cheek.

But so it goes: it's over now – as far as these things ever are. My father was full of remorse, my mother's bronchitis cleared up, the twins passed yet more exams and got their names and pictures in the papers as infant prodigies. The student medical centre decided I had an eidetic memory, and fortunately a high IQ to go with it, so I could make sense of the reams of information which assaulted my brain, otherwise I might have developed serious adjustment 'issues'. My case (anonymously of course) made the *Lancet* and a medical column in *The Times*. No mention was made of the gang bang scandal which so nearly got me sent down. And little Robert weathered the family storms and grew up un-traumatised, so far as anyone could see.

My mother explained my father away to me by saying that men do strange things when their daughters leave home: they get panicky and think youth and freedom are running out. So? She can forgive him but, though I miss the friendship, I will never forgive Jude.

Evenings at the Club

MEMBERS PAID THEIR ENTRANCE fee and signed in, and leered at me as I sat topless in whatever threads or lack of them had been selected for my evening's role. They bought drinks at extraordinary prices, and the club made a profit. They could dance with me and if they wished to pursue and upgrade the intimacy would consult Clive, or Audrey, or both, and pay the tariff, one half on demand, second half on delivery.

A snapshot, a film still, then it starts rolling: the husband and wife team, Clive and Audrey talking to a couple of clients, father and son from the look of them, both big-boned, brash and confident. Parents' Day, I thought? The father looks as if he might be from the working end of the oil industry.

It must be Thursday, because Audrey's wearing a violet caftan. They all look over to me. They're haggling. I am suddenly self-conscious. No sign of Alden or Ray. It's easier to sit around in public with naked boobs when they're with me: I don't feel so exposed. I particularly hate walking into the bar on my own when there are a lot of customers in there, and they all turn to look, and wonder how much I cost, and whether I'll be worth the money or not.

Clive beckons me over with a nod, and I get up and walk towards them. I am wearing a long flouncy skirt in transparent voile, and red sandals and that's all. There is a moment's hush in the bar as I walk by. Then everyone starts talking again. It is actually quite a lively place; a lot of people just come to talk and drink and hang out, and for some of them I'm just a sideshow. The casual boast, 'I was at the Divan Club the other night' can make the most boring people seem more fascinating to most respectable company: or so the boasters told themselves.

Another snapshot, and again the characters start moving: Father has shown son how it's done. (Son knows pretty well by now how it's done, or at least how he does it, but father doesn't know that.) Girl on knees, grab hair, pull mouth onto cock, bang cock into mouth, choke if necessary. Girl onto bed, part her thighs wide, stare intently, lubricate with KY (lucky old me this time) and – in it goes. No time to spare for natural lubrication. Dad's member is a monster: girl is meant to gasp in awe, girl does – and she means it. Fourteen inches? Son wants his turn. Now, and he means now! Dad tells him to fucking wait. Son tells him he fucking won't. Dad tells him he fucking will. Dad turns me over, makes me kneel, and starts shoving up my anus.

Son waves yet more monstrous prick before my eyes: sixteen inches – can such prodigies exist?

That's down my throat now, really stretching my lips, pumping in and out with the use of my hair as the handle. I gag. Dad tells Son to get the fuck off his case, can't he see Dad is trying to fucking concentrate. Son says what's the matter, Dad, got a prostate problem? Dad says Son's a little douchebag compared to his elder brother, always was: no class, no fucking manners. Son sloshes on some more lubricant and tries to drive his monster dick in next to his dad's. I cry out, I wasn't expecting that; I wriggle my bum away from them both. Son tries to drag me back. Dad flies into a fury and begins to beat Son up.

'You're gonna fucking learn to fucking wait your turn!'

The son is silent. I look round. 'You stupid old prick, you're past it!' he says, but he's waited too long. Bleats of reassurance from me, roars of rage from dad. Squeals of defiance from son. Bam, crash. Happy families! Father and son together get me on my face on the bed. Enter at speed Lam – to whom I attribute the knack of walking through walls, being of the Higher Light Realms of Sirius Two, the Dog Star – and he lightly tosses both men against separate walls. So he's an alien, so he's not: maybe this is some Tibetan martial art, or not – I'm not about to quibble.

Enter Clive and Audrey at the run: they blame me for 'making a fuss' and being 'unprofessional', tick off

Lam for 'direct physical intervention action against clients,' and offer father and son a full refund and another girl. Dad just goes for a refund.

Cut to postscript: I am relating this vignette to Alden and Ray over a full English breakfast I've cooked for us. Alden takes particular care with the application of a dollop of mustard to a grilled organic chipolata rather than meet my eye. But my tale quite stirs Ray up – he actually goes to his canvas and starts adjusting the little mirrors. Though I notice he doesn't quite pick up his brush, it looks like progress.

What was meant to take two weeks stretched into four. The Lukas workshops are waiting for the prototype new generation of post-Bluetooth widgetry to be delivered: Bluebeard. My days, and even more so my nights are a blur, sharpened into focus by more sporadic snapshots. There's one of me walking through St James' Park with Phoebe, being happy. The sky is striped red to the west: starlings wheel. In the next we're sitting having coffee by the bandstand, watching Sergeant Pepper's baton coaxing euphony from glinting trombones.

I had not recalled Phoebe's existence at all, until a fleeting memory was triggered by the first picture. Phoebe the transsexual, the she-male, the man-woman. She was another permanent hostess; she had a delicate smile, and looked wholly female with her straight dark hair, luminous blue eyes and pretty C-cup breasts, but she had male genitalia. She was very popular with certain of the clients, mostly the closet bi and gays, but on lesbian nights she really came into her own. It all comes back. I strapped on a dildo; they are awkward to use and always made me feel slightly absurd, and lunged, while Phoebe just glided about proudly, charmingly, bestowing pleasure, a reassurance to nervy women who were soothed by her breasts and fascinated by her member. Good times were had by all. All sex toys demonstrated by Phoebe and me could be purchased after the performance.

Phoebe was serene, a walking, living revelation of how it is possible to be all things to all men, and women too. She delighted in herself, in her all-things-to-all-people-ness. She was kind to me, and she explained human nature to me; always generously, and with forgiveness. I told her about Jude once, and she said, 'It must have been hard for her, because you had everything, and she had so little. You were pretty and she wasn't. She thought having your father might right the balance.' I didn't tell her that I was really Vanessa, because all that other world of Oxford and Kant and PhD's would have been so alien to her, it would have frightened her off and spoiled our friendship. But I could see that Vanessa's world wasn't all that much to be proud of. Phoebe was just as beneficial to mankind, and womankind, as I was.

Things she said come back. That she was an important part of God's creation. That gender ran in a straight line from extreme male to extreme female, with room for all sorts and mix ups in the middle. That people like her enjoyed short life expectancy, no-one knew why, other than that those the Gods love die young. 'The flame burns brightly and quickly,' she says, 'and then burns out.' She shrugs. 'Who wants to grow old anyway?'

Scenarios

AND STILL THE LUKAS bed was stuck in the workshops – a woman employee had a baby, someone else's girlfriend had a baby, a flood in north east China delayed a delivery of electronic chips. Clouds open in China, and in Soho a butterfly helplessly flaps its wings. Me.

In the meanwhile Alden and Lukas obtained their various gratifications at my expense. My guess is Alden had decided his way out of the tantric trap was through voyeurism: and Ray thought he might as well exercise some found Golden Dawn powers as he waited for his Muse to return. We went out of doors, lunching on the grass. I was 'under will.' Perhaps Lam preferred indoors, for he is absent from these snaps, and only returns when we're back in marble halls, when he swoops down to rescue me from being held under to drown.

Snapshots. Green fields and warm sun, long grass and wild flowers. I am Europa, daughter of Agenor,

King of Tyre. I dance naked with my handmaidens, garlanded only by flowers. Zeus sees me, must have me, changes into the form of a handsome white bull: my girls flee in alarm but I stand my ground – he approaches me, pawing the ground, I am no longer frightened: I place my garland round his great jowly neck, and before I know it he's upon me, and I'm so small and he so animal, and big—

Snapshots. A seascape this time. I am Andromeda chained to the rock, waiting for the dragon to come. A dot in the sky, then nearer and bigger, blotting out the sun, leathery skin and gleaming eyes, breathing fire and thrusting penis: I scream, I struggle to no avail – and then a rush of wind and Perseus with his winged sandals swoops down, and the dragon's slain just in time, and I am unchained – and rewarding my hero as custom demands, on my knees while the water laps around my legs and the little white waves froth and bubble around my mouth: Alden planned those ones, no doubt, proud of his A level in the Myths and Magic of Ancient Greece.

Snapshots. These will be Ray's creation. He read a lot of science fiction when he was boy. I am the young daughter of space colonists on a far planet with three suns. Disobeying my parents, I wander away from the stockade to dally amongst strange and beautiful plants and whispering rocks. The alien approaches, giant, hideous, deformed, claws and probes instead of fingers, a yawning, toothy, greedy, slavering mouth: I try to run but a tentacle reaches out and curls around my waist and he draws me screaming to him and lopes off with me to his lair where others even fouler wait. They strip me, explore me and probe my body, finding pain and pleasure in every orifice. No longer virgin, I am at their mercy. Shades of Dr Bardsey. I am part pleasured, part destroyed, orgasm will kill me, I know it will. I die of pleasure.

And then a sudden escalation of event. Now we're on a grander scale. More people are involved, as is I suppose some other like-minded organisation, or film company. Money is spent. This time the narrative is continuous, memory is joined up, though blurred. It is not so easily wiped, deleted. But it still has the texture of dream.

It's a Tuesday. We left the house early. We're on our way to a grand country hotel in Sussex. There's to be a wedding. We travel down in Loki's taxi. Alden faces me in his wheelchair, Ray sits next to me. I ask who the bride is and Alden replies, 'You are, my dear,' and Ray turns my face to his with one finger under my chin, looks at me and says, 'Joan, you are eighteen.' It is really sweet to be eighteen again: I am so full of trust, and tremulous excitement about the future. I am a virgin. I am conscious of the little tight pinkness of my pussy. I can't even say cunt. Ray asks me to say it and laughs at me but I just can't say it; I shake my head. 'Joan's gone,' he says. 'We have Tess here.'

Alden tells me I am from Ireland, where I was

schooled by cloistered nuns, am a good little girl who has never had a boyfriend. I have come to London to enroll on a nursing course and I have been terribly lonely, but now at last I have met a dear man I love so much, and who loves me. He has untold wealth, his name is Jasper, and Ray adds that he's a baronet, a Knight of the Realm.

'Sir Jasper has proposed to you, and you have accepted him,' says Alden, 'and he has given you a diamond engagement ring!' I can hardly believe I am so happy. Humble little me, married to Sir Jasper!

My parents have got wind of our plans and are close behind us on the next flight from Knock, but Sir Jasper says we must get married at once before they arrive and try to stop me. I agree. So many difficult people, all trying to stand in the way of true love! I am to believe everything Sir Jasper tells me is true, because I love him and love means trust.

All the arrangements have been made. Sir Jasper's mother has even lent me her own wedding dress and gown, which will be waiting for me at the hotel. All Jasper's side of the family have been invited, and his friends too – and when the cab pulls up, there they all are, in their wedding finery: white ties and tails, and beautiful picture hats.

But I only have eyes for Sir Jasper, the man I love. He kisses me and murmurs words of love, I sigh and tell him of mine. Jasper's mother and sister come to greet me: they take me to one of the bedrooms: and there's my wedding dress. A glorious, full tulle skirt and a tiny satin bodice, all beaded with pearls. I am bathed and scented, my pussy is shaved – so intimate, but they say it is the custom! – my hair put in rollers and my face made up: pale, pale foundation, just a touch of rouge. The lights are so bright in here! Spotlights shine down, but they say they need good light to get the details right. And then it's time for the wedding dress – Jasper's mother is smaller than me so it's rather tight – but there's a little matching bolero which makes it decent. Out come the hair rollers and on goes the lace veil – adorable – falling from a diamond tiara. It covers my face unless I push it aside. Was ever a girl luckier than me!

The priest who will marry us comes in to see me in my finery. He wears a dog collar and crimson robes: he is rather bald and old and fat, like Friar Tuck. But he's so kind. He talks to my about my duty of obedience and trust and how many things may seem strange to a convent girl like me, but I must accept them. My husband will be there to guide me. The mother and sister get a fit of the giggles and I wish they wouldn't. He blesses me and leaves.

A blink: a blur: we're back to snapshots. I stand before the altar in a church. This is a little confusing; weren't we in an hotel? But it must be a church; there is stained glass, and candles and the smell of incense. And my friend the priest is officiating. He's very clever: he knows Latin. In Nomine Dei Nostri Satanas Luciferi

Excelis, he intones. My dress is simply lovely: lots and lots of white tulle everywhere. Beside me stands Jasper. My day, my special day. I can't see all that much because of the veil. I don't recognise the hymns. They aren't what we sung at school, being rather dirge like and throbbing. 'It is the evening of the day, your pleasure is fulfilled: you, our Lord of Ecstasy.' And 'Be with us now, oh blessed child of Samael and Lilith.' Sir Jasper slips the ring on my finger and stares into my eyes. Soon we will go to the honeymoon suite. He is so tender and loving.

But first we must have the photographic session. Everyone seems to want to have their picture taken with me. Some of the guests are wearing rather odd gear for a country wedding: tight, black and shiny outfits, hooded gowns with unfamiliar symbols embroidered on them. But here is Jasper, whispering what smart clothes everyone is wearing: isn't that an Armani suit: that hat can only come from Harvey Nicks. And looking again, I see they are.

Cut to the honeymoon suite. I am the virgin bride, alight with eagerness. He comes in the door, closes it behind him and walks towards me, arms outstretched. So handsome! But so bright in here – why is it still so bright? – but Jasper is pushing me back onto the bed, throwing my dress over my head in a great enveloping mass, pushing my legs apart. I struggle and scream, the veil is ripped aside, the priest is behind me, wearing only his dog collar, his hands into the breasts which no man has seen before – Jasper now casually ripping the pearl bodice of his own mother's wedding gown – I am shamed, so shamed. Now his mother and his sister are there, they hold me down, laughing, the pearls fly everywhere – the priest turns my face to him, his fingers force my mouth open – Jasper's hands are in me – a sudden vision of Dr Bardsey – I am screaming but the veil is pushed into my mouth – and the sound rumbles back into my lungs, and I hear someone say 'how's that for a gurgle?'

Cut to: I am bent over the marble bath, still in a great welter of cloth and the best man and the photographer are attempting to get into my pussy together, and I can see the shadow of the camera: and my nose is an inch away from water and there are people all around, laughing and talking and excited. 'Brilliant, terrific reaction shots. Did you see the expression on her face!' And Vanessa is back with me suddenly, saying what is all this nonsense, this is going too far – what have you got us into – and I am struggling to get free—

But my head is dunked into the water and my veil floats to the surface. Brussels lace, Chantilly – Venetian point – Vanessa knows exactly what it is, how old, where from. Joan has been keeping expensive company, prepared to pay a lot for props, high production values. But Vanessa is extremely put out. Joan has let her down. Vanessa is a vocational girl, not a whore. Meanwhile Joan is just about drowning, struggling for breath, blue in the face while she is rammed from behind: her head is lifted from the water: she struggles for breath – 'If I die, you die,' Vanessa snarls at Joan. And down my head goes again – then suddenly I can breathe again because once more my saviour Lam has pulled my head out of the water and scattered my assailants.

Snapshot: I am lying face down on a hotel carpet, still coughing up water, choking, though someone quickly gets my face turned to the camera so as not to miss a thing and I am beyond fury, trying to strike it out of the way. 'Great,' says someone, 'great! Did you get that?' And I collapse, exhausted by the effort, and I can see that lying there wet and trembling, bedraggled and half dead, surrounded by all that damp wedding gown, I make a great not too simulated shot. The extras are already cavorting in some orgy scene in the background. The cameras keep rolling.

Lam is now wrapping me in a soft towel and patting me dry, tenderly, and when I ask where Ray and Alden are he says,'They go home. Not their show.'

'Oh thanks a million, boys,' I say. 'Fuckers.'

'Leased you out,' Lam says.

'Shits!' I shout. Lam does not condemn my language.

On the way home in the taxi Loki passes me a carton of OJ and a sandwich. It's chicken and lettuce in wholewheat bread and butter, not margarine. I am really touched, and grateful. Lam either doesn't understand human appetites – he may even be doing a crash course in them, majoring in sex, to take back to the

Dog Star – or is human, and under orders to keep me hungry, on the grounds that hunger gives a girl a more vulnerable and eager look. Then at least the instructions haven't yet travelled down the chain of command as far as Loki: 'Keep her famished.'

I bet the rest of the cast of hundreds from the party settled down after their Black Mass to a really good lunch from the film caterers' trailers I had noticed. I didn't get any. But I suppose I should be glad they didn't decide on a postprandial human sacrifice, unsimulated, and were shooting a tamer Ravished Bride/Drowning Fetish script this time. Girls in the porn scene do sometimes just disappear. The police may look into it but leads are few and far between.

Loki's good Samaritan gesture of the sandwich did more to bolster my spirits than any of Ray's subsequent attempts to overlay trauma with an 'under will' memory of what a blissfully glamorous day I'd had. Phoebe says small human kindnesses, if they come hot on the heels of major blows to the spirit, can counteract a lot of the damage done.

Suburbia

FROM TIME TO TIME Clive and Audrey would take me out to suburbia: we'd travel in their grand Mercedes to 'real' homes, where we'd act out the rather second-grade scenarios for which the porn public, they were convinced, had developed an appetite. Phoebe told me that Adult Video News had recently run an article on changing tastes in porn, in which it was claimed that films with low production values were currently doing better than the high grade stuff. High could just be too graphic and detailed for the many. Viewers liked something explicit, but at the same time muzzy and homey, more 'real', more like their own lives. I didn't suppose Clive and Audrey actually read AVN, reading was not their thing, but no doubt word got round. There I'd be, on the road, with an amateur camera man and two or three extras following on. Alden and Ray kept out of the way: these particular outings being too cheap and tasteless for artists of their quality. If Lam was somewhere about he kept himself to himself.

A light or two would be set up wherever, in leafy avenue or identikit housing estate: the awful pattern of crimson stair carpet, chosen to not show the dirt, as one sprawled face down, the hard ridge of the cheap kitchen table digging into ones buttocks or breasts, became alarmingly samey.

I would play the heroine. Local lads and laddettes would play supporting parts, or occasionally they'd ship in some pros. But Viagra and Cialis can make porn stars out of the boy next door, or his over the hill grandpop.

There were various scenarios I got to know rather well. There was 'If you won't I know someone who will.' In this the reluctant wife/partner is woken in the middle of the night to find her husband/partner taking his pleasure with a strange girl at the foot of the bed and obliged to be an onlooker. I tie her hands to the bedposts and he then abandons me and forces her. Bedposts are quite a rarity these days, headboards being the thing, but bed restraint systems are readily available. These slip under any bed and provide leashes, rings and cuffs. 'That'll teach you to refuse me!'

There was 'obliged to fuck the landlord to pay the rent, the whoever to pay the gambling debt, the college fees,' etc. Boring to me because the plot is so minimal. Once the reluctance is established, the girl proceeds to noisily enjoy what happens next, which is any position any one can think of with as many men as can be enjoyed by one woman at a time. 'That proves it, any woman can be bought!'

In the lesbian version, the landlord is a woman: in the gay version all participants are male. In the dominatrix version I stick on a dildo and fuck and generally oppress the male, but it doesn't come naturally.

There's the 'be nice to my friends or else,' scenario. I am the wife ironing the shirt or cooking the dinner expecting her man home from the pub. A knock at the door, she opens up, and he's on the doorstep with six of his friends. They need entertaining. She must oblige. They take her from room to room so there's no space unsullied. They tie her to the cooker, to the central heating boiler, to the work bench in the garage. 'Don't think you're special, you're not.'

And so on. The revenge of the man on the uppity woman. Always a best seller. I, man, am stronger than you, woman. You may make more money, have more friends, gain more respect, but I am stronger than you.

Lam Juggles

A ND I'D GET HOME and we'd settle down, to supper
and the TV, and Lam would do juggling tricks
with eight oranges, one for each of the stellar Gateways,
and I'd see them flash in and out of existence, into
space and back again, as far as Betelgeuse and back.
Or that's what Ray told me was happening. 'See what
giant hands he has!' says Ray. 'To him an orange is
an apricot, and just as well. Maybe a planet is an
orange...'

And I see the giant hands. And Vanessa starts up in
my head about Betelgeuse, the red giant, whence all
the trans-mundane intelligences have their birth: she's
running down a page in a publication called *The Oneness*, and I, Joan, have to stamp her down because
Vanessa will not for one moment accept that Lam is an
alien just because Ray says he is.

'Actually Lam doesn't really come from Tibet,' says
Ray. 'I was only having you on, Joan. Nor is he an
alien. He's from the Dogon tribe in Mali. They all look

like that there, and juggle with oranges because of their hands.'

'Don't talk such nonsense,' Alden says to Ray. 'The poor girl is confused enough already.'

I am having a hard time with Vanessa today; since the second incident with a bath she's been quite stroppy. She's back and whizzing through the pages of a work written in 1950, by the anthropologist Marcel Griaule, with help from the Dogon tribe who knew more about Sirius and its unseen star companions than could reasonably be expected. Its title is 'Un Système Soudanais de Sirius'. Power devolved from Betelgeuse to Sirius, says Vanessa, at least according to the Thelemites, and a being from the double star was sighted by Crowley in 1918—

'Oh shut up, shut up,' I cry. 'Too much information!' and Alden and Ray look quite put out, thinking I am talking to them which of course I am not. Ray puts me under will to calm me, and we all go to bed together which is probably the best thing that can happen. Vanessa hasn't been shopping for a week or so and the Bipolar Two part is getting quite difficult. Alden still can't come and Ray still can't stop himself, but it's cosy and friendly and I don't mind at all. Or Ray says I don't. And at least Vanessa's gone again, the snarky bitch, I'm glad.

We're up in the attic on the sofa. Alden's hum is on the loudspeaker. The tone has changed. The pitch is lower. I have a distinct impression it's something to do with Bride in the Bath. This is because of something Alden says. 'Listen to that,' he says proudly, 'it's good. That's what the gurgle input does. That was some gurgle, that was.'

That was the death cry of the virgin he was talking about, at the hands of Sir Jasper and the false priest. The rattle of the death of hope as the bridal veil is thrust down the maiden throat. But Alden didn't even stop in his flow: he is talkative and animated tonight. When Lukas finally delivered the newly-equipped bed rejigged with Bluebeard Alden would be able to map pitch, duration, intensity, velocity and envelope; determine loop length, sample rate, and so on, of similar sounds, and subject the lot to granular synthesis: the new special synthesizers from China would allow him to involve light and intensity movement. Or something. I'd switched off by then, and so had Ray, who yawned, though I daresay Vanessa was listening. But I'm feeling sleepy. I often am, these days.

We're up in the studio again. Lam is juggling oranges again.

Fruit-bearing trees originate on Sirius, Ray tells me, according to a lecture on the Transcendentalists he'd just been to at the Southgate Centre.

'He must be missing home,' says Ray.

'But you said he was a Dogon,' I say.

'Same thing,' says Ray.

'Do stop all that crap,' says Alden. He makes a speech. 'You're a natural hypnotist, that's all it is.

Fourth Path, my arse. Joan's a happy little sex slave, a sub to my dom, a bottom to my top, not a route to higher powers, not an approach to the transcendental, just a help in getting some rather important atonal music written. Stick with the lectures on Japanese rope bondage, leave the rest to me. You get more of a hard on down the Divan than up at Southgate with the dreamers, not that that's saying much. Nor is Lam an alien, he's the guy who pushes my chair about and helps me organise my sex life. You haven't touched that fucking painting for days.'

But the oranges glitter their reflection into all the little mirrors on the canvas, ninety-three of them, and suddenly the whole room seems ablaze, throwing back flashes of colour as the oranges whirl, reds and oranges, mixed with the blue of the base to add purples, from each to each, back and back into infinity. And even Alden seems quite awed and is silent.

And in the silence of my own head Vanessa is starting up again about the number 93. Why was Crowley so fascinated by it? Was it just because he happened to rent rooms on the fourth floor at No. 93 Jermyn Street, above Paxton's, the famous cheese shop? Vanessa's over-heated mind whizzes through the references. Aleister Crowley moved in to No. 93 with his new wife Rose on March 25th 1907, the Great Beast 666, founder of Crowleyanity and preacher of the Law of Thelema. He was 29. His life had already been marked by excess and odd events. He had written peculiar but much-admired poetry, he had alarmed society with his odd views on sex and religion, he had gathered a crew of literary occultists round him – W.B. Yeats, Arthur Machen, Saki, Synge, Jepson, Wilde – and artists too – Marcel Duchamp, Nina Hammett, Epstein – and quarrelled bitterly and publicly with most of them. He had already founded the Argentum Astri, Inner Order of the Thelemites: the Outer Order having become too petty and ordinary for its founder. He had won renown of all things as a mountaineer: in 1903 he had even been approached by the famous Dr Jules Jacot-Guillarmod to accompany him on the first expedition to Kanchenjunga, the third largest mountain in the world, in Nepal. He had accepted. The team used the Singalila approach. Crowley led the trek. Four of its members failed to survive, swept away by an avalanche at 25,000 feet. (According to Crowley; others said 21,000.) Rumours abounded. The porters had wanted to turn back: their mountain gods were thunderous and angry. But Crowley, having his own hotline to his own powerful entities, insisted the party went on. The mountain gods won. Crowley fled and left his men to die. And all he had to say about it was 'their disobedience resulted in things going wrong.'

Vanessa's knowledge beats in my head like some frenetic bird desperate to get out. I wish she'd shut up. I want to concentrate on the dancing of orange light. Ray's tiny strokes of black have begun to cavort and tangle through the air. The hum is getting louder:

Alden has turned the volume up. These are my own shrieks and screams and *cries de joie*, my own terror and exultation, my degradation and my exhilaration, channelled and booming through the bowels of the earth, now vibrating the bluey-orange-purple air. I cover my ears but the whole room trembles. The light thrown back from the painting is now moving towards the blue glow of a billion computer screens, in the infinite complexity of their making, the darting of the synapses of the brain echoed in the darting of the pixels, a billion tiny sticks of black, the peoples of the earth, writhing and copulating, the Bride Stripped Bare by her Bachelors. They bring the Bride new gifts in the name of Bill Gates, Lord of the XXX sites, newly crowned king of the universe, God of Gods, whose servant and priestess I have become. I am the Scarlet Whore of New Babylon, the face of computer sex and my nation is Babel, and I am as mad as Vanessa. I cannot keep her split off from me for much longer.

She is pinching me, she is urging me. 'Joan, Joan,' she is saying, 'Aleister's wife Rose died in a mad house.'

'Well, that'll be your doing, not mine. You're the mad one, everyone knows, I'm perfectly sane. I'm the laughing, happy little one,' I snarl back at her. But she won't be quiet.

'Listen to me, listen to me, Joan. It says here the Scarlet Woman, Crowley's whore, was slain by constant copulation with a he-goat!' and at that I, Joan laugh. The nearest thing round here to a he-goat would be

Ray, and Ray is not exactly going to make me die from sexual exhaustion. And Alden can't be a goat: he hardly has the legs for it. If only he were. But his plunging and plunging, and his lack of coming is, I decide, oddly unsatisfactory for me and a source of resentment. Which is I guess why Vanessa keeps making her manic entrances: that, and the lack of shopping. I haven't been shopping for ages. There hasn't been time, I've been too busy whoring.

The lights stop circling, the room stops vibrating. Lam has put away his oranges. Silence. Then Alden's cellphone beeps, which breaks the trance and he answers it and it's someone from the Lukas workshop saying the bed will be delivered on Friday week. Such is Alden's pleasure at this news that he is delivered to my bed again and continues plunging but to tell you the truth I'm so bored I fall asleep mid-thrust and have to be woken by Lam's long poking finger prodding my shoulder.

Living sacrifice

THE DIVAN'S CAMERAMAN WAS fired, I don't know why. Perhaps pure professionalism got the better of him and he started producing good films. The outings stopped and I was back to the more humdrum and immediate duties at the Divan. Ray and Alden seemed to have lost interest in what I was doing and seldom came along. I was sorry about that: I preferred it when they were around. Clive liked me: Audrey increasingly didn't. I put it to Alden and Ray that I needed a rest and a holiday, and anyone could do what I was doing at the Divan but they said I should work out two weeks' notice like anyone else. After that the bed would be back and we could go back to the old ways.

We were now at the end of August. People were coming back from holiday: the clientèle at the club changed: fewer foreigners looking for holiday excitement: more businessmen who'd spent dull weeks abroad with their wives and families: gays with their hearts broken looking for solace, in particular looking for Phoebe, though many straight men liked her as well.

Also, Health and Safety officers were sniffing around the Divan. As a precaution activities in the annexe were being more discreetly arranged. No-one objected to bare bosoms, so long as they were properly licensed, and dancing was okay, so long as there was no live music, only canned: it was just that fire exits had to be in order, and there could be no cockroaches in the kitchens or we'd be closed down overnight. So far as the authorities were concerned there were no back rooms to the club at all: the annexe simply didn't exist, and I daresay money changed hands to make sure it never had and never did. But everybody was being very careful. Perhaps that was why Ray and Alden weren't around so much – busts could happen and they wouldn't want to be there when they did.

My arguments that nobody paid me, I worked for fun and love of the trade, or that I was 'under will' and liking it, wouldn't cut much ice with raiding police. And there'd been an incident a couple of weeks back, when they'd been called out to us, which made everyone nervous. An alarmed punter, bursting in on what he thought was a genuine group rape in the bar after hours, had dialled 999.

It was actually a scenario in which Phoebe and I played victims, the sex was consensual and no-one underage, so would be legal enough in a private home. It was just that the Divan wasn't one, and they took entrance money. We were two innocent young tourists to be dragged from our bar stools by football hooligans, tied up and set upon to cries of 'let them have it'; 'give it them good and hard'; 'down their throats,'; 'cream their faces'; 'roast 'em on the spit'; 'slam their shit holes', and so on, while Phoebe and I moaned with pleasure or alarm – 'oh that's good, so hard, so big'; or conversely, 'don't, don't, please, it hurts': whatever in fact seemed to be required.

The police took two hours to come, by which time the participants had climaxed and calmed down, rearranged their clothing, folded and put away their football kit – scarves, woolly hats and T-shirts – Manchester always a favourite – and gone home. There was nothing to hide and nothing to be seen but the police are not fools, and there was a lot of writing notes and taking of numbers.

These days, alas, I could turn up at the club merely to bare-breast dance with the punters, while even wives and girlfriends looked on, and that would be as far as the action went. On other nights the back rooms would be opened up and business would be much as usual, just less public. A couple of nights a week there was lap dancing: the game then was for the men to hide any overt sign of desire. The girls waggled their bums in men's faces, and taunted them, and the men had to keep their hands to themselves and disguise their erections, and the wives and girlfriends pretended not to be embarrassed. It seemed totally dishonourable to me. We'd show our breasts just so the men could demonstrate to partners or friends how little we stirred them: we, the loveliest girls in the world. Phoebe did not even flash her cock – that would have been vulgar, though sensational.

I said to Audrey once that it seemed daft to me: you could eat the dinner but not have the girl. Why not have the girl, and be forbidden the dinner; smell the garlic in order to resist the food? It would make as much sense. It was probably a Vanessa kind of thing to say and Audrey took added exception. Now she really had it in for me.

Until now I had been able to exercise a degree of choice. A slight distasteful shake of the head when a man came into the club was enough for Clive to steer him away from me. But now Clive, under pressure from Audrey, stopped doing that. Instead, he seemed to take pleasure in interpreting my 'no's' as 'yes please's.'

There is a certain kind of man I simply do not fancy: mid-fifties usually, self-satisfied, jowly, whiskery, flabby, smiling mouth and mean eyes. They're the ones who like to go for the Dungeon, and then try to take over from the dungeon master. They'll want you to bend over the leather 'master's horse' with your ankles wide apart along a spreader bar and your wrists handcuffed to it and leave you like that for too long so it really hurts: and only then fuck you. In actual fact not all that much fucking goes on in the Dungeon: it's usually a matter of situation, and the eroticism of a tied girl which people appreciate, women as well as men. In Japanese bondage sex is the ultimate aim, but in the West it's the idea of helplessness which appeals: what might happen, not what does. A skilled dungeon master, for all his cruel looks and bare torso, supervises carefully and will make sure the bondagee is safe and more or less comfortable.

Tonight the dungeon master was not in: so far as I was concerned this was an evening of drinking with the boys and should I end up in one of the bedrooms the Frith Street end of the complex then so be it. On the whole, membership of the Divan costing the earth, we had very few rough and unpleasant types in. Over-ingenious, yes: but seldom ignorant or rough.

I daresay one of my objections to going out filming with Clive and Audrey was simply snobbish – they were, frankly, people's films, and 'the people', as I found them in what were euphemistically called the suburbs, were often crude and competitive or simply dull and brutish in their sexual habits.

But tonight Mr M, of the smiling mouth, mean eyes and whiskery chin came in about ten-thirty, ordered a drink, sat down beside me and looked me up and down with lecherous eyes. Well, after all, that was why I was sitting there topless and smiling, in order that others should look at me speculatively and lecherously, and if they were lecherous enough, why then they would hand over money to the management. But he came too close and without invitation or permission tweaked a nipple with none too clean fingernails. I moved away pointedly and sat somewhere else. Audrey saw and shook her head at me. That was being rude to the clients: it was my job to be nice to them.

I moved yet further away. Audrey went and had a word with Clive. Clive went over to Mr M and had a brief conversation and Mr M simpered in my direction and nodded and Audrey went behind the bar, got the key to the dungeon, handed it to me and asked me to open up and bring back a pony girl mask. Pony girls and pony boys get harnessed up, the bit between their teeth, and asked to trot round and do their master's bidding, turn left and right and do what they're told, but it is a fairly soft option for down there.

True, the more decadent of the Russian aristocrats used to have naked peasant girls to pull their carriages, but I don't think they fucked them, it was just a pleasant sight. And even Aristotle was rumoured to be a pony boy and liked to be ridden by women. This may be, as Vanessa pointed out, beacuse there is in existence a 1420 etching of him by one Hans Bedlung Grien – *Aristotle riding Phyllis*, and they're both naked – but I reckon Phyllis is the Greek Goddess of the spring, trees, wisdom and women's secrets, not just some girlfriend, and that's how the rumour originated. At any rate ponyism tends to be out-doorish and to do with display and consensus.

So I trotted along the dark passages in my little red and white spotted rah-rah skirt and heels and nothing much else. I daresay I am by nature over trusting, but in my view this is preferable to expecting the worst of everyone. If you expect the best sometimes it happens. I unlocked the door, turned on the lights – red and spooky – and went over to where the gags and bits and saddles were kept. But of course Mr M was padding along behind me as I pranced along, and before I knew it I'd been pushed to the ground, and was tethered by the ankle to a chain, the other end of which was padlocked to an iron ring in the floor.

The dungeon is no place to be in the absence of a dungeon master, with a vindictive man who doesn't know the rules of the game. Mr M dropped the padlock key on the ground without even looking to see where it had fallen. Keys of all restraint items need to be kept in a safe place, with spares in known places. The whole point of SM dungeon games is that, in theory, there is only feigned coercion, and the submissive can get out of their quandary, whatever it is, at a given signal. Otherwise the police move in and close everyone down. But Mr M just let the key fall after it had done its job and trapped me, and his ignorance frightened me more than anything.

I did not like the look on Mr M's face, or the way he was stripping off. There were too many whips and paddles about, gags and masks, bondage ropes, cuffs and collars to inspire him. I did not like the look of his cock, which was half erect. He would be looking for means of making it come up full and strong and there was too much around to fire his imagination. I could not believe Audrey had done this: or that Clive hadn't stopped her. Or that she hated me so much she simply didn't care about Alden and Ray's displeasure, for displeased they would be. If Lam were really an alien he would be here to rescue me but there was no sign of him.

Mr M went off to examine the array of whips. Bad. I found the key – luckily just within reach, and stuffed it inside my shoe. He was coming back now with a full pony mask, neck restraints over one wrist and a bra over the other – the kind which confines the breasts while showing them, which you can tighten until the blood supply is restricted and they turn purple and ugly. If he got this lot on me I would be blind, deaf, dumb and helpless, open to assault from all angles and my breasts sore for days. He probably wouldn't murder me because he was a known member, and the Divan was strict on checking identities. I wasn't going to have a pleasant time: this was not outdoor-y, pleasant pony play at all. This was punishment time. And I was angry. At myself, at Audrey, at Clive, at Alden, at Ray, at Lam, at Vanessa for knowing best, at my parents for not saving me from myself, at my siblings for having the nerve to be born, at Dr Bardsey for taking my virginity so casually. Mostly at myself, I was truly, truly furious.

I pretended to weep and wail and sob for mercy, which hardened his dick considerably. I grovelled on the ground and let him put the bra on, crying 'no, no, no!' but before he had worked out how to tighten the restraints I squirmed round and gave him a good kick in the groin, with an extra twist to get his balls with my stiletto heel, fished the key out, undid the chain where it met the ring, and ran off dragging the chain behind me, down the corridor and into the bar and safety, where my flushed and agitated appearance caused quite a stir amongst the drinkers and their wives.

I ran through the bar and into the office, where Audrey, far from being her usual slimy solicitous self, advanced on me, slapping my face and shouting what was the matter with me, he was just a man like any other, I was losing her money, and she had her reputation to think of, I was to get right back in there, he was an important client. I slapped her right back.

That night I found Alden and Ray in fine good humour which was more than I could say for myself. The bed was arriving the following day, had been tested in the labs and worked: everything had gone right: it was practically a state of the art sound studio in itself. There was no need any longer for the old-fashioned camouflage of carved wood and hidden panels: wires were not required. Lukas's version of Bluebeard did it all.

My announcement that I had given up the Divan and was never going there again was met with indifference. My account of my brush with the sadist in the dungeon, Audrey's perfidy and Clive's irresponsibility, seemed to rouse very little reaction at all. I was within an ace of walking out on them and going back to my job at the Olivier. So angry was I, indeed, that I actually took from my bag the chain and cuff from which Phoebe had managed to extricate my ankle, which I had brought home with me to demonstrate the kind of danger I had been in, and hurled it straight at *The Blue Box*.

Little bits of mirror shattered and fell. Where they fell more glass shattered. It was if a tiny tornado had streaked across a trailer park collapsing everything in its path. I was horrified. But it got their attention all right. The chain lay on the floor. Lam picked it up and handed it to Alden. I thought for a moment he was going to use it on me and wished I was back in the dungeon as a pony girl but all Alden said was, as if thinking of something else – 'Well, that got a reaction.'

'I'm sorry,' I said. 'I'm sorry.' I was trembling. The Audrey episode was fading into insignificance. What had I done!

Ray was standing over his painting: he ran his finger up the jutting shards and there was blood on his finger. When he turned there were tears in his eyes. He looked wholly stricken.

'It'll be okay,' Alden said. 'It's only the mirrors. They're the easy bit.'

'But why did she want to?' asked Ray. 'I don't understand her. I thought she loved us.'

'I do,' I said, 'I do.'

Alden moved his chair up to the painting and ran

his finger down the sharp bits. He jabbed at the flesh until it started to bleed. He came back to me where I stood transfixed, wishing I could put the clock back, rewind, reset the computer of my life to a previous date, anything, to have my act of vandalism undone. How could I have done that! Alden made me kneel by his chair, to remind me that he was un-whole and I was whole and therefore owed him a duty, and put his finger in my mouth and I sucked the blood. It tasted pretty much like my own. 'Now I own your soul,' he said. 'By virtue of your own sin you become mine.'

Now I knew this was sententious rubbish even as he spoke. Vanessa was tugging at me, warning me. More of the language of Crowley Mania: the chanting of mumbo-jumbo, as if words had more power the less meaning they had: the humourless mumbling of the would-be necromancer, from the witchdoctor to the Thelemite via Mme Blavatsky. The use of ceremony, using blood, which is real, to control 'soul', which is an idea; the association of sex, the most loaded three-letter word of them all, which again is real, with another one, 'sin', or 'virtue' which are notional – and Vanessa had lost me and I shut her off. I was too tired and upset to work it out. Alden repeated it. 'By virtue of your sin you become mine.' If only it didn't have the ring of truth. Some dark, stupid part of me believed him totally.

I had played in to Alden's hands. But the victim controls his oppressors by his passivity. It was like being in Japanese bondage: if you struggle even silk ropes begin to hurt. Better to stay still; and quiet, and consent. Submission leads to the Great Orgasm in the Sky. Yet I had thrown my chains at *The Blue Box*, and defied my masters. This would not be the end of it. When Alden said that tomorrow I would go back to the club, apologise to Audrey, and obey her as I would himself or Ray, and that would be my punishment, I meekly said I would.

'Now clean,' he said, 'this room must be ready for tomorrow. And so I cleaned the mirror room and polished the glass, although it was all already clean as clean can be. I was on my hands and knees on the parquet when Ray came in and knelt beside me. He raised my head and looked into my eyes.

'I forgive you, Joan,' he said. 'I understand you. To need to love is to want to destroy. Love is the law. Love under will.'

I wished he did not have a plaster on his finger. It destroyed the image of the master artist busy restructuring the he universe. He went away. Presently Lam came in.

'Picture okay,' he said. 'Lam mend.'

Lam put me to bed and massaged me with his big fingers until the strength began to seep back into me.

'Lam mend Joan too,' he said. I had a friend. I slept.

A New Beginning

N O MENTION WAS MADE the next day of the incident with the painting. I was to look my best. I was sent off for the morning to have my hair streaked and a bikini wax. I managed a secret hour at Little Venice just to check the e-mail, throw away the junk circulars and brush out a few cobwebs. The place felt so unlived in: fabrics had lost their texture and colours their depth, as if I had mysteriously and unknowingly withdrawn some psychic support, and what once had three dimensions was now reduced to two. The minor Picasso, the Klimt and the Chagall stayed vigorous and voluptuous, I was pleased to see: they could do very well without me; I was a bit part player in their drama. *The Blue Box* would survive, but God, I'd been a vandal, a desecrator. How could I have done that?

I checked through the e-mails and fired several off in reply – reassuring my family I was alive and well, and telling friends I'd be in touch when time allowed. A letter from my college asked if I was going to enrol next term or not. It was to Vanessa, not to me. I screwed it up and threw it away. I prudently flicked through Wittgenstein to see if it made sense and thank God it didn't, nor did Vanessa leap into my head and start telling me what was going on. That was good. Let her keep her nagging Bipolarism to herself. As Joan, I wanted none of it. I could look after myself.

And let me not think about having to apologise to Audrey. Why should I have to apologise? She was in the wrong, not me. Why should I be 'under will' to someone as crummy and naff as her? What did that make me? But then I had all but wrecked *The Blue Box*. It was all too complicated. I didn't even want to think about it, so I didn't.

I came across some family snaps as I tidied up. I thought I'd show them to Alden and Ray. I wanted to be forgiven; I wanted to be included; I wanted them to realise I was real, had a family, a past, a history, a future. The snaps were of Robert, Alison and Katharine, larking about in the garden last time I'd been home. A garden is a garden and no-one could tell the pictures weren't taken in some council house in Essex. Joan's unemployable printer father might well have planted the odd hollyhock or clematis: such plants can be bought anywhere and are not reserved for vicarage gardens. There was no decking, mind you, which could be a giveaway but Alden and Ray were metropolitans – what did they know?

When I got home to Hampstead everyone was still

waiting for Lukas's people to deliver the bed. The delay made them tetchy and nervous. I bounced and chattered and giggled and tried to make everyone feel better. We had a late lunch in the studio. *The Blue Box* seemed wholly restored; as if the time had been rewound to before the tornado happened. Except the chain and leather cuff was draped over the strong pegs which supported the work on the easel. Why? – was no-one to be allowed to forget the incident? Ray had barely touched the painting since the last burst of creative fire, the Daisy effect having long since worn itself out. I counted fifteen squares still undone.

Alden and Ray seemed peevish because I'd been back to Little Venice without telling them, and I apologised; but I was beginning to resent having to check in all the time. I was family, wasn't I surely, not staff? They were generally edgy that day, no doubt about it. But they took a quick look at the snaps and then Ray started scanning and Alden was at the computer and before I knew it there were my siblings large as life and twice as handsome up on the computer screen, transported through time and space to the virtual here and now. The marvel of it got to me, and I'd have liked to have talked about it, but I remembered in time Joan was a sex-and-shopping girl and that sort of thing wasn't within her orbit. I'd have to be careful. Vanessa was hovering about somewhere, almost sane for once: perhaps her manic fit was over or at least easing? Soon it might be safe to let her back in, but not yet.

Watching them magnified on the screen like this, I actually felt quite proud of my sisters. Beneath the twins' Marks & Sparks navy sweatshirts and black tracksuit bottoms were hidden two rather graceful identical girls. They were certainly teen sized – it would take two of them to make one adult, but then there were two of them. Their eyes behind National Health owl glasses were wide and trusting as they smiled into the camera. Rather little mouths and thin lips but good regular tiny teeth, and clear, flawless complexions.

We had been playing netball and their hair had flopped out from behind their head bands, all fair and curly. They were growing up – finally. They were hand-in-hand, and their heads were turned sideways and up, showing clean cut, very delicate features. It was always quite uncanny, the way they moved together, turned their heads at the same angle, as if you were seeing double. Alden and Ray studied them for a long time.

'Don't even go there,' said Ray to Alden, but I knew he already had. I should never have showed them the pictures. In some people's heads innocence just exists for the plucking.

'I'll try hard,' said Alden. But he didn't mean it. They pondered some more.

'How old?' Ray asked me.

'Seventeen,' I said.

'Do they have boy-friends?' Alden asked me.

'Of course they do,' I lied. Let them not for God's sake know here was a pair of twin virgins, within reaching distance. 'They started young.'

'Call-centre girls,' observed Ray. I had to work out what he meant. Of course – I'd told them that the girls worked in a call centre, and Robert was at the local comprehensive. The trouble with telling lies is that one keeps forgetting one has.

Robert's picture was up on the screen now, poor spotty lad. But the acne did not show up too badly in the pictures, and I could see he had the makings of a good adult male. He had the fine family features, hair like mine, but blonde, and had been charging round the garden like a mad thing, playing football with our netball. He was naked to the muscled waist and sweaty. He was laughing and happy, smiling into the camera, and not at all his usual grungy, haughty self. He had a wide, full-lipped mouth and good teeth, like the rest of the family, but on a larger scale than the twin's.

'You've kept very quiet about him,' said Alden.

'He's such a pain,' I said. 'I try to pretend he doesn't exist.'

They asked how old he was and I said nearly seventeen.

'Bit old,' said Ray, and I asked if I could I have my snaps back, which was absurd because the images were now in the computer forever unless he chose to delete them, and then the front door bell made its sickly, new-age noise: the Lukas bed was back.

It didn't look the same at all. It was two thirds its original size – which was probably good because

Alden would have easier wheelchair access to whoever lay upon it. The posts were no longer wooden with caryatids but smoothly post-modern, in some non-conductive metal. It looked graceful rather than imposing. Lights gleamed: there were almost as many touch pads on the frame as on Alden's chair. And it had its own built-in mirrored ceiling. The mattress was a little harder than the one that went with the old bed: but no doubt there were now more sensors in it to go along with the direction-finding mikes on the posts.

The workmen went.

I lay upon the bed with my newly streaked hair, my new bikini wax, and thought happy thoughts and miserable thoughts to order, and faked the gamut of sexual sounds from orgasm to chokes to screams of rapture and terror. I thought I did very well but Alden was complaining of feedback and they fiddled around for ages, up and down to the music room where Alden worked, getting crosser and crosser with the technology that served them. It seemed to me totally fitting that the new process was called Bluebeard, inasmuch as Harold Bluetooth's son was Svein Forkbeard, both Danish kings who raided England in the tenth century – Vanessa knew that, but I didn't mind: she was being neither manic, nor intrusive, nor contentious. And I had never dared enter Alden's music studio, because the door was always closed, it had no handle and could only be opened from his wheelchair – as far as I knew. It was one of the rooms in the higher reaches of the house, and he liked to keep it private, even from me. A secret room.

Lam finally said, 'No echo in flesh. Echo in heart of Joan,' and it was true. Something had happened to me. I was going through the motions of trust but I did not feel it. I had showed them the pictures of my family and then regretted it. I had said I would apologise to Audrey but I resented it. I lay upon their bed and made noises but I felt stupid. The feedback I was producing was in my own heart, and somehow they had picked this up. I was 'under will' but jeering at myself for being so: I was double-emoting in response to everything I said or they did.

Lam was perfectly right, though I wished he hadn't said what he had, because now Alden and Ray looked at me coldly as if it was all my fault. But perhaps I imagined it out of guilt. I had reduced sections of *The Blue Box* to broken shards and they weren't going to forget that easily. I would have to earn my redemption. I resolved to do so.

The Pay Back

AND THEN IT WAS time for the Divan and for once Alden and Ray came down to Soho with me, just, I supposed, to make sure I apologised to Audrey. I was surprised they could bear to leave their precious bed. Lam stayed home. I'd chosen a long red satin skirt with a little pink lace jacket that stopped short of my breasts top and sides and was elegant while being excellently indecent.

Loki drove us in the black cab. I felt very comfortable and at home with Loki now. He knew everything about me and didn't seem to mind, or judge. He was the eldest of five children – the others were still back home in Berbera. He was a bright boy who'd got a church school scholarship and was living in Enfield with an aunt. He was on my side: he had given me a chicken sandwich at a time when I really needed it. We chatted on a bit about this and that through the open partition until Alden said he wanted to think and would we be quiet so I shut up.

I had to go into the office and say sorry to Audrey. She was wearing red and gold culottes which did nothing for her figure, a Goddess top which showed her fleshy upper arms to disadvantage, and stupid pointy green silk slippers. She wasn't at all gracious. I had slapped her: I could be arrested for common assault, as she pointed out. She seemed to have quite forgotten that she had slapped me first, and that after having handed me over to the mercies of a sadistic madman. Let alone that if I chose to go running to the police I could nail her on a dozen different counts. One of the annoying things about trying to work for people on drugs like cocaine is that they forget so much, other than believing in general you're in the wrong and they're in the right and can get away with anything. I very seldom take drugs myself, so I keep forgetting how much of so many people's behaviour is due to a chemical reaction in the brain. I tried to forgive her.

Ray usually took care to put me 'under will' before I went down to the Divan but tonight, what with the bed and the new sound system and the feedback he forgot about it. Alden always said it was unnecessary anyway: someone on the Fourth Path shouldn't be so insecure. 'Under will' was 'under will', it wasn't like an aspirin that had to be taken every four hours. But what with one thing and another I guess some of my normal passivity had deserted me.

Tonight, after being dismissed to the bar after a lecture by Audrey, and waiting for what would happen

251

to happen, a smirking man in his fifties, well-built if a little paunchy, beautifully-suited and satisfied with himself, asked me to dance. He gave a backward glance at his wife, who smiled bravely and tried hard not to look hurt, insulted and humiliated. Which she was. She was in her fifties: I was in my twenties. There is nothing much a woman can do about that. I stood up. I'd had to change. Audrey had told me to class myself up a bit, and now I just looked absurd. I was wearing her version of 'class' – which was a rather short pleated Burberry skirt, thick stockings and lace-up brogues, and a leather belt with a buckle which dug in to the bare flesh. Clive, who had taken over as the club costumier, had tightened the belt an extra notch so it made me look fat. Above that my bare breasts: not for the teeny-fanciers really, who like a girl body to be narrow and skinny, so the cock is more the master, proportionately, when it enters – but clearly just right, alas, for this particular client. Audrey is naff, but she isn't daft: you can't underestimate the public's taste, is as true about sex as it is about films.

Once on the dance floor my punter was erect within the minute and letting me know it. 'I just called to say I love you, I just called to say I love you,' droned the canned music. My nipples rose under his gaze. I couldn't help that either. Desire does not go hand in hand with liking. Far from it. He kept looking round to see how his wife was taking it, and grinning. I hated him. I hated the hypocrisy of it all. I hated her feebleness, how she just sat by and let herself be tormented. And I wanted to be fucked.

Alden and Ray seemed to have forgotten me. They were sitting at a table busily looking through the menu. I wouldn't be getting anything to eat. That made me even snarkier. That and being excluded. It was pathetic, the way I wanted to 'belong'.

'I have something in my eye,' I said. 'Can you take it out?'

'We'd better go where there's more light,' he said.

'Let's try the cloakroom,' I said, and we danced our way casually into the darkness outside the circle of light beamed onto the dance floor and out into the corridor and into the cloakroom. I knelt at his feet and zipped down his flies and his cock stuck out, and I wrapped my lips around the end, but he pushed and pushed deeper inside, over-excited, not settling into his own pleasure at all. I took my mouth away for air and he stood me up and leaned me against the wall and shoved my skirt up and was inside me in a second. He was hateful but it was wonderful.

But within the minute Alden's chair was there, and Alden's strong arms were battering at him, tearing him off me, hitting him round the head, with Ray bleating 'Don't, Alden, don't!' It is a fearful thing to be attacked out of nowhere by a man in a wheelchair; one doesn't expect it. My punter let out a fearful yell. I rearranged my Burberry skirt, and got a stray swipe from Alden which left my ear ringing. Audrey and Clive were there at the double, in their pantomime Ali Baba clothes, and the security man, and now the wife too, quite hysterical, and my poor punter wondering how he'd got into this. And now his wife was at him too, slap, slap, slap. Good for you, I thought. It was wonderful. What an uproar! What can happen if you act out of turn, of your own volition! Fuck Ray, I thought, and his ninety-three squares, and the flashing lights of the universe, fuck the Thelemites; this is real art; this is creativity, something where there was nothing before, and I'd done it.

Loki was sent for; I was bundled up and taken home in the taxi, in disgrace. 'Whore! Slut!' said Alden from his wheelchair. Well, I was glad he cared. 'Alden, be reasonable,' pleaded Ray from beside me. 'She does as I say,' says Alden, 'not what she wants.' And still I thought it was funny.

I was to learn otherwise.

'Find a dark street,' said Alden over the intercom to Loki. We made a detour here, a short cut there: we ended up somewhere behind the British Museum where the streets are quiet and a parked black cab will attract no attention.

Loki seemed to know what was expected of him. He got out of the front and came round to Ray's side at the back. Ray got out to let him in – suddenly panicked, I made a dash for it – and it was Loki who caught me and hurled me back in while Alden helped drag me around until I was sprawled opposite him with my neck cricked into the corner of the cab. Loki, my friend, always punctual, always polite, who gave me a sandwich when I was hungry, now pushing up my long red satin gown with business-like hands as if he'd been thinking about this for some time and had every move worked out.

'Only business, Joan,' said Alden. 'This way we recoup some transport fees.'

But what he meant was that I should see that he controlled even my friendships; that Loki thought more of getting his bill paid than he did of me. See how I liked that! And he was right. I didn't. Not one bit.

I struggled some more. Ray was somewhere in there too, bleating in my ear. 'Joan, enjoy: Joan, enjoy,' and Alden was saying 'Why the fuck should she enjoy, the disobedient little bitch?'

But then I thought, well, at least I'm getting to fuck Loki, who is much better looking than either of you two, and almost certainly better at it: that's what I did, that's how I won, I decided to enjoy. I stopped struggling – a matter of indifference to Loki, I thought: he was so strong and lithe he probably didn't notice I had been – and of annoyance to Alden, who was bending his face into mine, only inches away. My white skin, Loki's dark torso – Alden trapped there by his stupid legs, no Lam to help him: he was pitiable. Loki, silhouetted in the light of the antique gas street lamps which they have in the British Museum area, was gorgeous. It is a softer light than halogen, almost romantic. He didn't

255

kiss me when we had finished – and I didn't come – of course he wouldn't: this was not kissing territory; but he did thank me, as though I had given him a really good tip.

And then we all went on home as if nothing had happened, except that Alden was really quite frighteningly furious.

Lam was waiting up for us.

'Joan not behave?' he asked.

'Joan very, very bad,' said Alden. 'Joan taught lesson.'

Ray went straight upstairs to the studio. No doubt he got at least two or three more squares done. It must have been quite an intense evening for him too, from his voyeur's vewpoint.

'I'm not responsible for what happened tonight,' he said, as he went. 'I won't be. Joan, please consider yourself no longer under-will.'

'She soon will be,' said Alden. 'But my way, not yours.'

There were two of them, and one of me. One might be in a wheelchair but the other had big strong hands and was from outer space. Being 'under will' is not a one-sided game. I was enough Vanessa now to be kicking up a storm, but I still had many residual Joan beliefs, including that Lam was from the Dog Star Sirius, and not only that: Ray was on the Seventh Path down in Southgate, treading the way of the mighty which meant seventh level as well as seventh path, and trod in the steps of the holy Tathgata, whose face was the rising sun of thought eternal. What nonsense it all was, yet here I was, crouched on the floor of the mirror room, the cuff which had adorned the pegs of the easel back round my left ankle, and the chain – nasty rusty old thing it was – fixed to a thin metal ring in some smart new metal on the smart new bed post. The new bed was not going to be all that different from the old.

And I had been left alone to contemplate my sins. The mirrors threw back a sorry portrait of a wilful, disobedient, ungrateful girl. I had endangered everything by a single, lustful, vengeful act. The reputation of the Divan, the ego of the smug man, the contentment of his wife: I had betrayed and upset both Ray and Alden, abandoned the power of my dependency, complicated my relationship with Loki, and there was no health in me. And I had tried to damage *The Blue Box*. And – now I could see – what was almost worse, that I had damaged the quilt with the ninety-three patchwork squares. It was too big for the new bed and its hems trailed on the floor. Three of the squares were coming adrift; they needed to be mended. My fault. I had been told to take it down to the cleaners but I had thought that was a waste on money and wedged it into the washing machine and put it through. Another thing to be guilty about.

Lam came in, the alien from Sirius the Dog Star – the follower of Tathgata, who is universal. And oh God, not again: I'd thought she had improved, but Vanessa was in full agitated flood again as Lam padded around, fetching props, selecting whips, waving his tentacles: Vanessa was now quoting from the Great Parinirvana Sutra, the gospel of the four paths, in which the Buddha talks about the noble truth of suffering, an eternally abiding, unchanging, fine and essential awareness. Suffering is bad enough, shrieks Vanessa, but if they say Lam is on the Seventh Path then it's Dark Zen he's into, the worship of the self (Satanism) plus pure productive energy (*The Blue Box*) and once that ties in with Crowley mania and modern technology – *The Blue Box* being the outer and visible form of the triumph of the infinite complexity of all things, in other words representing the computer – why then, says Vanessa, we're in real trouble. It's bound to end up with someone wanting a human sacrifice – because this stuff is escalating: they're children, children, playing with fire like Alden playing with fireworks, and the black mass in the chapel was a mere early rehearsal – why won't I realise? She snaps away in my head. But what can I do about it? All I know is that this bed has a steel V-frame to which I am tied, facing the door, and a spreader bar for my feet and all directional mikes are pointed my way. Again I am left alone to contemplate. If that was Lam with the tentacles than I am definitely under will again. Vanessa doesn't save me, she makes things worse.

Perhaps now was the time to really talk? I could

tell Alden all about Vanessa, how she tormented me with her over-active mentation, so I'd had to take refuge in Joan. Explain how I hadn't really set out to deceive Ray and himself, just to entertain them. I must persuade Alden that actually Vanessa might bring more to their lives than Joan ever could; Joan could stop babbling and chattering and engage them in a proper conversation, on their own level. Wouldn't that be wonderful? Meet Alden fact for fact, reference for reference? I must convince them that they were better off with the vocational girl, Vanessa, than with the (mostly) willing whore, Joan. That once I could be true to myself Alden mightn't get the feedback echo which so annoyed him. His dreams for *Thelemy – The Murmur of Eternity*, would at last be realised.

But even as I tried to formulate the right words in my head I realised that it was hopeless: Alden and Ray would not believe me. I only barely believed myself. Vanessa was only Vanessa if she behaved like Vanessa. If Joan claimed to have a double first, a rectory for a family home, and be called Vanessa, Joan was lying or deluded. Vanessa was a figment of Joan's imagination: the girl from Little Venice with the good boobs and the easy, smiling ways, the thick reddish-brown hair which could be grabbed and pulled, the girl with the low self image that made her so ready and ripe for defilement, was simply Joan the tart. She was now the real one. Why make trouble?

Lam pads back in and out again, bringing me a pill and some water.

'Paracetemol,' he says. 'Joan needs.'

Joan would have to be punished, I realised that, and Alden meant to, unless he was just scaring me to death. I looked up at the mirror above, and could see the evidence of my crimes in three unstitched squares of white velvet and one of damask. I had put the quilt through the delicate wash; I'd had to stuff it in because it was so bulky but it was on gentle spin, and the cold water wash. But to no avail. I had also by mistake put in some red thongs. The quilt had come out palest pink. I put it through again at 30°, with bleach, and though the fabric returned to white well enough, it had lost body to a different degree in different of its patchwork squares, and where square joined square it had either stretched or wrinkled. Ninety-three squares. Bloody cabalists! All I could hope was Alden would not choose to notice now.

Ten minutes later Alden came in, without Lam, and chose the whip I least liked the look of, with the red lacquered handle, and nine thin red leather thongs.

He thwacked the whip through the air so as to frighten me with the sound. It did, but I pretended not. To cower and whimper would not help me now, rather the contrary.

'You mustn't mark me,' I said, 'that would be stupid.'

'You're the stupid one,' he said; 'You drive me mad

with your stupidity. Now see what you've made me do.'

He actually laughed, with a maniac laugh which would have impressed a horror film director, and I wondered what drug he was on. He turned on the hum, painfully loudly. He would be adding another track. He stroked between my legs with the tip of the whip and I squealed. He poked it a little in just to show he could. Then he took it out.

'You'll ruin your ears with that noise,' I said. 'You probably have already. You're probably as deaf as Beethoven by now. I hope you are.'

'You talk too much,' was all he said. 'And hear too much.'

It was a helmet I was familiar with. The sweaty black latex ruined your hair and the mouthpiece held your mouth open and held your tongue down and stopped you speaking and the padded prongs of the ear-pieces went into your ears and plugged them and stopped you hearing. It intensified sensation in other orifices and on a good day made you orgasm all over the place but I did not think this was going to be a good day. And with Alden with the lash in his hand and in the mood he was I did not need any sensation to be intensified. He put the helmet on, hurting my mouth as he stretched it wide with the metal bar, the scolds' bridle, as it's called, which fitted from ear to ear across the front of the helmet.

I was now in no position to answer back, explain,

speak at all. He raised the whip, held it there to the count of ten, and brought it down across both breasts. I lost all composure but it did me no good. He waited a minute or so, standing over me, whip raised until my muffled squealings died away.

'That's better,' he said. 'Now that was a real response.'

He unbuckled and removed the helmet: my mouth went back to its proper shape, though I could taste it was bleeding a little at the edges. I breathed, I heard, I could speak. I spoke.

'Radio 3 may accept it,' I said. 'Daisy O may play it at her opening because you blackmail her. But no-one in the world is going to want to listen to it.'

I shouldn't have said it. It was just too much of a temptation. Fury, usually diminished by the spirit of scientific and artistic enquiry, swept up through him. He caught me with the lashes on the ribs, over the breasts, under them, across my thighs. I screamed. I lost all sense of irony. The touch pads glowed, the steel V became a wheel, folded, turned me, bent me; now it was the cane across my buttocks, where at least he could inflict no real damage, only pain and humiliation. I screamed and wriggled but Lukas's ingenuity kept me in place. And then again, and again, streaks of pain, until I forgot there'd ever been such a state as pleasure. Pain alone was real, and all consuming.

'That's enough, Alden,' said Ray's voice, 'that's enough. I can't stand this bloody noise. Are you mad?'

The sound suddenly ceased and the cane did not come again, and I was unbent, turned, but still held. I was conscious of my tear-swollen face, my muddy, mascaraed eyes, my sweaty hair, my reddened body, and I hoped he was sorry. At the same time I felt purged, quiet, content and punished. The sin, though I could scarcely remember what it had been, was atoned for. The smarting was already fading, just so long as I stayed still.

I wish I could give you a better account of myself. How I plotted to murder him or burned the house down: have him exposed as an art fraud, a pornographer and a drug peddler. I didn't. I'm afraid it doesn't work like that. I was just the more anxious to please him. Vanessa was so disgusted with me she went into a deep cover which at least allowed me to sink into a languid submission without her alarmist interruptions. Though I may have been deceiving myself, and she too was simply cowed and terrified. We shared the body, after all.

I was released from bondage, the fine metal struts were retracted, my poor stiff body laid on my side on the bed, and Alden lay behind me. Once again he thrust and thrust, while my bruised flesh cried out in protest, and once again he almost, almost came, and didn't. And once again I thought it was my fault, and all I could be grateful for was that nobody had noticed the state of the quilt, where it trailed inelegantly on the floor.

I think Alden wept a little and apologised and said it was his love for me that had driven him to do this: and it was the first time that he had mentioned the word. I was so happy to hear it, I turned and clung to him, and kissed his strong, solid torso all over and felt so sorry for his poor legs I cried for him and no longer for me. He said I was never going to the Divan again, and I was so grateful.

Quiet Seas

WE SETTLED DOWN: WE healed: we were quite domestic and cosy now the storms had passed. Work on *The Blue Box* went slowly, but it went. Ray reckoned that if the art movers could come on September 21st, the Autumn equinox, the piece would be ready for installation in Daisy's gallery on the 24th, the day before the official opening. Alden accordingly booked the best, and most expensive, specialist art movers in the business.

Alden spent a lot of time holed up in his Bluebeard room working on his acoustics. In response to general demand the hum was played no more than once or twice day. It triggered a quite strong reaction in me: that is to say my bum began to hurt and twitch, and also under the ribs where a particularly nasty lash had got me. I didn't need Vanessa to tell me this response was Pavlovian.

'Cat o' nine tails,' Lam said. 'Nine unlucky.'

Arts-Intrinsick was on schedule with the gallery

opening: Daisy had not insisted on the parquet floor being re-laid. She had not nagged or bothered Ray at all as to the completion of *The Blue Box*. She trusted Alden and she trusted Ray. Invitations had gone out. She brushed away little problems: it would all be all right on the night.

I had quite gone off sex. Whether this was the fear of the lash, or Alden and Ray deciding they didn't want to risk any more freelance action on my part, I don't know. I shopped though: Ray handed me cash and I just got on with it. Loki would take me, wait outside the shops or circle the block, and bring me home again. We only referred once to the British Museum incident, as I had registered it in my mind; and to tell the truth what happened afterwards had obscured a lot of its detail in my memory.

Loki remarked lightly that Mr Alden was running up quite a bill again, and I said I'd mention it to him, and Loki said no, don't do that, I could pay in kind any time: but I didn't follow it up as once I would. Just thinking about it made my bum hurt. But it was wonderful to be able to spend again – the feeling of shopping bags stacked up against one legs in a taxi, the rustle of tissue as one shifted on the seat seemed so satisfactory.

Lam went away for a week: he was teaching an advanced course in Portsmouth. Ray and I between us performed the carer's duties. We managed without Lam. Indeed, we could almost have been said to be living normal lives. Other than that I was summoned up to Ray's studio from time to time, and he would lie me naked at the foot of his canvas, and study me until another of the thin lines went on the canvas. Every tiny, tiny stroke a person, an act, an excess, laid one against the other in complexities only he understood, mirrored to infinity if he got it right. No wonder his spirit sometimes failed. Sometimes we went to bed and just slept. I felt very mature. I was looking good these days: early bed, restful nights, and I was glad to say my eyes were as bright, my hair as glossy and my skin as glowing as it had ever been.

We were doing well, I suspect, the three of us, without resort to Ray's magic words and Alden's he-who-must-be-obeyed stance. They weren't needed. Alden had found a timeless way of subduing me. And without Lam it seemed there was no excess. His apparent passivity egged others on.

My room began to look rather like my place in Little Venice only without the books. I went on paying my rent: Alden said I should. I had rather hoped he'd tell me to give up the flat and move in with him properly but he didn't. But I thought if I just hung in there it would happen in the end. After mid-September, perhaps, after the En Garde gallery had opened and Alden could concentrate more on matters of the heart. They seemed to have forgotten about my family photographs, and I was glad of that.

Sometimes I would go down with Alden to the

warehouse where Daisy's artworks were accumulating, flown in from all over the planet, and I would make lists, check off inventories, and help work out whether any tax was applicable. Though these were simple enough tasks, Alden seemed quite impressed that I could do them. He himself, when it came to lists and forms, was a terrible muddler.

When I bumped into Lady Daisy in the warehouse she didn't recognise me. She was wearing a good plain cashmere jumper beneath through which the shape of her nipples showed and an asymmetrical skirt, its hem elaborately and annoyingly uneven. She was relaxed and looked far prettier than she had when first I met her. She walked hand in hand with Lord Toby O, her husband, who was much older and much shorter than she was but they seemed fond enough of each other, and I was glad. I didn't suppose they had much of a sex life, but no doubt she had her women friends. It would be a waste if she didn't. One of the warehousemen told me that though the project had got off to a hellish start, the Lady Daisy had turned out to be a pleasure to work with. I felt I'd achieved something.

I bought needle and thread and saw to the patchwork quilt, secretly. I'm good at sewing and I'm proud of my tiny little hemming stitches. The men were not the only creative people in that household.

Loki took me to see Dr Wondle, Alden's man in Harley Street. He was a dignified, white-haired man who asked me what drugs I took, nodded his head when

I told him, saying the great thing was to drink lots of water, which cleared the system of lingering toxicities. He checked me over, took tests, and pronounced me free of anything nasty. I complained to him of what I described as fluctuating memory, and he said surely that was no bad thing. Most of us have things in our mind that are better forgotten. He said I seemed not only the glass of fashion but the picture of health and asked me to give his regards to Alden and thank him for sending along such an admirable specimen of humanity. I wasn't sure I liked being described as a specimen but was glad to have got away without an internal examination or worse. I wouldn't have put it past Alden to have plotted to sell one of my kidneys if need arose: and then I thought that's a rotten thing to think about the man I love. A little flicker of Vanessa, surfacing again. I shrugged her off.

To complete the picture of domesticity we even sometimes had a guest for dinner. His name was Bernie. Alden dismissed him in private as a rich star-fucker, an art collector who wanted to touch the hem of Ray's garment: when he was there Alden was all over him. Bernie was very good looking, and very gay, with that kind of protected, solid, polished, tanned, well-manicured look that hangs round such people like an aura. We get a lot of them at the Olivier. He took very little notice of me, other than to look me up and down in a quizzical kind of way when Ray described me as his muse. I think he had assumed I was with

Alden, when actually I was with both of them.

Bernie would sometimes come with his boyfriend – a French North African, I reckoned – very young, black, beautiful and sulky. Arts-Intrinsick was making over Bernie's place in Mayfair to house his growing collection of South American art. It was a big deal, and was going to fit in nicely after the work on Lady Daisy's show was done. Alden was in a benign mood, the more so because he had finally delivered his piece to Radio 3 where it had been well received, though he still waited for the overall programme to be green lit. But all were confident this would be the case.

Bernie brought round some stuff, a newly discovered hallucinogen from yet another 'rare plant in the rain forest'. Chemists were trying to synthesise it but running into trouble. Bernie was a consultant to a Russian billionaire, an oil oligarch, seeking to acquire great swathes of the world's art works – so such freebies came his way from time to time. Alden offered to give it a test run, since Bernie was obviously nervous. It was meant to deliver a blend of amphetamine and soporific with a peppering of the visionary, leading to easy, intensified sexual gratification. Ray stuck to ordinary black hashish on the grounds that he did not want his artistic judgment compromised so near to Day Zero. Alden and I tried it but it didn't do a thing for either of us. We decided the billionaire was being had: but neither Bernie nor his billionaire sponsor would be pleased to hear that, so we went along with their expectations and said it was great stuff. Well, you don't like to mess with oligarchs and Alden had a vested interest in keeping things running smoothly with Bernie.

It was a little lie, but one which was going to come back and haunt me. There is a kind of natural justice out there in the world: Alden and Ray went to great lengths to subvert it with their Ophidian currents, their Crowleyanity, their numbered Paths to Wisdom and so on, but they would have done better just to let things alone and accept them, not try to wrest power out of an unblinking universe.

Because there was then, suddenly – Trouble. It seemed the build-up of paint on the large canvas of *The Blue Box* was causing cracks to occur in the glue which held the wooden frames in place, so the mirrors themselves were cracking and in two cases had shattered completely: when one went it had a domino effect. Six would be affected. Lam could deal with the cracked glass well enough but the wooden frames had taken months and needed Ray's creative input. Ray stamped and swore and tore his hair; Alden said wait for Lam to get back and do it: Ray talked about authenticity and it was Alden's turn to say 'fuck authenticity, what about my opening?'

Work on the painting stopped. I felt obscurely to blame. The painting had a memory of the damage I had done: now it was repeating it of its own accord.

Worse, Radio 3 had not green-lit Alden's work: it had received only an orange light. Proceed with caution. The Programme's head of music, himself a rival minimalist composer of note, had suggested Alden 'make changes'. Alden was outraged, even if not all the news was bad: Daisy had heard the piece and loved it and it would be having its premier at the opening as planned.

But it was bad enough. And again, I felt it was my fault. I had failed to deliver. My passion and my pain had not been of concert standard.

And they looked at me, I, their muse, in a way that I knew I had to come up with something.

True Love

LIAM CAME HOME AND I was sent home for the weekend. Early September and just a hint of autumn in the air: the smell of bonfires drifted across common and woodland. I realised how much I'd missed my family. My mother asked me how my holiday had been, and I remembered in time I'd said I was going to Thailand. She wondered when I was going back into academia and I said I didn't think I was. She sighed and said it was a waste of a good brain.

Katharine and Alison asked my advice. They'd been reading Ovid's Art of Love in Latin. They wanted to know how to lose their virginities. They thought perhaps they were missing out on full appreciation of the texts. I told them that if they just stood around in pubs and did a bit of binge drinking it would happen soon enough.'We've tried that,' they said. 'Nothing happens.'

I was not surprised. They did look a little odd. They'd looked better in the photographs. In real life they were so pale, thin and flat-chested, you could hardly tell the difference between them and their background. And they hated to be parted. So different from myself. Could my parents have been telling lies? Perhaps I wasn't my father's daughter? Or perhaps the twins were not his?

'Dad's still having that affair,' said Alison.

'With your friend Jude,' said Katharine. 'You shouldn't ever have brought her home.'

'You shouldn't ever have run and told,' I said. The twins had done some detective work and found out Jude had just had a little baby. A boy. They had moved into a cottage five miles away.

'We think it's Daddy's baby,' said Alison.

'Jude calls herself Mrs but she isn't,' said Katharine.

'He visits her on Wednesday lunchtimes, while Mummy's taking midweek Eucharist.'

They wanted to know if they should tell our mother or not.

'No!' I said. 'Just shut up and perhaps it will all go away.'

They danced around on their skinny legs and called me Cleopatra, Queen of Denial. Why did they have to play detective? Why did they have to stir things up? I wished they'd get themselves boyfriends and turn into proper people, and not wear National Health glasses. But they couldn't even see anything wrong with them.

Robert was next. He came sobbing to me to ask my

advice. His zits were making him unattractive to women. Our mother was trying to cure them with homeopathic remedies which weren't working. I suggested he went to see Dr Barky who would give him antibiotics. He said he thought Dr Barky was gay. I said I really didn't think he was. Robert said he'd tried to get it on with an older woman but it hadn't worked. I asked him how much older and he said about your age. I said he should concentrate on young women, and ask Dr Barky for Viagra while he was about it.

Robert 'yes, but'-ed, as he had since he was small. Yes but, Vanessa, supposing I'm really gay? I said there's nothing wrong with being gay. He said eagerly did I think so? I said it saved an awful lot of money on child care. But perhaps he should wait and see what he was, he was only sixteen. The immediate and major worry was the acne.

He said yes but, Vanessa, Jude had said she didn't mind the zits, they should try again, but actually she rather disgusted him. He couldn't understand why women had to have breasts. He'd quite fancy me if I didn't have them.

'Did you say Jude?' I asked and he said yes, that was her name. He thought I knew her. He'd met her outside the local Garden Centre and she was crying because of some man. They'd got into conversation and she asked Robert to cheer her up behind the potting sheds. He hadn't wanted to, but she was so miserable he thought he ought. It hadn't worked.

It had for my father, more's the pity, I thought.

Robert said he was getting very neurotic about the gay thing. He kept thinking he had a dreadful smell coming from his arse and his friends avoided him. I said he'd probably been smoking too much dope. He said yes but Vanessa, he'd seen a documentary on television about borderline schizophrenia, and some of his symptoms seemed right. And so on. Yes but. Yes but.

I took the early train back to London on Sunday night. My mother didn't see me off at the station: she was taking Evensong, swanning around in white and gold vestments. I wished she'd take more notice of me, and my father too.

Parents never get it right. There's either too much of them or too little of them. And the visit had stirred up Vanessa.

The Siblings Come To Town

THEY WERE WAITING FOR me when I came back. I let myself in the door with a cheerful 'Hi, you guys! I'm back.' But the whole mood of the house had changed. The hum was booming through it at full blast: the sound now had a double thread to it: the low notes were lower and I supposed Alden had achieved his ninety-three hertz, greeting of the Thelemites, (ninety-three being the Gematrian, or numerological reduction of the Greek words 'Thelemy' – will, and 'Agape', love – Vanessa was back, all right. She reckoned Crowley rented rooms in Jermyn Street because the cheese shop happened to be at No. 93, and so it took his fancy and impressed others, even though it meant he and Rosa had to climb four flights to get to them). But now there was also a shriller note as well, overlaying and threading through the whole, which was to me rather horrible, putting me in mind of my time under the lash of the cat-o-nine tails. Perhaps, if this was the piece Alden had submitted to Radio 3, it was understandable that the head of department wanted 'changes'. Perhaps, as it was, it just made him uneasy. Perhaps the new piece delighted Lady Daisy because she was a more sincere masochist than I could ever be.

I would have preferred Alden to have been motivated by personal and sexual gratification, even at my expense, than the pursuit of the En Garde. This was the problem with going home: what seems normal in one place is simply not in another. One gets stirred up. But I was given no time to think about these things. Apparently I had done wrong. I was sent to my room with Lam, who stripped me, cuffed my hands behind my back and took me up to sit next to Ray on the blue sofa, with Alden facing me in his chair.

'Bad girl,' said Lam on the way, by way of explanation. 'Wash quilt wrong.'

It seemed the spectroanalyser – one of Lukas's developments, an instrument that combined the functions of both spectrometer and a spectrum analyser for low frequencies – had detected some red in the pure white of the quilt. White enough for the naked eye, that is to say, but not for Alden's sensors. They had pieced together what had happened. I confessed. A red thong in the washing machine by mistake. But I'd been told to take the quilt to the cleaners. So why was it in the washing machine? Disobedience!

'I mended it,' I said. 'No harm was done.' And then of course it came out that some of the squares had been shrunk and others stretched because of the thirty degree wash. I sat there while Ray and Alden gave me little cross pinches with their nails. But it did not get any worse than that. There was a cracking sound and another of the tiny mirrors on *The Blue Box* slipped out of its frame, and saved me, before it did.

Lam attended to it. Alden forgave me, but with a warning.

'It is very important, Joan,' he said, 'that you do exactly as we tell you. Not just follow some approximation of your own. You don't have the wit or wisdom.'

And he put a cigarette in my mouth, and when he lit it I could tell what was in it from the cedary smell: Bernie's new drug. It didn't do anything much, I knew, so I inhaled and held my breath. Lam untied my hands and gave me a silk wrap – a Zedzz organza with a few sequins, a snip at £99 – which didn't hide much but was better than nothing – and they put the family snaps up on the screen. And I knew what this was all about: what I was meant to come up with. And I wasn't going to be party to it.

But Ray did his old trick of looking into my eyes. He had advanced a path or claimed to have – rather to have shifted over via the fifth stage to the fifth sphere, so his power was intensified to the fifth degree. Oh my God, bleated Vanessa, don't say they're into Steiner. Steiner was a high initiate of Crowley's original OTO, before he diverted to the Rosicrucians. Stage five – the Mystic Death, the descent into hell. Bet that's what

279

Ray sees himself as going through. The torment of the artist on the way to the oneness. This Southgate lot, protests Vanessa, are renegades: all-purpose polymorphous occultists: anything will do. But she seems slightly mollified at the mention of Steiner: at least he wasn't into human sacrifice, only growing crops by the phases of the moon. Although Walther Darré, Hitler's Minister For Agriculture, who invented the term 'organic gardening' developed the idea from Steiner's 'bio-dynamics': Rudolph Hess was a fan, and the German Steiner schools were under his protection until he flew to Scotland. Shut up, Vanessa, thought Joan.

'Okay Joan,' says Ray. 'Holiday's over. You're under will.'

After that it's snapshots. Bernie and his companion have come round. Five men, one woman in a diaphanous gown. But of the men two of them are gay, one of them a potential alien, one of them unable to come and the other one a premature ejaculator; all are searching for the secret of the Holy Grail, as well they might. Bernie is disappointed that the rain forest drug isn't doing much for anyone: there is a lot of money invested in its research and development.

Bernie is having a hard time from his boyfriend Naz. Naz doesn't much like coming over to our house and lets it be known. He's bored and off-hand, and tapping his foot, and just wants to get out of there. Art's not his bag and he's not bothering to make Bernie think it is. This relationship's going nowhere, it's not hard to tell. It's run its course, and Bernie is going to be left feeling dull, stale and old unless he quickly finds some diversion. In the end money and the adoration of an older man is not enough. Enchantment, lust and excitement beckon, not to mention the call of the new. I know the feeling. Bernie was the one wanting to please: well, it is always the older one, isn't it.

Snapshot. Five men and one girl looking at photos of my little brother Robert in the garden, laughing and sweaty, half naked and with perfect teeth. And I'd just been worrying about the twins.

'You're pathetic,' said Naz to Bernie. 'If you think I'm going to be jealous of that. I don't believe I'm gay anyway. You just told me I was.'

'I suppose you want her, then,' said Bernie, indicating little diaphanous me, with distaste. 'Presumably that's what she's here for.'

I could see that it probably was, and also the rain forest drug wasn't as hopeless as they said, because my interest in things of the flesh was quite revived.

'I'm not as hetero as all that,' said Naz, and got to his feet and walked out, and I applauded gently. I like it when others show spirit. But then Naz wasn't under will. I seemed to have remarkably little choice, living under law, the law being love.

Snapshot. Me meeting Robert at Paddington.

Snapshot: Robert wandering amongst our grandmother's art, my paintings, the Chagall, the

Picasso, the Klimt – he has quite an eye for a painting – my scented lingerie, my dresses, my jackets, my scarves, my mascaras, eye colour, concealers, all my littered lovely female mess: my Wittgenstein, my Cathexis, still unopened.

Robert scooping up a great armful of garments and throwing them all in the air and laughing. Robert at my dressing table putting on lipstick, patting his hair, deciding no wig: pulling out drawers, pulling on panties to hold himself in, smooth his front of unsightly bobbles, constrict him.

'I reckon I'm gay,' he said. 'Or perhaps I'm a girl.'

I said, 'You don't know till you try.'

'I don't go for all that marriage and children stuff,' he said.

I said, 'My boyfriend has asked us out to dinner tonight to meet some friends of his,' and Robert said that was okay by him, there wasn't much food in this place, was there? 'Robert,' I said, 'but you have to do me a favour. Play it plebeian, not public school. I've told them you're a comprehensive boy, our dad is an unemployed retard, mum's a social worker and we live in a council flat.'

'That's fine by me,' he said. 'More fashionable.'

Snapshot. We go out walking down by the canal in the evening. He is fetchingly pretty in my pale pink flouncy blouse and a peasant skirt with a tight gold belt. It wasn't a woman's taste: it was what a man thought a woman's taste was. I'd helped him with his eye-shadow and mascara. Two coats, no smudges. Some concealer for the acne but it wasn't too bad.

'Feels really good,' he said, my little teenage brother, stumbling on heels, head high, little bosoms improvised out of rolled up socks, buttocks out, pretty face turned to the low sun. Men looked after us. I could see it was a turning point. What was to become of him? He'd scraped through his exams. What then? I supposed he could join the Soho *demi-monde*, that subfusc world of men and women of dubious sexuality, who frequent the clubs and the street corners, thinking about sex-change ops, talking to therapists, staring into mirrors, dolling themselves up, thinking about nothing except the impression they make. Well, it was his life.

Snapshot. Dinner at the Ivy. Very grand. Alden, Ray, me, Bernie, Robert, Lady Daisy and Lord O, puffing and snorting and spluttering when he spoke. She looking at me a little puzzled and saying, 'I'm sure I've met you somewhere before. Do you paint also?'

All of us having caviar – the last of their Beluga, imports now being banned – Bernie saying there was nothing else worth eating on the menu. Ray wincing: he and Alden were treating the rest of us. Bernie choosing the wine.

And Bernie looking at Robert and Robert looking at Bernie: and the two of them falling in love. I've seen it happen once or twice before. Two people meet, their eyes hold, and they know their lives are going to join, whether it be for a night, a week, a year, for life. Across a crowded room, everything just slips into another gear, another dimension, the Dream Time. Though of course it is possible for at least one person to pretend. But this was genuine: I'd give it at least five years.

Robert recovering first. Bernie, moon-eyes, pouring him champagne. Their futures sorted, just like that. Robert would learn about art, money, power; move on when he had learned all he needed. Bernie would be left behind, but that would be his fate whoever it was. I had won the old man another few years, which he didn't deserve because he thought nothing of me, and let it show, but never mind.

Lifting champagne glasses to the En Garde gallery, opening Tuesday, a week to go. Well, not quite – it's already Thursday. *The Blue Box* to be put in place on Sunday. 'Isn't that cutting it a bit fine?' from Lord Toby. Daisy patting his hand, and saying, 'Don't be such a fusspot, Toby. We must trust Ray.' Ray saying it was completed, except the varnishing: I knowing otherwise – one square still to go and another two mirrors cracked today.

Ray picking up the bill – but there's something wrong with his right hand. The fingers won't clench. Bernie taking the tab from Ray, saying: 'No, please let me do this.' Bernie holding Robert's eye, soppy and daft. Robert's cheerful, bright smile. Robert 16, Bernie 53, I guessed, but given an age of consent, consent can get given. The time is right. Robert takes the baton from me and runs with it.

Bernie saying, 'Can't thank you enough for inviting me, Alden. Thank you Ray.' For my little brother Robert, the freebie, or loss leader.

Stress And Paralysis

SNAPSHOTS. PANIC STATIONS. RAY'S right hand, paralysed. The clock ticking. A week to go. Mirrors cracking and springing as fast as Lam can mend them. Only one square left to fill in with tiny lines to complete the universe, but the apparent unlikelihood of its achievement. Alden's chair going round in circles as he loses control of his touch-pads in his agitation – I've never seen this before. Dr Wondle summonsed urgently. Diagnosis: hysterical paralysis. The cause: stress, sexual repression. No wonder they have him as a doctor: private doctors always tell you what you want to hear.

Vanessa's voice loud and clear in my head. She says the poststructuralist concept of subjectivity is suggestive of a self that is both stable, and unstable, knowable and unknowable, constructed and unique. Crowley's pivotal magical experience was when the Scarlet Woman copulated with the goat and it was the goat that died. What is Alden's pivotal experience going to be, as he follows in the footsteps of the master, seeking ultimate self-realisation? Desperate people do desperate things: be careful. Vanessa bows out with a cheery, 'Take care, God is good, keep rocking!'

Alden's persecuting Ray by telling him he has the name of a private restorer who'll come in and get the piece ready in no time. He'll simply copy into the waiting Box 93 what's in Box 1 and that will complete the circle. Hysterics from Ray: threats of suicide: an actual physical attack on Alden which has to be fended off by Lam. I am back cleaning and scrubbing and getting under everyone's feet but somehow it feels safer at floor level. A telephone call from Robert saying he's in love, he's in love, he's in love, he's in love with a wonderful man. I am rather sorry for Bernie: his emotions will be shredded at some point.

And Ray's poor right hand dangles from his wrist, useless, just as his cock dangles from his balls, useless. If only the one worked, the other would too.

A telephone call from the BBC: they're hoping for delivery soon. They have a change of schedule. Can Alden have the piece in its finished form within the week? Alden says yes, and stares at me. What does he want from me now? Some deathbed howl? We watch some porn films to see the state of the market. We watch family snaps of the twins on the lawn playing netball.

'They're virgins, aren't they,' he says. 'You were telling porky-pies?'

'How would you know that?' I ask, but he just shrugs. I say yes, actually: he wins, he's right. He doesn't pursue the matter any further. He just waits. I know him by now. But there isn't much time to take time, and we both know it.

I do what I can for Alden, I really do. I lie down, crawl about, crouch, sit, blow, suck, twirl, everything a girl with a practiced repertoire can do for any man without the use of his legs, but a strong upper body and an alien assistant. I squeal, grunt, scream, choke, laugh, delight, chatter, and come: 80% is genuine. Still he doesn't come: the gods of Tantra win.

I do what I can for Ray. I lie in his big low divan with its heavy silk savonnerie spread, naked and next to him at his request: he's crying and needs comfort, his nose is running and he's snuggled into goose-down cushions in the foetal position, and the sheets haven't been changed for ages. I do the rest of the house but not the studio (nor the Bluebeard room, of course). It's very Ray-ish and fairly disgusting but I'm sorry for him. I wear nothing but he's not interested. His penis lies small and cosy against his balls and refuses to so much as twitch. That's okay by me, though not by Alden. Alden wants Ray's soul and Ray won't let him have it. Alden sees Ray as an extension of himself. Ray in the meanwhile won't have Alden in bed with us. He says it's unnatural. The paralysis is his punishment for sins of lust. My sins, he means, Ray just mostly watched.

Even as Ray and I lie there in the dark there's a tiny pinging sound, and I know another mirror's gone. I wonder if the same thing is happening to the quilt in the mirror room – whether the patches are disintegrating yet further. I decide to go down and see.

Snapshot. Me creeping from the studio and tiptoeing downstairs to the mirrored bedroom with my needle and thread. A couple more patches have come adrift, but maybe it's not too bad, not terminal. The quilt ought really go to be professionally restored, but I can't face the uproar consequent upon my suggesting it. I sit on the floor to get to the worst frayings and comings-apart which are round the hem. The mirrors throw back reflections: I'm there reflected unto all infinity – naked girl crouching with needle and thread. I don't like the room at all any more: nasty things have happened here. Once it was pure and light and naughty and experimental. Now something else haunts it.

Snapshot. Alden's chair, the swish of its wheels on the carpet. My ears are tuned to the sound by now. Alden in a rage, or is it simulated rage? Something has happened.

Lam follows on behind.

'Vanessa!' he says. 'Liar.'

He seems to be crying. There are tears on his cheeks. So, I am discovered. Robert had blabbed. Well, it was bound to come out. I am not Joan, the girl he can despise, I am Vanessa, the girl he must respect, love for her mind as well as for her body. If a man can love

Joan surely he would love Vanessa more? It will all be all right. If only he had not said Vanessa's name as if he hated her.

Alden presses a touch pad. The hum starts up: the latest, horriblest version with my howls upon it. Another touch and the metal bars begin to come down to form the V. Lam is looking for whips. I fear for my life. I offer Alden the twins.

Snapshot. Vanessa writing out place names. Florists are bringing in flowers, masses of them.

Vanessa: How do you spell Mikhail?

Alden: M-i-k-h-a-i-l.

Vanessa: As in an oligarch?

Alden: As in an oligarch.

Vanessa: And Bernie?

Alden: B-e-r-n-i-e. I thought you knew how to spell. You might as well be Joan.

So we can laugh about it now. The twins are coming to dinner. They're staying the night at the Dorchester, all expenses paid by Alden. Bernie's oligarch is coming. He has to be soothed because of the fiasco with the rainforest drug. No-one likes to look foolish. If the oligarch is pleased, favours will flow down the line once more. Everyone will benefit. Everyone is excited and confident. They know the night augers well.

Caterers are providing the dinner. All I have to do are the place names. Ray is out of his sofa bed, taking a bath, shaving, enjoying all the things a man can do with his left hand. By tomorrow he is sure *The Blue*

Box will be complete, all ninety-three squares done, three years' work borne fruit. I think he expects an apotheosis. Tomorrow, tomorrow all will be well, he will be assumed into Heaven. Alden has spent most of the day in his Bluebeard room. Occasionally he comes out to wind me up about my double first.

'Philosophy!' he exclaims. 'Your father a Latin scholar, your mother a vicar! What a little minx you are. Laughing at us all the time, I suppose?'

I say laughter was not really all that high up on my agenda. Oh, I was growing up.

Snapshot: Katharine and Alison, in a taxi with Vanessa, from Paddington on their way to Hampstead, and Alden's mansion on the hill. They look awful, negligible, wearing the shapeless navy blue in which they hope to stay invisible. They have one small, old-fashioned leather suitcase between them, with (they say) all their finery in it, which they have chosen themselves. I'm rather worried about this. I am wearing jeans, heels, a plain white top and my Lacroix jacket and look gorgeous. They haven't even noticed.

Alison: We've been reading the Minmermus Elegies.

Katharine: 7th century BC. Very early texts.

Alison: Our tutor says it would help if we could only feel, not just think. It's a matter of interpretation, not just translation.

I can't concentrate. What am I doing? Why?

Katharine: Don't worry about it, Vanessa.

Alison: We know what we're doing.

Katharine: We brought white dresses for defilement.

Vanessa: Defilement? You've been asked to a dinner party.

They look at me with sceptical eyes and laugh. What can Bernie have told them, Robert? What can Robert have told the twins? But Robert won't be there tonight; he's back at Eton.

The twins meet Alden, and politely admire his wheelchair and his house. They are not shown all of it; not the mirror room, for instance. They are gauche, have no social graces. They ask Alden about his accident and whether it has affected his potency. He tells them no, though he has some residual psychosomatic difficulty. They hope stem-cell technology will soon be able to help him.

I ask Alden how he finds them, and he says it's as well the oligarch speaks very little English.

They go up to the studio and meet Ray and admire *The Blue Box*. They point out that one of the squares is still blank and ask if this is accident or design. Ray replies, 'Act of God.' Alison counts the squares and tells her sister 'ninety-three', and Katharine says, 'I see, a greeting.' Alison asks Ray if moving the piece is going to be a problem. They are introduced to Lam and Katharine says, 'LAM? Isn't that the acronym for lymphangioleiomyomatosis?'

Lam says, 'No, Lam breathe well. Good air on Dog Star,' and sidles off smirking.

The long L word is for a very nasty, usually fatal, lung disease which affects fertile young women. The twins, as I do, like medical dictionaries. Their eidetic skills are probably twice mine. But I don't think they have Bipolar Two. Their troubles, if such they be, lie at the autistic end of the mental disturbance scale, which is uncommon for girls. But they have each other, and a great capacity for enjoyment.

They change in my room. The transformation is astonishing. They wear simple cream silk shifts over their thin, almost hipless bodies. For once I am able to see their legs, which are long and slim. They wear no bras and no panty line is visible. Their breasts make slight bumps. They might as well be wearing nothing, but the effect is graceful and innocent. They move as one. You'd think you were seeing double. By the time most identical twins are seventeen tiny changes in environment will have worked to make them at least distinguishable from each other, but not with these two. They're not so much individuals as one walking brain with two bodies.

I go and change for dinner. Joan's still tripping round in my head la-la-ing, which is the only way I can describe it. La-la-la, all's for the best in the best of all possible worlds. She's trying to make me wear a bright red satin thing but I don't want to upstage the twins. I go for pale pink, more big-sistery, and not too much make-up.

Proper formal dinner-time at Alden's table. I really

go for this. Forget the Divan; forget the scenarios, all that's another life, a kind of sideline. This is the real thing. White linen, silver cutlery, crystal glasses – Riedel, I was pretty sure. Primroses. Flown in from where? Geothermal greenhouses in Iceland – a special order. Mikhail the Oligarch, with Bernie at his side, has arrived in a limo long enough to block all traffic trying to get round South End Green. The chauffeur drops them off, doesn't even try to park. Two security men sit just inside our front door. They are armed with automatic weapons.

Alden sits at the head of the table: I sit at the foot, we are a married couple. When we have solved his sexual problems he will forget his need to make music out of experience, and we will settle down like other, normal people. Ray will go off and live somewhere more suitable for a famous artist, such as LA, and I'll use the studio as a nursery. Alden will have stem-cell treatment and we won't need to have Lam around. I feel warm inside, owned and appreciated. Alison and Katharine sit next to each other, Alison perched on the left of her chair, Katharine to the right of hers, so their hipless bodies touch. They are wearing their big owl glasses. Why can't they get contact lenses like anyone else? I am embarrassed for them. Don't they know anything of how to behave? They seem so untutored in the ways of the world. Ray sits next to them, using his left hand to guide his right. Lam, who stands behind Alden's chair, comes over to cut up his food. The girls are concerned for him; they coo and murmur in their twinnish way, and put morsels of food into his mouth; he seems quite pleased by the attention.

Sitting opposite are Bernie and Mikhail. Mikhail takes up two places. He's like a much cruder, larger, glossier, heavier, more uncouth version of Bernie. Caterers flap around serving minimal portions of allegedly gourmet food. Mikhail refuses it, but nothing seems to upset me. I realise I am under will, and probably have been since I left for Paddington. Ray calls me Vanessa now, not Joan, and for this reason, I suspect, I am thus more vulnerable to the way of the Fourth, or is it now the Fifth Path, the Fifth Stage, the Fifth Sphere? Or just to the eyes, as Alden would have it, of a natural-born hypnotist. Alden the new Crowley, Ray the new Mesmer, with his powers of animal magnetism.

Mikhail pushes his plate away, untouched. I am not surprised. Alden chose the menu: goujons of rhubarb, lentil and squid? I just nod and smile and ask the staff to bring bread, cheese, sausage – apparently he always brings his own with him – and raw onions. He sits and eats using a knife to pierce the food and bring it to his lips, and he chews, carefully studies Alison and Katharine.

I wonder if this vision of the oligarch is Ray-induced, or some flashback from the rainforest drug, which is more powerful than it seems, so stereotypical is his behaviour. 'Gross oligarch with crude table manners' – like some Boyar in an Eisenstein film? But a bit of chewed cheese splutters from his lips onto my cheek, and I can tell he is real: it's true. The twins don't seem to notice anything strange. I am sure it was never like this at home. I have to get them back home before something terrible happens. I try to stand. Ray pulls me back down and leans over to me and says, 'Vanessa, they are the Chosen of the King. Let it be.'

'It's all right, Vanessa,' says Alison. 'We're getting very well paid.'

'We know what we're doing,' says Katharine. 'But it's sweet of you to worry.'

That's all right then. Ten thousand each, it seems. They know the value for what they can offer – a double virgin defloration. They must have sorted it out with Alden while I was wondering about their social graces. Perhaps we do have the same father after all.

I am handing them chocolates from the Harrods box. I am eating myself. We agree they're a little on the sweet side and must be fearfully calorific but we like them. Mikhail hoists his bulk to his feet, knocking over his chair and breaking a couple of the Riedel glasses – two champagne flutes and one claret – and cries out something in Russian which I assume to be 'let's get to business!'

The sudden noise makes me start and wince: everything looks very clear and sharp. What has been going on? What is Alden is saying about 'little owls'? He has taken the glasses from their noses. Their eyes are wide and pale, short-sighted, startled and eager. Mikhail is stumbling round the room like one of those brown bears which break into houses in Alaska and toss all the contents about like rubbish. He is roaring just like a bear too, but I find that a bit hard to separate out from Alden's music. Lam herds the bear and the twins into the mirror room.

Snapshot. Alden is unlocking a door. We are upstairs. It is Bluebeard's door. I am honoured! His music room at last – what I have so wanted to see.

Bluebeard – Gilles de Rais, Marshall of France, friend of Joan of Arc, and master of the black arts. In February 1904 Crowley delivered a lecture – known to posterity as 'The Banned Lecture' – to the Oxford Poetry Society, claiming Gilles de Rais was a victim of a conspiracy of defamation: an example of how established theocracy always tries to destroy the free thinker. De Rais was a powerful force in French politics and military affairs until his views on sex brought him into disrepute. Scandal broke about his head and destroyed him. Ronald Knox banned the lecture, but Crowley published all the same. De Rais was said to have lured children to his castle in Brittany where he sexually abused and murdered them. His cellars were found to be piled high with broken bodies. He was hanged in 1440 and his body burned. Five hundred years later Crowley was to die, broken by scandal: rumours of sexual abuse, black magic, human sacrifice, to be believed or not believed according to your fancy. And

Crowley has his admirers clearly, since he is listed by the BBC among its Top One Hundred British Heroes, so selected by popular vote.

So is Lam an alien from Sirius the Dog Star, a magus from Tibet, or a person with glandular difficulties from Surbiton or Leigh-on-Sea – which would I prefer to believe?

Good wife, don't ask what it is your husband is doing tonight, don't seek to go where you're not asked – in case you find out more than suits you. Then you too must die. Bluebeard's wife is rescued by her brothers in the nick of time. I wondered, as we trooped into the music room, Alden, Lam, Ray, Bernie, myself – who I could trust to be my brothers?

Of course it was not just a music room. Oh Vanessa, Queen of Denial! How could you not know? What did you think those blazing lights were all about? All those mirrors for their crafty reflection shots? There was music equipment here of course there was, banks of it twinkling away, for synthesis and analysis, spectrograms and spectrographs, and graphs leaping up and down over computer screens. But its main function was as a digital film studio and a very sophisticated one: lights, cameras, editing equipment: discs stacked high. Few leads muddling everything up: the new Bluebeard technology. Why would it be otherwise? Two technicians are setting up. They are in white coats but they have their backs to us so I can't yet see their faces. Someone makes good quality film in here: as near to life as can be. Viewing chairs are arranged around the square, and the square is the mirror above the Lukas bed. Only it's not of course mirror from up here; look down and you see clear glass.

Alden has been making high quality porno films. I am a film star. No wonder I'm not allowed out and about too much. And a seat in these hospitality chairs must bring in a pretty penny.

A film is being edited at the moment. Round the room are screens with extracts from my life in the bed, my life in the Divan, my life in the Scenario Suburbs. The quality is variable. The dungeon scene where I kick and flee is practically unusable because of the lighting but new technology is amazing and I daresay something can be rescued. The Bride in the Bath sequence where I drown is awesome in its *verité*. You get a real reaction from me. The monster cock slides into my helpless bum as my mouth spews up water. You don't get much of that on the net though the whole nation endlessly searches; sex 'n' violence in the same shot. Some of these set pieces would be allowed. Lots wouldn't. Something for everyone; every need catered for in a competitive market. In and out, in and out slide the monster cocks, close up, medium shot, long shot. Isn't that the tennis star's penis, in and out of my mouth? Young Hasan's face in extremis? Loki takes me pressed up against the corner of the cab: lots of other hands in shot to show there's company. They have cameras even there. Every one of my taxi journeys, to the shops, to home, to the Divan and back, there on film for cutaways. Europa ravished by the Bull is charming. I see Daisy's body in the lesbian scene but not her face. We weren't in a flowery field in the sun, just on a carpet under lights. Mine is there, clear as clear. I look so happy. The bondage stills are beautiful. I make a great damsel in distress. And I'm not acting. I believe every minute of it. The joy, the peace after orgasm, the slave's trust and adoration, all there. And now the whipping, the pièce de resistance; I writhe and scream: I watch the red weals form, the gag dig in, the mouth bleed. They are all watching me watching myself. Alden is smiling.

The technicians turn to look at me too. I don't think it can be Max from the Olivier – how could it be? The long jaw, the lugubrious face? Even that a set up? Joan known for a fraud from the beginning? Is that Luigi from the Bound Beast and Bumpkin? Shaker of nutmeg? Can't be. I am in shock. I see what is not there, surely. I will wake soon. And Robert, what about Robert? The twins? What have I done? I turn to escape, save them, but I am caught and turned back.

'Enjoy, Vanessa, enjoy,' says Ray. 'You're the girl who loves sex; it's your vocation.' But it's beyond that. They have their cameras on me even now, I realise that. Title: 'Forced Witness.'

I am sat in a chair to see what is happening down below. My wrists are fastened. The lights go down up here: the many screens grow blank. Time for the next

300

film. Just the one light as they record my reactions, test my responses, one last bar for Alden's masterpiece, one last line for Ray's *Blue Box*.

The lights brighten on the scene below. Alden is directing from up here in the control room: producer, director, composer, art dealer, designer, star – the Renaissance man who can do it all, except fuck to closure. His talents are wondrous.

Katharine and Alison lie on the bed in their cream dresses, side by side, bodies touching, skinny-limbed, scarcely wider when laid together than my single body ever was. No cushions. The dresses, in this light, are not as good as I thought. The seams are badly sewn: it's cheap stuff. A pity. Alison's left wrist is fastened to the left bedpost and Katharine's right wrist to the other, but the ties are long. They have freedom to move – they can turn to each other, embrace, kiss and fondle, though this is not primarily an incest film. Incest has a great following. I so seldom got as much freedom of movement, I am almost envious.

They seem relaxed and unworried. This may not be so bad. I will not play into enemy hands; I will not give them the shots they want: I will not give them torment, horror and distress. They can have my delight, my fascination, the exhilaration of the Vocational Girl, the seeker after the pleasures of the flesh, what can never be contained in language or on film, or in dance, or song, or music, or painting, in porn, or any other means, though so many try so hard. What sex feels like, what it is, when mind and body give up their separate ways and travel the same path. I lean forward to see better. I smile. That is all they will get from me.

For three minutes or so the twins just lie there, waiting, expectant. Title: 'Deflowered Twins'? It has all the makings of a classic. Cut, says Alden.

The twins look up at the mirror and I am pretty sure they know they are on film. I am just an innocent compared to the rest of my family. I expect everyone knew about my father and Jude. I was the only one who never guessed.

Alden the director decides this is not the response he expects from me. He pinches my nipple and takes me by surprise so I yelp and wriggle but only for a moment. Too bad, another few frames to intercut. Unwilling Witness, stock footage, to be cannibalised in many films, Alden's own, or else sold on, some just within the law, some well past it, depending on the market served.

'Don't be too rough,' Bernie says. 'She's Robert's sister.'

I am happy for Robert. All that is going to be all right. I have not done too terrible a thing. Bernie cares. A tear rolls down my cheek: it's a tear of simple happiness. Can you imagine the rarity? The lens moves close. Everyone's delighted. A genuine tear in high resolution can be used and re-used all over the net, flung from one computer to another: Roussel's dream comes true. One bite, a trillion bytes. A trillion pixels multiply on blue boxes everywhere, sourced by that single human tear, the organic and inorganic at last united. The infinite complexity of mirrored forms: what is this but chaos theory; science and the arts united. One tear rolls, the universe laps it up. Ray comes up close to me. I can feel his erection. Astonishing – Ray, the hapless lover! They so seldom try just being nice to each other, these people. He licks the tear off my cheek. That too is filmed.

Down below the great brown bear lumbers in. Actually he is surprisingly fast and light on his feet. He wears a dark yellow silk shirt and a red belt, good against the white background. My sisters seem to display almost no colour at all, with their short wheaten hair, pale skins and eyes. Mikhail's chin is black and stubbly, the mouth coarse. He seems to fill more space than he should, to have an unreasonable intensity of being. He exudes charisma. You can see the balls and the penis as he moves, heavy and hairy. He has the energy that comes with power. Power translates into star quality on screen. He stares down at Alison for a while. His eyes move to Katharine. He prefers Katharine. He rips the dress off her, one long tear from neck to hem. Perhaps the dresses were not so badly chosen after all. Cheap material rips easily.

Both girls stare upwards, helpless, give little moans of terror. They are acting: I know they are. They have the family blood in them. They will ask for copies of the film when this is over, along with their money. I am pretty sure Mikhail has no idea he's on film. I doubt that Alden and Ray will have the courage to release it

– though they might be tempted to simply transpose another head onto the oligarch's body. Even so – a wart, a birthmark, a tattoo? He might get to know, and nasty sudden deaths could happen. That would clean up the world a bit.

Or perhaps he just won't care: why should he? Truly powerful men do not care what others think. He might take it as a compliment; distribute the footage through his footballs clubs around the world. Look at me, the man who de-flowered two English virgins, me, the most powerful man in the world! Who is to say which way it will go?

Alison's turn to lose her dress. She squeals so he thrusts it in her mouth. The penis has risen now, pushing the yellow silk out in front of him. It seems enormous. The girls' eyes move to look: they do now seem a little alarmed, but they lie there; thoughts of Ovid and Catullus no doubt make them brave. I look, but keep my expression impassive. Waste of good film, up here. Down there it's different.

Now Mikhail lies between the twins. He has to separate them to do so. It's like dividing two chopsticks. They don't like that. But for this occasion they do have to acknowledge they are two people, not one. He mounts Katharine, and with one casual giant hand lifting her buttocks in the air, pushes his whole body forward to enter her. She cries out: I try not to wince. He withdraws and now it's Alison's turn. Another cry from her and then he's back to Katharine. He has great energy and no subtlety. The deed is done. There is not much more to it. It was their purity he required: the exhalation of some virtue into the air for him to breathe in and be revitalised.

He elaborates a little by flopping the twins on their fronts and pulling them onto their knees and going in there, first this one, then that one, to make his mark. He leaves their mouths alone. Cissy stuff. The climax is as noisy and triumphant as ever I have heard: it is inside Katharine. They will fake a money shot. It's all over within ten minutes, but the technicians can easily sort that out, simply repeat frames.

The twins are deflowered at their own request. They will be able to pay for the next couple of years' tuition. Ovid will, or will not, spring to life for them. They are not impetuous: they are not likely to follow in their big sister's footsteps along the paths trodden by the Vocational Girl. I hope not. I can see that path runs far too near the banks of the canal, the edge of railway line, the fringe of the motorway, where just a push can be the end of you. There are too many truly nasty people about. Alden is one of them.

At least he never came in me, out of me, or indeed at all. There's an odd comfort in that. Someone presses a cloth over my nose and mouth from behind. I refuse to struggle or flail about, because I can still hear a camera whirring. Fuck 'em! I breathe deep and pass out. There were no brothers to come to the rescue. Why would there be?

Party

I AM STRETCHED OUT ON the blue sofa. Ray is working at his easel. He moves calmly and efficiently. The hysterical paralysis is over, it seems. No doubt I and the twins have contributed in some way to this release of artistic energy. A kind of double-echo, fed-back voyeurism, unwanted on a sound track, but stimulating enough in real life.

I have a very bad headache, but I am alive. I had thought perhaps I was in a snuff movie. But I am a movie star: why would they want to get rid of the star? The girls who star, briefly, in snuff movies don't have my looks or graces. They're the ones nobody wants, the rejects of society and their own families. The deformed, the poor, the sulky and sullen. They get snuffed, tortured or mishandled to death for the sake of some good footage, a source of excitement to others. Do these girls get a look in, in Ray's portrait of the universe? Probably not. His is an up-market view, as much a rarified luxury as is Alden's *Thelemy*

– *The Murmur of Eternity*, designed to appeal to those so satiated by extremes of technology they no longer listen out for the real music of the spheres: a baby, a bird, rain on the window.

This morning the eternal murmur, in its newest – perhaps final – version, is playing in my ears as I wake. It sounds slightly less dire: the pain in my head has subsided into the background and there's a kind of airy trill running through it; I reckon it has breathed in, modified, and is now breathing out, the twins' first act of love. Whatever it is has healed Ray's hand. I wish I was happy for him, but I am not.

So Alden reckons that with me the film stops before the death of the body. Thank you, Alden. For me humiliation is enough: death of the spirit. Show me my past, laugh at me, trample my ideals, make yourself some money. Oh, I am humiliated all right. You have seen to that. I am well and truly paid out for being Joan. If that was Max at the sound console last night, if Max moonlights as a film technician, why then Alden had played me for a fool from the beginning. And yes, that was the tennis player, that was young Hasan: famous and notorious cocks without faces: try to guess who?

The suites on the fourth floor of the Olivier are fitted out with cameras. Who's that fool of a girl, thinking she is doing good? None other than the Olivier's tame whore, Vanessa. Alden's victory over me is complete.

'Better now?' Ray, discovering that I am awake. His world has not come to an end, just mine. He's excited, thrilled, and triumphant. He's working again! His normally tentative voice is strong and deep, as if a great surge of new testosterone now flooded through his bloodstream.

'Vanessa,' he says. 'I've so nearly finished! A couple more strokes and I'm free of the whole thing! The magnetic forces stream from Betelgeuse to Sirius, the wild horses of human passion will be harnessed to the chariot of the Spiritual Sun.'

His hand is better, and his spirits, but his head has taken a turn for the worse. I was glad. They could lock him up too. After the police had finished with Alden.

'Ah, you lovely, lovely thing,' he said, 'I read rebellion in your face. Look into my eyes.'

I close mine quickly but it's too late.

Snapshots. Ray is fucking me on the sofa. On and on, the long mean thing goes in and in, and on, as if each thwarted attempt in his past now had to be made up for. (Which comes first, I wonder, the painting or the sex: which begins it all, the body or the mind?') He pauses from time to time to congratulate me. 'You're so wonderful, Vanessa, I can never get enough of you. Like the sea, always different.' And so forth; then it resumes.

I remember how Crowley's woman Leah died from exhaustion, from fucking a goat. Or was it the goat that died? They won't let Ray die, that's for sure: his one last thin black line must be put upon canvas, so the next Leap Through The Universe can be taken. He's saving completion up, like the icing on a cake. On and on. They're all such silly little boys: if only they were not so dangerous.

Snapshot. I am in my room. I am being dressed and anointed. A wreath of flowers, tried for size. A long white muslin gown. I recognise my two attendants as the bride's mother and sister from the Black Mass scenario. They've abandoned the wreath and have my hair in rollers. The sister is heating the hair with a dryer. I wish she wouldn't do that: it is so bad for the hair. She burns my scalp. I tug my head away; she slaps me. I am amongst enemies. Don't react, don't react. The cameras are everywhere: in this room too. What have they watched, what have they seen? I get a little extra burn on purpose from the sister, but don't protest. What these women need is a good straightforward fuck: if they had proper normal sex lives they wouldn't be so malicious. Audrey's problem too, most likely: the sex is too fancy. Clive? How can you get a straight fuck from a man in pointed gold silk slippers and mauve pantaloons?

Snapshot. The mirror room, but not a mirror in sight. It's been draped with purple velvet hangings. They look old and dusty to me, fit to make you sneeze. The Lukas bed has been contracted to the size and shape of an altar, but lying north to south. There's a pentagram painted on the floor around it. Now how are they going to get that off? I've spent so many hours cleaning this floor.

I don't like the look of any of this. There are black candles everywhere, stuck into cheap wrought-iron stands, flaking rust. Alden has always saved on props. Should Satan think he deserves better, he will probably take his revenge. Good.

Guests mill around as at any cocktail party: some are naked, dressed in black latex, or wear witchy gowns with symbols on them. I recognise faces: cameramen, actors in the scenarios. Audrey, Clive. Ray, all in black, grinning. There's a tall blonde, naked: it's Daisy, Lady O, her husband Toby, withered and old, also with no clothes, and shrivelled little testicles, by her side. Dr Wondle, Loki. Bernie, Naz. No Robert, thank God no Robert. If I ever get out of this I will warn him.

Is everyone in this? All, all Thelemites? The Southgate breakaway branch, the renegades too? I think that's Matilda Weiss, with her stiff botoxed face that still bears the lines of complaint. Can't be! Was that a set-up too? The bride's mother leads me and puts my hand in Alden's.

Alden's torso is naked other than a goat's head medallion hanging round his neck and a blackish red cloth draped over his knees with an upside down cross badly embroidered on it. Where does one buy such things? I remember a lawsuit. A store in Minneapolis selling love potions: 'The law is not made for experts but to protect the public, that vast multitude which includes the ignorant, the unthinking and the credulous, who, in making purchases, do not stop to analyze but too often are governed by appearances and general impressions.' Aronberg et al. v. Federal Trade Commission, 132 F.2d 165. There's a voice in my head. It's the simpleton: Joan, 'Stop it, stop it, Vanessa. Think! Help us!' Yes, I can see this is fairly drastic. You don't have to be a virgin to be a sacrifice. The dying gurgle of the Scarlet Whore of Babylon would fill a sound-track just as nicely.

Only Lam, behind Alden's chair, is dressed in white. Polo neck. It seems as indecent to think about his lower half as it does about Alden's. Just a seam at hip level, like a plastic doll.

Alden says to me, 'Just one last note from you, Vanessa. One last chord for me.' As I thought. 'But you were brilliant,' he adds. 'So brilliant! I owe you a great deal.'

It is never nice to be spoken of in the past tense. The smell of incense is heavy. Background music turns in to foreground music. *Thelemy, Lust for Life*, the latest unheard, virgin version, renamed and re-mixed, bass-heavy and throbbing. He'll have to work some more on it before tomorrow's opening, or nobody's going to buy anything: they'll just want to go home. But the guests are singing along to it, chanting. It occurs to me they've practiced.

I see the picture from above. The wreathed girl being led to the altar. Who can she be? I remember now, she's the Hotel Olivier's tame whore Vanessa, the one who told herself and everyone she was 'doing good'. That sex was a fine and lovely delight, a gift from the Almighty, the Good God. I mount the steps. I lie upon the altar. A bright, bright spotlight shines down on me. Scissors cut my gown down the middle; the fabric is draped around me. It won't be enough to sop up the blood, or perhaps they mean to drink it? Probably. I am naked on the altar, except for white silk shoes with high heels, the throwaway kind people wear for suburban weddings. Yes, this time it is a snuff movie. It's my real death that is required: my sacrificial blood to feed the home computers of the world, to keep Google and the porn sites sated.

Alden raises the knife. He is not going to stab. He will slit my throat. The life expectancy of a porn star is not great at the best of times. 'Shemhaforash,' he intones. 'So God spoke when he created the world.'

The Scarlet Woman, the Whore of Babylon, butchered to make a Thelemite holiday! It will be necrophilia. The last resort. He will burst within me, finally, explode. Dead, I will not destroy him. I cannot laugh at him or even with him. I can never compare him with anyone else, and find him wanting. I will not be Vanessa, I will not be Joan, I will be nothing: he will come, the consummation devoutly to be wished.

The knife is poised, long handled, well-balanced, the easier for a man in a wheel-chair to wield. The knife's familiar. Normally it hangs from a magnet in the Crabtree kitchen. Alden has found his solution. He will complete his composition as my power moves into him: he feels no guilt: my body- and soul-death will be immortalised in his music: I am the muse, he the artist. Alden will blaze through the firmament as Liber AL, the star foretold, as revealed to poor mad Crowley over three consecutive lunchtimes in April 1904 by Aiwass, minister of Hoor-paar-kraat, the Sun God, whose kinsfolk are Lords of the Earth. Through the whore's death Alden will be made physically whole. Riches and powers unknown until now will be his. The whore must have accumulated a great deal of other people's life-force during her days in the Divan; that no doubt was what she was doing there, accumulating the stuff. It's just now she has to hand her takings over. Probably Aiwass is in this dismal room right now. Light glints off the blade.

'Oh mother, save me now!' That's Joan bleating: I, Vanessa, am far too proud to murmur.

'Aiwass, aiwass, aiwass,' chants the crowd.

'Do what thou wilt,' cries Alden, 'shall be all of the Law!'

'Shemhaforash!' they reply. 'Shemhaforash!'

'Mummy, Mummy!' cries Joan.

I am my mother's daughter. I want to pray. But to whom? Who is there?

'St Michael,' my mother tells me. 'Pray to St Michael!'

'Why him?' I am bewildered. Surely St Michael is the patron saint of grocers, mariners, paratroopers, police and sickness?

'St Michael guards the body of Eve,' she whispers. 'Quick, quick.'

She's right. The Revelation of Moses section in the Apocryphal Gospels.

'We're hardly Eve,' I say.

'It hardly matters,' says my mother. 'He lives next door. For God's sake, Vanessa!'

And of course she's right. St Michael's, my mother's church, the church on the hill, the boy next door.

'Shemhaforash!' they cry. 'Shemhaforash!'

'What thou wilt be done!' cries Alden and now the knife glints at my throat.

'St Michael,' I pray, 'please help! I know I've been bad but we're neighbours.'

There is a sudden savage gust of wind which blows the door open, and the candles out. It is pitch black, save for the beam of light on to the altar. That goes out too. A power cut? A peal of thunder crashes over Parliament Hill. St Michael, God's enforcer: in charge of all nature, wind, rain, thunder, lightning? Alden's touch pads glow in the dark. A peal of thunder crashes over Parliament Hill. The guests squeal and panic. 'The great sow takes the hindmost!' shouts someone, and they scatter. I can hear them though I can't see them. A harsh breathing, as of the sow rushing through, but it might just be the sound of cameras dying for lack of electricity.

All is confusion. I ease myself down from the altar. Obviously I must run. I don't know whither exactly because the house will be sealed, and Alden's touch pad controls the exits, but at least I know the house as the others may not. I've made my way from bed to bed in the dark often enough. Everyone else is milling and squawking. I grope my way to where I hope the front door is. Slimy things brush my face, as on the Ghost Train at Disneyland. I feel for my Lacroix jacket on the peg – and it's there. Everything is going to be all right. And Lam is holding the front door open for me. Lam, my brother, is nodding me through. A gleam of light comes from his eyes, or seems to.

'Good girl,' he says. 'Live happy.'

I have to know, even now.

'Lam, where do you come from?' I ask.

'Me Tzaddikim,' he says. 'Righteous one. Thirty-six of us. Watchers,' and he laughs uproariously. My betting is Tibet, and some glandular deficiency. But Joan is egging me to on get out of here. God, how she will panic!

And I am out in the street, without a purse, no money, after midnight, just a jacket which barely covers my crotch, miles from home, in white shoes with high heels but the thinnest of soles, and for a moment I contemplate going back inside. They can't really have been serious! People don't do human sacrifice. And that's when I feel for and find the twenty pound note folded small in my pocket, and know that if I can only find a cab I can get home. One comes along. It is not even Loki's. It has a proper identifying plate from the

315

Public Carriage Office, number 299929: twenty-nine nine, nine twenty-nine, I say to myself.

The twenty-ninth of September is the feast day of Saints Michael, Gabriel and Raphael, Archangels.

I am back in the world of the non-Thelemites. I will never go back. I want to live.

A Scandal

I SEE IT ON THE TV. It is not the Twin Towers, it is not the Waco siege, it is not Princess Diana confessing adultery but it will make minor TV history for years. It is the opening of Lady O's art gallery in her London town house down the road from Mrs Thatcher's. The arts media is there in force. The footage is very dull at first, apart from the commissioned piece, *The Blue Box*, by the up-and-coming conceptual artist Ray Franchi, all mirrors and glitter, which quite takes the camera's eye. And the music is said to be interesting, but the sound system isn't all that good – Lady O must have taken her eye off the ball at some stage – and someone is heard to complain it sounds as if there was something wrong with the central heating.

And then the extraordinary happens. It's all there on film. A couple burst through the security cordon, each wielding a cricket bat. One is a woman in long robes wearing a dog collar, as if she was a woman vicar; the other looks a perfectly decent man of the school-teacher variety. The woman goes for *The Blue Box* with the bat: glass splinters burst everywhere: the man just lays about him, getting the sound system, sculptures, paintings. The art crowd dive for cover. Mobile phones are pointed. The couple flee before the police arrive.

The twins, I guess, went home and told. Probably boasted. My parents did their parental duty.

And that's it. There seem to be no consequences. The police do not prosecute. They may know a thing or two about Alden. Modern art is not popular. People just laugh. As when the Momart warehouse in Leyton burned to the ground and no-one thought that what was lost was of any value at all. Good riddance to bad rubbish, it was universally agreed. The O's faces, comical in their surprise, were on too many cell phone cameras to be ever taken seriously ever again. They abandoned their art patron activities and I believe went to Africa where they try to save wild apes from extinction.

As for Alden, the BBC never played his piece. It was too closely associated with scandal for their comfort. They don't like anything which attracts too much attention. Alden will end up like Crowley: blaze across the sky, the promised star Liber AL, just to burn out. Every generation or so Aiwass needs a victim to suck dry. It was Alden, not me.

And Ray? Ray lapsed into obscurity, as happens to so many artists who take themselves too seriously. At any rate I never came across his name in any publication again. Nor did I hear from Lam. I tried to get in touch with the Southgate Branch but it had disbanded.

When next I went home we sat around the table – Mother, Dad, the twins, Robert and me – and none of us said a word about any of it. We're like that. I went off and did my PhD with Professor Freddie Wilques, whose wife had left him. When the college health centre once again suggested I go back on lithium, I didn't.

FINIS